New, exciting and di

These are fast-moving
events which lead up
'breaking' of an exclus
a typical tabloid newsp

Since graduating from university in the mid Eighties,
Neil Bartlem has explored many different aspects of
professional writing from staff positions on newspapers
and magazines to public relations and advertising for
household name organisations.

SOCCER ACE GUNNED DOWN

a newspaper novel

by

NEIL BARTLEM

SOCCER ACE
GUNNED DOWN

First published in 1993 by Tabloid Books,
12 Beresford Drive, Southport PR9 7JY

ISBN 1–874652–03–1

This is a work of fiction. The situations and
scenes described, other than historical events,
are all imaginary. None of the characters
portrayed is based on real people and any
similarity to any person living or dead is purely
coincidental.

Cover picture: Tangent Photography, Neston,
Wirral.
Models: Helen Jeffrey, Salubi

Cover design: Pheon Graphics, Southport.

This book is set in 10pt Plantin by Chippendale
Type Ltd., Otley, West Yorkshire.

Printed and bound by Cox & Wyman Ltd.,
Reading, Berks.

FOR MUM AND DAD

ACKNOWLEDGMENTS

My heartfelt thanks to everyone whose encouragement sustained me while writing this first novel, especially Julian Desser and Sarah Waddell.

Even now he was aroused. At the very edges of her mouth a sly smile lingered like a wicked memory.

Her face was astonishingly beautiful; her eyes impenetrable as if they were absorbing light, sucking the watcher in. It was an expression of pure animal desire.

She was entirely naked, kneeling on a bed among crumpled sheets with her slender arms clasped behind her head, lifting the hair from the nape of her neck.

The motion of her arms raised and tightened her breasts with their dark nipples.

But wherever attention briefly wandered – to the soft perfection of her lips or the exuberant bush of ebony hair between her thighs – it returned almost immediately to that iron lascivious gaze and its unmistakable promise.

Looking at her, Simmons felt just the same as on the first night they made love. There was a coiling and uncoiling in his guts and the blood was hot in his loins.

But there was a sense of desperation, too, of embarking on a journey he could not possibly complete.

With clumsy fingers, he let the photograph drop onto the table. Smaller now, she continued staring intensely up at him, her breasts still thrust aggressively outwards, encouraging him to touch them and taste their sweetness.

One by one, he flipped a dozen more photographs down as if he were playing a surreal game of cards.

He remembered himself behind the camera, clicking in compulsive self-defence, only the lens protecting him from the white-heat of her passion.

The colours seemed to grow more garish in each shot – the billowing whiteness of the bed sheets, the crimson interior of her sex as she offered herself to the camera.

And then, suddenly, there he was, the camera yielded up and switched to delayed exposure. She was pulling him down onto the bed, towards her and into her. He was inflamed.

With infinite delicacy, his black arm reached out to her

and was stark and shocking against her paler flesh. His eyes were closed. Hers were burning.

Tears welled in the eyes of Simmons. Looking again at those images, he felt suddenly stupefied, amazed at everything that had happened.

He realised he had been playing the game on everyone else's terms. Now it was time to start again, with a fresh set of rules.

Without savagery, he tore each of the photographs in two and tossed them into an ash tray. He lit a match and touched one of the pictures with the flame. It blackened and curled, giving off swirls of dense grey smoke, and gradually all of the photographs caught alight.

With a sense of liberation, Simmons left the house, the scent of the burning pictures still acrid in his nostrils.

It was a balmy early evening in late summer. His Victorian country house lay at the end of a lonely lane, its shape dominating the landscape.

In the west, the neatly ordered patchwork of hedged fields gave way slowly to suburban straggle and then, right at the horizon, to the spreading grey smudge of the big industrial city of Bradcaster.

Simmons' feet crunched on gravel as he moved towards his Mercedes convertible, one hand fumbling in his jacket for the keys.

Just then a figure materialised from the shade of a big yew tree just a few yards away.

Sensing the movement, Simmons glanced up and for a moment an expression of puzzled recognition creased his features.

He screamed: 'No! No! Please God! No!'

He flung his arms out in supplication and terror.

Although deafening, the first shot seemed to take place in a dream. He saw the black malevolent shape of the gun raised high and watched the hammer fall in grotesque slow-motion.

He was gasping for air like a drowning man, wanting to shout out again but no sounds would come.

The second shot crashed into his shoulder, spinning him round, and real time supervened. A searing pain exploded onto his senses and he clutched at the wound, saw the blood run crimson between his fingers.

Again and again and again he heard the shots, further and further away each time, and felt the bullets smashing into his soft body.

He hit the ground, sprawling. His face crashed into the stones and one eye stared up blankly. He could no longer think.

The pain and the noise receded until finally he was engulfed in a rushing darkness.

There are times when eight yards can look as narrow as a needle's eye. For Dave Stewart, captain of Bradcaster City Football Club, this was such a time.

Heart pounding like a jack hammer, he caught the ball tossed by the referee and placed it precisely on the painted white circle in the penalty box.

He seemed to have grown huge and awkward; he was absurdly conscious of the air rasping in his lungs as he fought to calm himself.

Defenders and scavengers from his own team were tensed at the edge of the box. The goalkeeper was staring right at him, tossing his arms and snorting like an enraged gorilla. His gaze was boring right inside Stewart, searching out his self-belief, daring him to keep his nerve.

He was conscious of the huge chasm of silence confronting him, as the massed ranks of Bradcaster fans with their blue banners held their collective breath in an ecstasy of anticipation.

A hundred yards back, Stewart heard the jeers and

whistles from the rival fans at the north end. He stepped back ten deliberate paces, his eyes fixed on the ball. Then he lifted his eyes to the goal.

It was like looking down the wrong end of a telescope. Yet bizarrely, the goalkeeper loomed large and threatening between goal posts that had shrunk to the dimensions of a toy.

Perched high in an eyrie in the west stand, several dozen pressmen gazed down at the lonely figure dressed in royal blue, his white shorts smeared with mud.

'A tenner he misses,' said Colin Gregory, sports reporter with the tabloid Daily World. 'He looks like he's shitting himself.'

It was the last minute of normal time. Bradcaster were losing one-nil to a breakaway goal after applying constant, frantic pressure for the whole of the game.

If they lost today, they would be propping up the rest of the First Division.

Stewart began his run. Reaching the ball, he swung his leg in a clean arc and hit it firm and true. There was a thump of leather on leather and the ball flew high past the keeper's outstretched left arm as he leapt towards the top corner.

Evading his fingertips, the ball clattered into the cross-bar and spooned harmlessly up into the Bradcaster crowd. There was a low groan, as of an animal in pain.

Gregory let out an ironical laugh. 'What did I tell you?' he asked nobody in particular. 'Useless bastard.'

Down on the neat green floodlit rectangle, the figure in blue had slumped to his knees on the turf, head in hands.

Beside him a gaggle of opposition players was dancing delightedly around their goalkeeper. Then came the cruel, piercing shriek of the referee's whistle and the game was over.

Unbelievably, Bradcaster City had been beaten again.

All around the ground there was an angry, exasperated murmuring that grew in volume and intensity. Thirty thousand Bradcaster fans, many from the toughest and poorest parts of the city, had had enough.

A chant began with a few isolated voices and swelled to a crescendo as the crowd picked up the theme, loudest of all among the Southsiders whose terrace was to be razed at the end of the season.

The tune was familiar enough but the words they bellowed out with all the breath in their lungs were starkly different.

'Sack the Board,' they chanted endlessly, faces contorted with rage. 'Sack the Board, sack the Board, sack the Board . . . '

A boy no more than ten years old, bedecked in royal blue and white, leaned over the mouth of the dressing room tunnel and spat ferociously at the retreating back of a Bradcaster player.

A great gobbet of spittle settled between his shoulder blades. The boy's eyes were full of unshed tears.

A dozen or so fans from the Southside had vaulted the barriers and gathered in the centre circle. They continued the chant, thrusting their arms aggressively at the glass-fronted directors' box in the east stand.

They were herded away without protest by policemen who were almost sympathetic.

Among the media men, Gregory had a telephone jammed between his right ear and shoulder, his neck twisted sideways. He was rummaging through his jacket pockets.

'Yeah, yeah. You ready?'

He produced a crumpled packet of Marlboro and flipped open the top. He extracted a cigarette and slipped it between his lips.

'Hold on,' he said through clenched teeth.

He lit the Marlboro with a dexterous flick of a Zippo lighter and sucked deeply.

'Christ, that's better. OK? First para. Bungling Bradcaster City reached rock bottom . . . no bottom, you silly sod . . . as angry fans invaded the pitch to tell club bosses – colon, open quotes – in God's name, go. Full stop, close quotes. New para.'

Now pushing 40, Gregory was an old hand.

The Daily World's chief soccer writer in the North, he kept an especially close eye on Bradcaster City. Win or lose, the club nearly always made good copy for the tabloid's sensation-hungry readers.

Over the years, Gregory had built a tight network of contacts within the club, despite his readiness to put the boot in from time to time. They recognised in him a real knowledge of the game and a kind of faded integrity.

As Gregory rang his story through, the sounds of anger and unrest faded as Bradcaster's fans streamed off the terraces and out into the dark backstreets of the city.

At the north end, the opposition supporters had been held back by the police. There were no songs of victory.

They were huddled and silent, aware that the situation had become violent and unpredictable. It was a walk of two miles through narrow streets to reach the train station.

And then, carried on the still air of a late autumn evening, came the sound of shattering glass. There was a terrible roar of approval from the mob, punctuated by more crashes.

The chanting started again but this time with a deeper undercurrent of hostility that made the blood run cold.

'You're go-ing home in a fuck-ing amb-u-lance!'

They repeated the rhythm by clapping their hands menacingly.

'You're go-ing home in a fuck-ing amb-u-lance!'

A wave of panic ran through the fans still inside the

ground, as through animals in a stockade. Instinctively, the crowd compressed, eyes wild, squeezing closer and closer together for reassurance.

It was midnight before the police regained control of the city.

There was a trail of wrecked cars and smashed windows. A pub landlord was glassed in the eye, slicing his retina in two. The casualty ward of Bradcaster Royal Infirmary was kept busy until dawn treating the wounded.

There were 147 arrests.

Since the glory days of the late Fifties, when they won the Double and reached the final of the European Cup, there had been many disappointments for Bradcaster City Football Club.

The apparently endless wait for a new trophy. A scandal involving back-handers to players. A long and bitter line of sacked managers.

But there had never been anything quite like this.

It was the blackest and most humiliating day in the history of the club.

Sid Graveney, a big man in late middle age with a broad Lancastrian accent, had a reputation for speaking his mind.

From humble beginnings in a local market, he had made a fortune from a chain of butcher's shops which now stretched across England.

Every single pork pie, every hot dog and burger sold at Bradcaster's home games was provided by the Graveney empire.

When a Bradcaster player pleased him, a Graveney meat wagon would roll up on Sunday morning with enough legs of pork and topsides of beef to fill his freezer to the brim.

His largesse was legendary. So, too, was his temper. He could forgive ignorance or incompetence but never lack of effort.

He was a colourful, tumultuous personality with an appetite for life. He also owned a quarter of Bradcaster City Football Club.

Just at the moment, that was a considerable liability.

Graveney was beginning to regret the moment ten years ago when he agreed to bale out Bradcaster. He had never expected a decent return on his investment; football wasn't like that.

But neither had he anticipated the sheer aggravation, the backbiting and hostility, the grinding unstoppable descent into insolvency. Unwittingly, he had booked a passage on the Titanic.

Graveney gazed pensively down from the directors' box onto the scarred turf below. It was the morning after Bradcaster's fans had rampaged through the city.

Still ringing in his brain was the faraway echo of the crowd chanting for his sacking. Despite the hour, he held a half-full tumbler of whisky absently in his hand.

He turned away from the window with a curious mixture of sadness and rage in his eyes. This was not the usual bluff loss of temper but a slow-burning, intense passion.

'This club is finished, Arthur,' he said. 'We've got the worst players for 30 years and we're up to our eyes in debt. Half the fans have stopped coming and the other half want to smash up the town when we get beat. And everyone thinks it's all our fault.'

He snorted with disgust and took a big slug of whisky.

'Sack the fucking Board! Who else do they think would do this job? I sunk millions into this club without a snowball in hell's chance of ever seeing it again. And all I get is aggro. Ungrateful bastards.'

Arthur Redwood, chairman of the club, said nothing. He had learned over the years it was better to let Graveney talk himself out.

Now nearing 70, with a shock of grey hair and piercing

ice-blue eyes, he was immaculate in dark blazer and striped regimental tie. He sat behind a great expanse of mahogany table in which he could see his own reflection, face stonily impassive.

Graveney was continuing in quiet fury, almost unaware of his presence.

'I used to stand on the Southside when I was a kid. Never missed a single home game. How many of those chanting morons could say that? Now we've got to knock it down and build a flash new stand with shiny plastic seats. It will never be the same. We've got to shell out ten million quid just to ruin the place.'

He shook his head in pain and bewilderment, and drained the whisky glass. The alcohol burned his throat and for an instant his mind fogged over.

Then he looked at Redwood with clear gimlet eyes.

'Arthur, if we're not in the Super League next season, we can kiss this club goodbye,' he said.

'If the satellite boys get the rights, just our share of the television money would keep us going. Could be a couple of million a year. But if we go down, it's just a share of sweet fuck all.

'The players aren't good enough, Arthur. You should know that better than anyone. We need a goalscorer but we're hocked up to our eyeballs already. What the hell are we going to do?'

Redwood spoke softly for the first time.

'McNally is a good man. He'll turn things around. We'll just have to learn to be a bit more patient.'

'McNally? That bloody clown!' exploded Graveney and laughed bitterly. 'I'd sack him tomorrow if we could afford the compensation. He's got no imagination. Our players can run all day but they can't pass the ball.'

Redwood stiffened slightly. Now there was a hint of irritation in his voice.

'Look Sid, let's get a couple of things straight, shall we?' he said. 'You don't have the authority to fire McNally under any circumstances. And you voted, along with the rest of us, to bring him here. So let's give the man a chance, for goodness' sake.'

Redwood was not a man who lost control; he indicated his displeasure by subtler means. There was no one at Bradcaster City, Graveney included, who didn't respect him and even fear him a little, despite the increasing frailty of his age.

Graveney was stung but wouldn't back down. Instead he tried a craftier, more wary approach.

'OK, there's nothing wrong with McNally,' he conceded. 'He's a tough lad and he does his best with what we've got available. But this club has always had a reputation for playing good football, even when the results weren't right. Now we're not even losing with dignity.'

He paused and looked hard at Redwood, searching him out.

'Look at that side you led out in the cup final in '59. Quality all through the side and you made them play football that was a joy to watch. I was there, just a bit of a kid on the terraces, and it was the proudest day of my life. McNally will never create a team like that if he's here until doomsday.'

Silence fell for a moment.

Then Redwood said quietly: 'You could be right.'

There was the faintest hint of desperation and hopelessness in his voice.

Graveney pressed home his advantage: 'You know damn well I'm right. Come on, Arthur. Between the two of us, we run this club. We've got to sort this out.'

Redwood squeezed his eyes with thumb and forefinger and for a moment looked his age.

'What exactly do you suggest?'

'Sack McNally. It's the only way.'

'No, Sid,' said Redwood, shaking his head slowly. 'He's been here less than a year. It's just not fair.'

Graveney looked utterly exasperated. His stolid, fleshy features were creased and suffused with rising colour.

'Oh for God's sake, don't be so naive,' he stormed. 'What's fair got to do with it? It might cost us a couple of hundred grand to pay him off but what can you buy for that? We're stuck with the players but we can chop the manager all right.'

Redwood smiled wearily. For a moment he looked decades younger and then his face relapsed into a ravaged cragginess.

'You can't run a football club like a butcher's shop, Sid. It's a question of loyalty. And who do you think would apply if we sacked McNally? Just the usual bunch of losers and Flash Harrys. It would be a waste of time.'

Graveney no longer struggled to conceal his anger. He was on his feet, his face shoved within inches of Redwood's.

'Don't patronise me, you old bastard,' he shouted, his voice cracking with emotion. 'You played a different bloody tune when you came crawling to me for money. If this club goes bust, it will be on your head. Remember that.'

Redwood remained seated, his eyes locked onto those of Graveney, utterly self-possessed. His inner strength made the big man look florid and foolish. Graveney sat down again abruptly, ashamed of the outburst, looking at his hands.

He seemed suddenly childlike. But Redwood knew that he was right about one thing at least.

The vultures were gathering above Bradcaster City. And unless he could rekindle the dying spark of life, Redwood himself would be their first victim.

SAD CITY SLUMP AGAIN

Sack the Board, demand fans

by Colin Gregory

BUNGLING Bradcaster City reached rock bottom as angry fans invaded the pitch to tell club bosses: 'In God's name, go.'

Last night's 1-0 home defeat by mid-table Newcastle Wanderers plunged once-proud City to the foot of the First Division for the first time in living memory.

Their dismal start to the season now contains just one victory in 11 games and already the spectre of relegation is haunting the stricken club.

A last-minute chance to save the game fell to Bradcaster skipper Dave Stewart after he was upended in the box.

But his kick slammed against the crossbar with the keeper

beaten and rebounded to safety.

The final whistle came just seconds later and was the signal for a pitch invasion by disgusted fans from the Southside terraces.

They burst through a police cordon to stage an angry demonstration below the Bradcaster directors' box, where club chairman Arthur Redwood watched stony-faced.

With turnstile attendances already slumped to an all-time low, this latest inept performance has thrown Bradcaster City into crisis.

Top of manager Dougie McNally's shopping list must be a top-class striker. His team dominated most of the match but their powder puff attack never created a clear-cut opening.

With the brave new world of next season's Super League beckoning England's elite teams, Bradcaster City are staring instead at a footballing wilderness.

The fans have sent a warning to the bosses of Bradcaster. Arthur Redwood, the hero of City's golden age, would do well to heed it before it is too late.

Below his hotel window, the beautiful Georgian city of Bath spread out in front of Augustus Simmons, lit by a mosaic of street lamps.

The sinuous black shape of the river flickered with occasional reflections. It was a still, crisp evening. Voices lifted from the restaurant across the street.

In the darkened room, Simmons had his head bent over something which he was squeezing with both hands. He was making little coaxing noises in his throat. Suddenly there was a bang and wetness gushed over his fingers.

'Ooh!' a girl's voice squealed excitedly. 'Champagne! What have I done to deserve this?'

A shape detached itself from the darkness and moved to where he stood at the window.

'Nothing yet,' he said.

The girl had one shoe dangling from her little finger by its strap. She waved it about, giggling.

'What do you mean?'

Eyes wide and bright, she leaned onto tiptoes and tilted her face towards his. But instead of kissing him, she simply settled her head on his shoulder like a child.

In the half-light, Simmons could see the black roots in her metallic blonde hair. One of the shoulder straps had fallen off her cheap dress, revealing a pale expanse of skin and the angular shape of her collar bone.

She could not have been more than 17 years old.

'Gus?' she whispered, her voice low and breathless.

Simmons was conscious of her young body clinging to him, her breath warm and moist on his neck. He was stiffening and he knew she could feel the growing pressure on her belly.

'Mmm?'

She giggled again, then nipped the underside of his chin gently with her teeth.

'I've never been with anyone famous before.'

'I'm not famous.'

She moved still closer, grinding against his hardness.

'And I've never been with a black man either.'

Simmons felt a swelling emptiness under his ribs. Grabbing a fistful of hair at her neck, he pulled back her head until she was staring up at him.

Then he kissed her, hard and dispassionately at first but with increasing softness and tenderness. She went still and small.

Simmons still held the champagne bottle in one hand. It was cool and damp with condensation.

He held it to the girl's mouth and her fingers tightened around his at the neck of the bottle. She parted her lips and made a sound that came from deep inside her.

Tilting the bottle, she drank copiously, champagne spilling over her face and soaking her dress. She pulled her mouth away from the bottle, laughing, and the wine gushed into her hair.

'No more, no more. I'll choke!'

She broke away from him, eyes dancing. She was backing off but her sweet body and the damp strands of hair kissing her cheek drew him on.

'Don't you dare!'

She was still laughing uncontrollably as Simmons let the champagne bottle fall and moved towards her. Scampering backwards, she slipped and fell in a tangle of limbs.

In a moment, he was on her, biting her neck, tearing at her dress. He was silent and predatory.

The girl was giving out high-pitched moans, responding, urging him on. At one stage, she even called out his name in ecstasy and longing.

It was a name he hardly recognised, as though he were a stranger watching his own love-making. Sometimes it was hard to believe what he had become.

In the morning, he woke to find her thin arm draped

across him. He noticed that her crimson fingernails were chipped and broken.

A seeping sense of guilt was invading him. Near the window, the champagne bottle was lying on its side in a puddle. The girl's dress lay all torn on the plush cream hotel carpet. Nearby, one of her high-heeled shoes had been tossed carelessly. There was no sign of its partner.

Now bathed in early morning sunshine, the room still had the musky scent of sex.

Hoisted up onto his elbows, Simmons stared blankly at the remnants of the seduction. When he was picking up the girl, he had felt curiously powerful and potent, testing the limits of what his fame could achieve.

Now it all seemed merely pointless and banal.

The girl stirred in her sleep and his whole body grew tense. Steadfastly looking away from her, he sensed her eyelids flicker open and was conscious of her breathing, deep and regular. In a soft and slumberous voice, she spoke.

'Do you want me to go?'

For a moment he paused, then said simply: 'Yes.'

'OK.'

The girl raised herself up, exposing her small delicate breasts. She rubbed her eyes and smiled with a kind of innocence.

'I didn't expect you to ask me to stay. It doesn't matter.'

Unwillingly, Simmons caught her gaze. Her lipstick had rubbed off and her mascara had run. She looked painfully young and vulnerable.

'I'm . . . I'm sorry,' he whispered. 'It's just that . . .'

His voice tailed away into an uncomfortable silence.

'It's all right, honestly,' said the girl encouragingly. 'Do you think I didn't notice this?'

She leaned across him, rubbing her girl's breasts across his muscular hairless chest. Her fingers found his left hand and held it up for inspection.

'I knew the score.'

Against his dark flesh, the gold band shone in sharp relief. Embarrassed, he snatched his hand away.

'Look, let's drop it,' he snapped. 'Just get your clothes on and fuck off.'

He turned his back and, in a few moments, he felt the girl slip from the bed and heard her struggling back into her ripped dress. She searched for maddening minutes for her errant shoe.

Then with a soft click of the bedroom door, she was gone. Her sudden absence was like a dead weight in the room.

A host of images was clamouring in his mind. The girl's pale shape as she arched beneath him. A bare shoulder where the strap of her dress had snapped. Her greedy mouth as she gulped the champagne.

And then, unbidden, his wife's face swam into view, shocked and bewildered. Poor Melanie. She had never done anything to deserve this.

But that, thought Simmons, was probably the problem.

The Bradcaster Herald was the biggest selling regional morning newspaper in the country. It was part of the fabric of life in the city.

It was staffed by more than 100 journalists, more than some of the national dailies. It was read by nearly a quarter of a million Bradcaster citizens six days a week.

When anything happened in the city, a tale of vice or tragedy or corruption, it was the Herald that legitimised it, made it real. It was the pulse of the lifeblood of the community.

That made its editor, Rex Thorneycroft, a powerful man. The Herald was a brave, campaigning newspaper feared by the petty town hall tyrants, slum landlords and pimps, drug pushers and brutal policemen.

But just now Thorneycroft felt anything but powerful. He felt instead like a naughty schoolboy, caught in the act of something unspeakable and called to the towering presence of the headmaster.

He was troubled with the same emotion every time he met Michael Conrad, the same withering of his spirit. And, as always, he was full of anger and self-loathing.

Conrad had walked into Thorneycroft's office and immediately made it his own. A hush had descended in his wake as he moved through the newsroom.

At first glance, there was nothing to mark him out. But a closer look revealed certain trappings – the perfectly tailored Armani suit, the exquisite Patek Philippe wristwatch.

Then something of the man himself would emerge. The quiescent power of a 50-year-old body in perfect shape, honed each day. The casual arrogance in the way he held himself.

Above all, the smile and easy laugh betrayed by intense steel-grey eyes that seemed to hold no reflection, the inflexible jawline. This was a man utterly in command of himself, with the innate ability to control others by sheer force of will.

'Thanks for making time to see me at such short notice, Rex,' said Conrad easily. 'I know this is a busy time of day for you.'

It was nine o'clock in the evening and Thorneycroft should have been organising his splash story for the last edition.

'That's all right,' he replied, without quite managing to eliminate the resentment in his voice. 'I presume it's something pretty important to bring you to Bradcaster. We don't see a lot of you up here.'

Thank God, he wanted to add. He was already beginning to feel uptight. Conrad had a reputation for taking pleasure in firing his staff in person – apparently at random and always unexpectedly.

As sole owner of Conrad Regional Newspapers, a publishing empire which embraced 30 major cities in Great Britain, Northern Ireland and the Irish Republic, he could do pretty much as he pleased.

'Actually,' said Conrad in his smooth, cultured voice, 'I came to talk about football.'

Thorneycroft was caught off guard. An expression of frank puzzlement leapt across his face.

'Football? What on earth do you mean?'

'Perhaps I should be a little more specific.'

Conrad settled deeper into his leather swivel chair, fingers drumming absently on the arm rest.

'I am interested in one particular football club.'

'Which is?'

'Bradcaster City.'

As he always did in conversation with Conrad, Thorneycroft felt unsettled, struggling to ascribe motive, second guessing the thrust of the argument.

'I'm afraid I don't understand.'

Conrad smiled but no warmth touched his eyes.

'You may not be aware of this but each day I read every single newspaper that I own. You know I think the Herald is a fine paper. But I am curious about your stance on Bradcaster City. You seem very supportive of the regime there – despite their recent, ah, difficulties.'

'Arthur Redwood is a decent man. He doesn't deserve all the flak that's flying around. Sometimes football fans have a short memory.'

Conrad waved a hand dismissively.

'Oh Rex, please. He's living on past glories. The club hasn't won anything that matters for over 30 years.'

Thorneycroft was irritated.

'Why the sudden interest in Bradcaster City, Michael?'

he asked with unaccustomed sharpness. 'And what exactly are you getting at? You didn't come all the way from London just to talk about football.'

Conrad opened his palms in a gesture of conciliation. His steel trap smile flashed once again.

'Look, you know I leave my editors to their own devices. I am simply making a suggestion, please don't over react.'

In a harder tone, he added: 'But this newspaper has a reputation for straight talking. Maybe you ought to take a tougher line on Bradcaster City.'

In mid-sentence, Conrad rose abruptly to shake Thorneycroft's hand with a grip of iron.

'Listen to the voice of the people, Rex.'

That was the end of the conversation. As Conrad swept from the office into the newsroom, he clapped a reporter on the back and, still walking, tossed out jocular phrases of encouragement. Everyone was staring into their computer screens.

When he had gone, Thorneycroft allowed himself an ironical smile. At least he still had a job.

But the long knives were out for Arthur Redwood and Bradcaster City Football Club. And he was to be the unwilling chief assassin.

'Come on!' Dougie McNally's raw Glaswegian voice knifed through the air. 'Get your fucking heads on it!'

It was a cold, damp morning in early winter. Bradcaster City's training ground was set amid a featureless tangle of industrial scrubland. Around the perimeter of its four pitches was a ten-feet high fence of razor barbed wire.

Above this decaying landscape, the sky was as black as night. A thick, chilling drizzle had set in and was gnawing its way into the bones. McNally's mood was as foul as the weather.

'You're all a bunch of fucking pansies!' he screamed. 'No wonder we're bottom of the league. You make me sick.'

The tracksuited manager was standing in the centre circle, with a row of footballs lined up in front of him. Forty yards ahead of him, his first team was scattered in the penalty area, five defenders marking five attackers.

McNally had spent a hour thumping balls as high as howitzer shells into the box. With their backs to goal, the attackers were at a perpetual disadvantage.

Almost every time, a big defender would rise and head the ball away or it would be claimed by the goalkeeper. But occasionally there would be a ricochet – the ball spinning off a shoulder or an outstretched boot – or a moment of indecision.

And the ball would end up nestling in the back of the net.

The sheer grinding monotony of the tactic was making the players refractory and mutinous. There were continual whispered oaths.

Some of their duels were turning into niggles of increasing viciousness. Elbows were flying, shirts being yanked, attackers sent sprawling into the mud by clumsy challenges from behind.

McNally sent yet another ball looping into the area. Dave Stewart, the captain, was underneath it, watching its trajectory with his marker breathing down his neck.

As the ball dropped, Stewart was backing into the defender, who was shoving hard with his chest, his arms snaking over Stewart's shoulders, holding him down.

Jostling for position, the players became more and more frenzied, arms flailing. Losing control completely, Stewart jerked his elbow back hard into the other man's face and felt a crunch.

The ball missed them both and bounced harmlessly through to the keeper. As Stewart turned, he saw his marker flat out on his back, blood pumping from his nose. He was groaning softly.

The rest of the players looked on in stunned disbelief. Even Stewart himself wore a shocked look, unable quite to comprehend what he had done.

McNally was running across the turf.

'What the fucking hell is going on?' he bellowed. 'Jesus Christ!'

Reaching the injured player, McNally bent down and lifted up his head to survey the damage. Fresh blood was smeared all over his face and had copiously stained his jersey.

'Don't worry, laddie, you'll live,' he said, coolly assessing the shattered nose. 'Get back inside and get yourself cleaned up.'

He dragged the player to his feet and pushed him off in the direction of the changing rooms, giving him a clip on the buttocks as he went. The player moved slowly and unsteadily, shaking his head to try to clear his senses.

Rounding on Stewart, McNally's voice was icy: 'What was all that about, Dave? You're supposed to be setting an example, for fuck's sake.'

Stewart's arms hung limply at his sides but his expression bore the signs of swelling anger.

'He was all over me, boss. You could see that.'

'It looked to me like he was doing his job.'

'He was asking for it, I tell you,' said the captain in a low voice.

'He'll be out for at least a fortnight. He's the only decent fucking centre half we've got. And you break his nose.'

McNally gave Stewart a hard, contemptuous look.

'You stupid bastard,' he spat in his brutal Gorbals accent.

Stewart's eyes blazed with resentment: 'Look boss, what did you expect? You spend all morning hoofing the ball into the box so we can fight over it. Larry was right up my arse every time. He just had to go, he was getting on my bloody nerves. What was the point? It had nothing to do with football.'

There were murmurs of assent from the other players, who were standing around with hands on hip, sensing a confrontation.

'Well you'd better get used to it,' said McNally. 'Because that's the way we're going to play from now on.'

A look of astonishment spread across Stewart's face.

'Not Route One?'

'That's right, laddie. I'm not going to let this club go down. If that's what I have to do, well, too bad.'

Stewart shook his head slowly. 'You just can't. Not at Bradcaster. You'll get lynched.'

McNally gave a bitter and cynical laugh. He made a dismissive gesture with his hand and started to walk back to the centre circle.

After a few paces he turned and shouted back to Stewart: 'I'm not putting my arse on the line just to play pretty football, Dave. You keep losing and I'm the first one to get screwed. You're going to have to pull your guts out and bang the ball in where it hurts. First time, every time. That way, we might start to win some matches.'

Reaching the churned-up turf at the centre circle, he pulled another half-dozen practice balls from a net and lined them up alongside the rest.

'OK,' he called out. 'Let's try again, shall we?'

With a mighty punt of his right leg, he sent another ball spinning high into the penalty area.

'And this time, make sure you get it fucking right.'

It was ten minutes to three on a Saturday afternoon in December.

A 20,000-strong crowd was packed into the stadium of Second Division Bristol United. A pale wintery sun barely warmed the air, as shivering fans thrust their hands deep into coat pockets or passed around steaming Thermos flasks.

All around the ground, there was a buzz of anticipation.

Bristol United had been a workmanlike mid-table side for a decade. Occasionally, they had flirted with the drop into the Third Division; even less regularly found themselves on the fringes of the promotion race.

But, by and large, fans had grown used to solid and unspectacular consolidation.

All that had changed this year. Now the team was pushing strongly for a place in what next season would become the Super League.

There was a single reason for this transformation of Bristol United from also-rans to pace setters, a change which had caught the imagination of the whole city and boosted home game attendances to full capacity.

His name was Augustus Simmons.

Just at that moment, he was emerging from the players' changing room, suffering the familiar constriction in the pit of his stomach, the gnawing of nausea.

Simmons was at the back of a shuffling Indian file of United players, their studs drumming on the tiled floor.

They were moving down a corridor towards a rectangle of light. It was the gateway to the chanting of the crowd, which ebbed and flowed in waves down the tunnel.

Simmons shivered momentarily. He was holding a football, his long fingers wrapped around it in an almost sensual caress.

As they neared the end of the tunnel, the players speeded to a trot and then to a run. The clatter of boots was deafening.

The crowd erupted as the first United player emerged blinking into the watery sunlight, a great roar that engulfed the stadium and swelled massively into the air.

Simmons rushed through a forest of arms at the tunnel's end. Leaning over from the concrete steps of the stand, they were reaching out to touch him as he passed just as the devout might touch a saint.

He hit the turf and lengthened his stride, all grace and silky power. The cacophony in the stadium grew still more intense.

His nerves forgotten, Simmons seemed to float on the noise as he tossed the ball in front of him and, from the very edge of the penalty area, smashed a shot high into the roof of the net.

The crowd began to chant his name in a huge, rolling wave of sound, bass notes that reverberated behind the ribs.

'Sii-mmm-oo-o! Sii-mmm-oo-o! Sii-mmm-oo-o!'

As his team mates mingled around him, flicking passes to each other, exchanging banter, Simmons remained aloof. He jogged slowly across the grass, turning sharply occasionally or bending to stretch his hamstrings.

After the first surge of adrenalin when he burst onto the pitch, he was now completely focused within himself. He could no longer hear the crowd, although it was as noisy and vibrant as before.

The referee called the two captains into the centre circle for the toss. The opposition called correctly and elected to play north, away from United's Kop End and its fanatical supporters.

Standing with the ball at his feet, Simmons was suddenly aware of a wall of sound before his concentration cocooned him again.

The referee sounded a single shrill note on his whistle to start the game. Simmons tapped the ball forward a couple of yards to a team mate standing alongside him and sprinted hard into the heart of the opposition defence.

Immediately, he was picked up by a big combative central defender. Simmons turned, looking for the ball, and felt his marker tight against his back, jostling him.

The United midfield still held possession, fending off a couple of lunging tackles. Then the ball was threaded through along the floor to Simmons, 30 yards out, ducking and spinning to try to lose his marker.

Controlling the ball instantly with his instep, Simmons turned away and just at that moment the big defender came sliding in. His exposed studs smashed into Simmons' standing leg just above the Achilles tendon.

The force of the challenge sent Simmons hurtling into the air, his feet arching above his head before he crashed heavily onto his back. He lay writhing on the ground, hands clutching at his calf, his face racked with pain.

The referee gave an angry blast on his whistle and came dashing over, already reaching into his breast pocket for a yellow card. The defender was smiling ruefully, palms open to the referee in a pantomime of innocence.

There was tumult among the packed United fans, who were yelling abuse and clutching their faces in horror and disbelief.

'Sorry ref, I went for the ball,' pleaded the player. 'He was just too quick for me.'

The referee brandished the yellow card with a straight-armed gesture, bristling with affronted authority, and waved him away. Instead the player strode over to where Simmons still lay supine on the ground.

Bending over him, he clapped Simmons on the shoulder in an apparent act of apology.

Then he leaned still closer, his back to the referee, and hissed into his ear: 'Look out, black boy. Plenty more where that came from.'

After prolonged treatment, Simmons was able to rise gingerly to his feet, testing his tendon and grimacing.

Each time he placed his weight on his left leg, a white-hot shaft of pain shot up his calf.

Simmons spent the rest of the first half hobbling harmlessly in midfield, trying to run off his injury. He touched the ball no more than half a dozen times.

Without his cutting edge up front, United looked impotent and aimless. Time and again, moves broke down at the edge of the penalty area for want of a telling run into space.

Gradually, the opposing team took a stranglehold on the game, controlling midfield and breaking swiftly down the flanks. A ragged United were relieved to reach the interval with the game still scoreless.

After ten minutes with an ice pack clasped to the back of his leg, Simmons was moving easier in the second half. He resumed his place at the head of the attack, making darting diagonal runs, pulling his marker all over the field from the touchline to the six-yard box.

The big defender was beginning to tire. Each time he received the ball, Simmons seemed to have a yard to spare, to turn or to lay the ball off. Suddenly yawning gaps were beginning to appear in the opposition defence.

Waiting at the near post for a corner, Simmons jabbed his elbow hard into the ribs of his panting marker.

'Enjoying this, you fucking donkey?'

It was just five minutes from the end when the decisive moment arrived.

Foraging deep, Simmons took the ball direct from his own central defender. Spinning out of one tackle and shimmying past another, he found acres of space gaping in front of him.

Now he was running at pace at the heart of the defence. Forty yards out, the cover was converging on him. But at the last moment, he flicked the ball wide to a team mate at the corner of the box.

It was the perfect one-two, the return steered behind

turning defenders. Hurdling another challenge, Simmons surged into the area and saw the goalkeeper rushing out, spreading himself.

He delayed the shot for a fraction of a second, just enough for the goalkeeper to fall and commit himself. Then, instead of the blast that everyone expected, Simmons scooped the ball over the prostrate body.

It dropped, bounced against the inside of the far post and settled gently in the back of the net.

With a sweet, arrogant smile of triumph, Simmons turned away with one arm raised. He took a long, deep bow in front of the Bristol United dugout.

It was a goal of genius. Everyone in the stadium knew they had witnessed something extraordinary. The crowd was electrified. Even the opposition supporters were smiling, shaking their heads, applauding.

At that precise moment, in north London, a referee brought another football match to a close.

Playing away from home, a new-style Bradcaster City had just lost five goals to nil, their heaviest defeat since the Thirties.

Arthur Redwood did not normally sleep late. A former Army captain with a distinguished war record, he had never shaken off the habit of rising at six o'clock exactly.

But this time his internal clock had failed him. It was the Monday morning after Bradcaster's disastrous expedition to the capital.

He had travelled the long journey back up the M1 in the players' coach, which was as quiet and sombre as a hearse.

Dougie McNally had sat alone, his jaw clenched and eyes as dark as night. Among the players, there had been no horseplay, no conversation at all. They had simply stared out of the window as the motorway unfurled

34

or closed their eyes and pretended to sleep.

No one had dared to look at Redwood.

All day on Sunday, Redwood had left the telephone off the hook. He needed time to absorb the significance of what had happened and, as he always did in times of crisis, withdrew into himself completely.

Right into the evening and the early hours of the next day, he had brooded.

One room of Redwood's house was devoted to memories of Bradcaster City Football Club. Rows of glass-fronted cases held replica trophies, shirts, scarves, pennants, signed footballs.

There were also dozens of photographs in gilt frames. Redwood at Wembley in 1959, taking the FA Cup from the Queen with an expression at once stunned and ecstatic. A team photograph from the same period, the players standing rigidly to attention with their Brylcreemed hair and voluminous shorts, Redwood discreet in the background in a long coat and trilby.

In this room, in the house where he had lived alone since the death of his wife 12 years before, Redwood had created a kind of shrine to Bradcaster City.

Here he had agonised for hours and hours. He knew he was surrounded by mere relics of the past, the glories of three decades ago. His achievements had grown musty with age.

When he had finally taken to his bed, he slept only fitfully, waking every hour bathed in sweat. Near dawn, utterly exhausted, he had fallen into a deep and dreamless sleep that lasted almost until noon.

Disturbed by this break in routine, he rose and washed punctiliously in cold water, splashing his face to awaken his numb brain. He dressed and, moving downstairs, replaced the telephone handset in its cradle.

Almost immediately, it began to ring shrilly. Redwood

puckered his brow and paused for a moment before he picked it up, without speaking.

'Arthur, for Christ's sake, what have you been doing? I've been trying to get through all bloody morning.'

It was Sid Graveney. To Redwood, his voice seemed to come from far away, as if he were shouting from inside a locked room. Graveney sounded panicked.

'Have you seen this morning's Herald?'

'No, not yet,' said Redwood. 'Why?'

'Just read it, Arthur. All over the front page. Just read it.'

The line went dead.

A sense of foreboding began to settle in the pit of Redwood's stomach. He had the Herald delivered every morning and a rolled-up copy was jammed into his letterbox.

Feverishly, he seized it and yanked it out. The spring-loaded flap slammed shut. He smoothed out the creased paper and looked at the front page.

His own face stared back at him above the caption 'Arthur Redwood: too old to cope?' The photograph, taken during a recent illness, had been deliberately chosen to make him look haggard and frail.

A huge banner headline dominated the page. It read, simply and starkly in bold capitals: 'NOW REDWOOD MUST GO'.

He stood motionless for a long time, reading the editorial over and again until it seemed like a cruel litany. He had never felt so crushed, such a sense of betrayal.

They said he encouraged the club to look backwards. That he was no longer in control of a manager who wanted to win at all costs. They said a fresh broom was needed to sweep away the rubbish of the past.

For the first time in more than 30 years, Arthur Redwood felt the icy fingers of doubt caress his spine.

Maybe, just maybe, the Herald was right.

SIMMO IS NOT FOR SALE

Big clubs get 'hands off' warning

BRISTOL UNITED boss Bill Waddell has acted quickly to damp down transfer speculation about British football's latest wonder boy, Gus Simmons.

Simmo's sparkling solo effort on Saturday was his tenth goal of the season and several First Division outfits are said to be keen to snap up the youngster.

But last night Waddell issued a 'hands off' warning to the big boys: 'There is no way Gus Simmons is for sale,' he declared. 'He is a vital part of our promotion plans and any manager thinking of approaching him will be told where to go in no uncertain terms.'

Yet with Simmons' contract due to expire at the end of the season, Waddell is surely putting on a brave face.

There is no way humble

Bristol United can match the kind of deal Simmons could command at a larger club.

The 22-year-old black star only broke into the United first team midway through last season but he made an immediate impact. His dream start to this campaign already has the pundits dubbing him football's outstanding prospect.

Yet doubts about his temperament persist. He has clashed several times with Waddell over his growing taste for the champagne lifestyle and was once docked a week's wages for skipping a training session.

Simmons himself was reluctant to comment on the transfer rumours: 'I just want to help Bristol United get into the Super League,' he said.

'This sort of talk just makes it more difficult to concentrate. As far as I'm concerned, I am a United player and that is the end of it.'

When Sid Graveney was worried, he would get in his car and drive. Not aimlessly, but with single-minded intent to the same part of the city each time.

In north west Bradcaster, there was a ragged square mile of back streets which contained fast food joints and massage parlours, cheap hotels and dubious nightclubs.

It was nearly midnight as Graveney's black 7-Series

BMW nosed slowly down the streets. Rain was falling in a great slanting sheet. The shop front lights created a pale wash of reds, blues and yellows in the puddles in the gutter.

It was like a late night in any big city, anywhere. A couple of drunks slumped at a bus stop. A gang of lads crossing the road, all macho swagger in their ale, laughing and swearing.

Then Graveney saw two girls sheltering in a doorway, right under a street lamp. One was still in her teens, straggly dark hair plastered around her face, which was foxy and watchful.

She wore a cheap unbuttoned raincoat and beneath it a tight black mini skirt, exposed as she stood with hands on hips. Her pale bare legs reflected an amber glow from the light.

The other girl was slightly older, her features harder, more aggressive, as her eyes swept the street. A red lycra dress emphasised the jut of her breasts and an incipient roll of fat at her midriff.

Graveney's car halted opposite the doorway and the electric window of the BMW hummed down.

Leaning across the passenger seat, Graveney craned his neck to look up at the girls, who had stepped forward into the rain.

'Are you working?'

'Might be,' said the elder of the two with a broad Bradcaster accent. 'What are you after, love?'

'How about the two of you? In the car.'

The tarts exchanged glances and the younger one shrugged.

'A hundred quid. We'll do what you like but it's got to be with a johnny.'

'Get in the back,' ordered Graveney curtly. 'And for God's sake keep your heads down.'

39

He sped away and gradually Bradcaster's streets gave way to industrial wasteland and finally to bleak moors. Graveney relaxed visibly.

He broke a leaden ten-minute silence, glancing over his left shoulder into the back of the car: 'What are your names then?'

'Never mind that. Where the fuck are we going?'

The girls were getting restless. They were shifting uncomfortably in their seats and peering into the deepening gloom.

'Don't you worry,' coaxed Graveney. 'Just trying to find somewhere nice and quiet. We don't want to be disturbed, do we?'

He pulled the BMW off the road and ran it 50 yards down a farmer's dirt track. He turned off the engine and killed the headlights. The inside of the car was bathed in pale, phosphorescent moonlight.

'Right, mister. Money up front or you get nowt.'

She thrust her open palm over his shoulder. Graveney reached into his breast pocket for his wallet and counted out five £20 notes into her hand.

'All right?'

'Ay. What do you fancy?'

Graveney pocketed the car keys.

'I think I'll join you.'

Within moments he was between the girls on the back seat, breathing heavily. Already the bulge of his erection was visible.

'We don't do kissing, OK?'

'I don't want to kiss you, you dirty slag. Why would I want to do that? Just keep your lip buttoned.'

Graveney turned to the younger girl, who had remained silent throughout the journey.

'You,' he said. 'Take this off.'

He tugged at her raincoat. Wordlessly, refusing to look

at him, she slipped it over her shoulders and wriggled out of it.

'Now your top.'

This time she fixed Graveney with her eyes, a look which seemed to search out the very quick of him. Still she did not speak.

Artlessly, she pulled the top over her head. As her arms straightened, her breasts lifted and tightened, the nipples hard in the cool night air.

'Oh, lovely,' whispered Graveney involuntarily.

He reached out to touch her with trembling fingers and cupped each breast in turn, massaging their soft shape. His breath came in short gasps. She held each of his hands at the wrist, neither encouraging nor preventing the caress.

'Suck me,' said Graveney to the other whore, without sparing her a glance.

As he continued squeezing the breasts of the younger girl, her partner slowly unzipped his fly and reached inside for his hardness. He shuddered as her fingers closed around his shaft.

She eased it out and, as she did so, bent her head into his lap. With no preliminary, she engulfed the head of his penis with her warm mouth, one hand still clasped tight around the base.

Graveney's eyes were closed. One of his hands strayed from the girl's breasts, across her bare downy midriff, reaching for the inside of her thighs.

By now the other tart was taking him deeper and deeper into her mouth, her hand working furiously. He could feel her sharp teeth rubbing on his glans and beyond them a moist, accommodating softness.

Graveney's fingers crept inside the girl's mini skirt. He searched out the tight bud of her clitoris and rubbed it gently with tiny circular movements.

She made no sound but began to rotate her pelvis in time

41

with the motion. He parted the lips of her vagina and thrust a finger into the warm tunnel.

Graveney let out a low groan of pleasure but still the girl stayed mute. Unconsciously, his hand began to pick up the rhythm of the tart's head bobbing in his lap, faster and faster.

He felt an unbearable tension cramming his senses and his body was racked with deep, shuddering spasms, each more intense than before.

Just at the right moment, the whore withdrew her mouth and his semen spurted all over the car's dark upholstery, creating a milky stain.

Graveney slumped back, panting.

'Oh God,' he kept repeating. 'Oh my God.'

In the faces of the girls, there was no hint of pleasure, simply disgust and contempt. Immediately they began rearranging themselves, tugging at clothing, ending the transaction.

In a still, small voice, Graveney heard himself say: 'OK girls, let's get you home.'

Once again he had tasted the bitter fag end of lust. It was like a sickness inside him, a dependency that needed constant gratification.

But it was the only thing that made him feel truly alive.

The headquarters of Spacelink, the satellite television company, was a massive construction of glass and tubular steel in London's Docklands.

Rearing up from the side of the Thames, more than 20 storeys high, it was incandescent under a bright winter sun, its myriad windows shimmering and glinting like the facets of a huge jewel.

Michael Conrad was gazing out across the river from the top floor of Spacelink Tower, towards Rotherhithe and Bermondsey on the south shore. On the water, pleasure craft bobbed like toys and a huge dredger moved idly down the centre channel.

Conrad was sitting at the head of the boardroom table, while men in slate-grey suits and tastefully flamboyant ties waited in silence.

Still staring out through the plate glass window which dominated the office, he said in a dream-like voice: 'So how much will it cost?'

The silence grew uneasy. One of the men cleared his throat and replied: 'Of course, we don't know what ITV will bid. But we might need to put as much as £250 million on the table, maybe even £300 million. It's hard to say exactly.'

Conrad turned abruptly away from the window and his voice hardened.

'You must have some idea, for God's sake. Do you expect me to bid blind?'

The man looked acutely uncomfortable.

'Well, our contacts suggest they are pretty desperate to get the Super League rights. Their ratings at the moment for live Sunday football are good. The word is they will go as high as they can afford.'

'Which is?'

There was a hesitation, long enough for the man at Conrad's elbow, Spacelink managing director Tom Haslam, to cut in smoothly.

'Michael, you know it's unpredictable. It depends on how optimistic their forecasts for advertising revenue are. There's no way we can second guess that.'

'Let me put it another way,' said Conrad. 'How high can we go before we get a nose bleed?'

Haslam paused, then replied: 'I honestly don't know. The Super League wants the deal to be over five years. We might sell another three or four million dishes in that time but, frankly, the market isn't expanding as we hoped.'

'So how high can we go?' repeated Conrad evenly.

'I would say any more than £150 million would be a serious risk to our cash flow position. Things are volatile at the moment.'

For the first time, Conrad looked directly at Haslam, whom he had poached from one of the biggest independent TV companies to run Spacelink. Haslam held his gaze.

'Tom, you know that won't be enough.'

Haslam shrugged. 'Probably not, but on the current forecasts we can't offer more. The banks just won't wear it.'

Conrad made a noise of exasperation.

'Then we shall have to change the rules of the game.'

Haslam's normally level temper was beginning to fray at the edges. This subject had been thrashed out many times before.

'What the hell do you mean by that, Michael?'

A quiet intensity had settled over Conrad. For him this was a moment of supreme truth.

He fixed Tom Haslam, one of his few friends, with a gaze that was almost compassionate.

'We launched Spacelink on a dream, you know that. We thought we were grasping the future, that every home in Britain would have a satellite dish. But we were wrong, Tom. We can never compete with the terrestrial channels for advertising, their audiences are just too big. We'll always be left with the crumbs.

'There's only one way to generate the money we need to be a major player. The people who watch the programmes have to be properly exploited. I don't just mean the movie channel. I mean the news channel, the main entertainment service and especially the sports channel.

'We send them out scrambled and if you want to watch,

you have to put your hand in your pocket. I want every single minute of our air time to be bought and paid for by the viewers. It's the only way.'

There was a stunned silence around the boardroom table. Almost casually, Conrad was proposing to overturn the strategy of the last two years.

Spacelink's marketing director Simon DeVere had grown increasingly agitated. He was squirming in his seat and compulsively screwing and unscrewing the top of his fountain pen.

Finally he broke in, his voice strident: 'For God's sake, what are you saying? We've spent millions claiming massive household penetration for satellite. Now you just want to chuck all that away. I am going to have to rethink the entire publicity and marketing campaign, right from scratch.'

Conrad's voice was like a steel blade: 'Well, let's just say that somebody will have to do that.'

DeVere's face slackened and collapsed. With darting eyes, he looked around the table for support but everyone was carefully avoiding his gaze. They were trying to absorb the changing circumstances, erect their own defences.

Haslam was shaking his head.

'Michael, this is not how we saw it at the beginning. If we go down that route, we'll always be a minority channel. Is that really what you want?'

'It will be a profitable minority. That is all I am interested in.'

Haslam looked hard at Conrad, deep into his impenetrable grey eyes. He knew this was his final chance.

He said simply: 'Michael, that isn't true.'

For a second, something visibly flickered within Conrad, something of his inner self. But then the look he gave Haslam left no room for any further doubt.

45

'Right gentlemen,' said Conrad briskly, turning away. 'Any further business?'

'I'm telling you Harry, this could be a big story. We've got to run it.'

Colin Gregory of the Daily World was getting impatient. He was in the surprisingly small and dingy office of Harry Walters, who ran the World's northern office in Bradcaster.

Walters was a tough Cockney who viewed his posting to Bradcaster as a demotion. Gregory, a northerner through and through, had always regarded him as an arrogant interloper.

Both men were smoking. Each had refused the other's cigarettes, although they were the same brand. A dense cloud of acrid blue smoke hovered above them.

'How can we be sure of the figures?' demanded Walters.

'Look, how many more times, this comes right from the top. Bradcaster City are on the verge of bankruptcy. They owe nearly £15 million. If they keep losing money at the turnstiles, they'll be belly up before the end of the season. The banks will just foreclose.'

Walters looked doubtful. He was shaking his head and pursing his lips in a way that made Gregory infuriated.

'How have they managed to make such a bloody cock-up of everything? It doesn't seem very likely, does it?'

Gregory had reached the end of his tether.

'Fucking hell, Harry, what would you know about it? All you're interested in is tits and shagging stories. You know bugger all about football.'

For a second a wave of anger swept across Walter's pale and flabby features. Then he threw back his head and roared with laughter, a genuine belly laugh that shattered the tension in the tiny room.

'Tits sell papers, Colin,' he said, his jowls still shaking

with cynical amusement. 'We're all tit men on the Daily World, even you.'

Despite himself, Gregory was beginning to smile.

'Right then,' said Walters with a magnanimous wave of his hand. 'If it's so bloody good, talk me through it again.'

Slightly mollified, Gregory continued.

'They got greedy,' he said simply. 'They realised their training ground was a prime piece of real estate, right in the heart of Bradcaster. But instead of selling it to a developer, they thought they could make even more money by building an office complex themselves and acting as landlords.

'The players got shunted out into facilities that would disgrace a Fourth Divison team and they razed the changing rooms and dug up the pitches.

'Half way through construction, the property market crashed. By the time it was built, they couldn't give away the space. Even now only one floor is occupied and it's a ten-storey building. It's turned into an absolute bloody white elephant.'

Walters was still far from convinced: 'But how come nobody knows about this? Bradcaster's accounts are public knowledge.'

'Of course they are, I checked them out myself. But the crafty bastards are disguising the real deficit by valuing the office complex as a major asset. In reality it's practically worthless and the whole club is disappearing up shit creek. Honestly Harry, they could go bang any day now.'

Gregory was growing passionate. This was one of the best exclusives of his career – the imminent collapse of perhaps the most famous football club in England.

But his frustration was growing too because he could sense something was bothering Walters. The editor was wearily rubbing the bridge of his nose between thumb and forefinger.

Finally he said: 'Are you sure this stands up, Colin? If we get it wrong, Arthur Redwood will sue. He can be a cantankerous old bastard.'

'Harry, I told you. This comes from a cast-iron source.'

'So why won't you tell me who it is?'

Gregory let out a long sigh of anguish and irritation.

'You know I can't do that. The conversation was totally off the record, that was the understanding.'

Walters gave Gregory a sly look.

'If your source is good, we'll run it. Not the back page lead but the front page splash, I promise you. But I have to know where this comes from.'

There was a long, tense silence. Gregory stared down into his lap, wrestling with himself.

Eventually he said softly: 'OK Harry. But I want your word that it will go no further than this room.'

Walters nodded.

'It was Sid Graveney.'

'What the hell is this?'

Gus Simmons squinted at the menu and then thrust it across the table, his finger pointing out a particular dish.

'Roti de Cailles? A brace of local quails, stuffed with smoked chicken and peach and served on a pool of Pineau de Charente sauce. Very nice.'

Steve Wilde craned forward, casting his eyes further down the list. He was dressed in a pale blue Hugo Boss suit and a Lacoste polo-shirt. The head waiter had already greeted him expansively by name.

'This is also superb,' he said. 'Foie de Veau, which is grilled calf's liver. The cognac and thyme sauce has to be tasted to be believed.'

'Oh God! I don't know how you could. A calf's liver. Yuk!'

Melanie Simmons was screwing up her frank, pretty

face in distaste and giggling like a schoolgirl. She had never been to a restaurant quite like this and she was full of gangling, nervous energy.

Wilde flashed her a smile breathtaking in its charm and emptiness. He was the ultimate public relations man: plausible, magnetic, polished.

He had a gift, which he ruthlessly cultivated, for making his companions feel like the most important people in the world.

'Melanie, my dear girl,' he murmured. 'You are much too sentimental. But why don't you try this instead, the Pot-au-feu de Faisan?'

Shyly, glancing first at Simmons for his reaction, she asked in her broad Bristolian accent: 'What does that mean? Do you think I will like it?"

'It's pheasant roasted in red wine. I tried it the last time I was here and it was beautiful, succulent.'

He rolled the word around his mouth with sensual emphasis, flirting with her. She lowered her eyes and smirked.

Simmons cut in abruptly, a little nettled: 'Do you get out this way much? I thought your offices were in London.'

'Oh, I'm a bit of a gipsy really,' replied Wilde smoothly. 'I go wherever my clients are. When I find myself in the West Country, I always eat here. It is a magnificent restaurant.'

La Belle Epoque was a meticulous recreation of a Parisian eating house, lit by ornate golden lamps and decorated with exquisite statuettes and hand-painted plates of fine china.

Where they sat, between a pair of marble pillars, a silken canopy stretched above their heads. Everywhere in the room hung heavy drapes in rich blues and greens.

'It is very nice,' said Simmons evenly. 'We're grateful for your trouble. But I already have an agent, I told you that.'

49

'Please,' said Wilde, holding up his hands. 'Let's not spoil our meal talking about business. Are we ready to order?'

He made an almost imperceptible gesture towards the head waiter, who was lurking discreetly nearby and appeared at his elbow instantly.

'Mr Wilde?' enquired the immaculate Frenchman. 'What would you like? Can we tempt you again with the Rable de Chevreuil?'

Wilde mused theatrically for a moment: 'Mmm, I haven't had venison for a little while. Yes, why not? My friend shall have the Foie de Veau and his lovely wife the Pot-au-feu de Faisan.'

He looked at both Simmons and Melanie in turn, playing the genial host to the hilt, completely in command.

'And can I suggest as a special treat we all start with the tartare of Gressingham duck? Alphonse here will tell you it is quite outstanding.'

The waiter smiled broadly.

'Indeed, sir.'

Simmons glanced at Melanie, who answered him with a helpless shrug.

'OK, that sounds good,' he said.

Now Wilde was studying the wine list, his brow furrowed.

'Something robust to drink, I think,' he said slowly, scanning the vintages. 'Do you like claret, Gus? How about the Chateau Brannaire Duluc Ducru 1983? I think that would do splendidly.'

Alphonse disappeared as subtly as a wisp of mist melting in the morning sun.

For the next hour, as dishes of extraordinary delicacy and beauty were consumed, Wilde kept up his relentless small talk. Shifting eye contact between the couple, he wrapped them in the warm and comfortable cocoon of his voice.

Three bottles of fine claret were brought to the table. Yet as Wilde splashed the wine with prodigal abandon into the glasses of Simmons and his wife, it was noticeable he took hardly a sip himself.

Finally all three sat nursing huge Armagnacs, swilling the rich amber liquid around their glasses, releasing the fragrance.

Simmons felt as though his brain was wrapped in cotton wool. Melanie, having first grown giggly and talkative with the wine, was struggling to keep her eyes open.

A dozy smile had spread across her features and lodged itself there immovably. Her chin was nodding into her chest and her eyelids quivering with the onset of sleep.

'Now Gus,' said Wilde. 'You are a very remarkable young man. You've scored a lot of goals and all the tabloids are talking about you. That's because they have recognised something important in you. It's called star quality.'

Simmons stirred himself to speak, his tongue thick and his brain uncooperative: 'I think you're bullshitting me. What are you getting at?'

'Simply that in this world you have to hold out for what you are worth.'

Simmons laughed and leaned across the table towards Wilde, his eyes unfocused.

'And what am I worth?'

'You could name your price, Gus. Think about it. Your contract is up at the end of the season. Pretty soon all the big First Division clubs will be beating a path to your door.'

Melanie said wearily: 'More money. We have too much money already.'

Wilde ignored her completely.

'Gus, a footballer's career is bloody short. I'm talking about sponsorship, endorsements, a nice fat signing-on fee. I know the agent you're working with now and he's a nice guy. But he is strictly small time, just peanuts. With my help, you could be the most famous black man this country has ever seen.'

Simmons laughed loudly again: 'My mum would be so pleased.'

Wilde wondered if the third bottle of claret had been a mistake. He looked hard at Simmons.

'Please, I am being perfectly serious. You don't understand your own potential.'

In a voice which was suddenly clear and steady, Simmons said: 'All right, Steve. We'll do it your way but a word of warning. Don't ever try to make me into something that I'm not.'

Bradcaster's town hall was a monument to Victorian confidence, an ugly but strangely impressive mock Gothic extravagance that dominated the city's skyline.

At night, lit by dozens of sodium lights, it looked like a gigantic fairy castle. But just a few streets behind it, the pimps and the pushers were part of a more sinister reality.

Inside the town hall was the vast and opulent council chamber, its vaulted ceiling at least 50 feet above a patterned marble floor. It looked and felt like the interior of a cathedral.

But tonight the space was reserved for more worldly matters. Long banqueting tables were draped in crisp pure white linen, glinting with silver cutlery and crystal glasses.

In the centre of the room, creating a vibrating hubbub of chatter and gossip, were more than 200 people. The men were ceremonial in black dinner suits and scarlet cummerbunds; their partners expansive and ornamental, shimmering in their finery.

This was the annual dinner of the Bradcaster Chamber

of Commerce, attended by all the wealthy and influential in the city.

The aristocratic and the self-made exchanged anecdotes. There were used car dealers and scrap metal merchants, bankers and businessmen, the famous and the notorious.

As usual, a pair of distinguished after-dinner speakers had been persuaded to address these notables. One was Arthur Redwood: almost a legend in Bradcaster, universally admired as a man of principle and integrity.

The other was media baron Michael Conrad. About him it would have been safer to say that opinion was divided.

Characteristically, Redwood had come to the function alone. He stood slightly apart from a small group of elderly men, the glass of white wine in his hand untouched.

He gave an occasional tight-lipped smile at some limp joke; he ventured the odd diffident remark before lapsing again into a broody silence.

As chairman of Bradcaster City Football Club, Redwood felt it was important to be visible at such events. But the crushing superficiality of social discourse made him uncomfortable.

If he could not speak his mind, Redwood preferred to say nothing.

By contrast Conrad was charming and voluble, holding court to a tight gaggle of hangers-on. At his side was his young wife Alexandra, in a tiered cobweb dress of lichen green and asphalt grey by Karl Lagerfeld for Chanel.

It was a supreme gesture of 'nouveau pauvre' chic, its pattern like compressed tin cans, teetering on the very edge of camp parody. She looked utterly unlike any other woman in the room.

Half-Italian on her mother's side, Alexandra Conrad had a sultry, heavy-lidded, indolent beauty. Her olive skin was flawless, her hair a cascade of raven-black that spilled over her shoulders towards the jutting V of her breasts in the tight bodice.

She was smiling but saying very little. Men orbited around her, mesmerised. She was quite magnetic but the allure stopped at her dark eyes, which were like a steel door being slammed shut.

Conrad was chatting easily, slapping men on the back, flirting with their wives, occasionally throwing back his head with a roguish roar of laughter.

Then he caught a glimpse of Arthur Redwood, who had sidled away from his companions and was leaning against a great stone pillar in a corner of the chamber.

For a moment the smile died on his lips and something hard crept behind his eyes. Then his face resumed its casual mask and, making his excuses, he slipped off through the throng towards Redwood.

Easing his way past a thickset councillor, he emerged suddenly into the space occupied by Redwood, who was momentarily startled.

'Hello again Arthur,' said Conrad suavely. 'They said you were the other speaker. Glad to see you.'

He thrust out his right arm in greeting. Redwood ignored it and nodded curtly.

His voice was icy: 'Mr Conrad, I can't imagine what we have to talk about. Please excuse me.'

He turned to go but Conrad caught his elbow with a powerful grip. Although Redwood felt each of the fingers digging into his arm, Conrad was still smiling.

'Arthur please, calm down. I promise you I have no control over what the Herald writes. Just for the record, I thought it was downright bloody unfair.'

The older man stared in frank disbelief at Conrad but said nothing. He felt the the fingers loosening from his elbow.

'Come outside with me for a second,' whispered Conrad. 'I have something I would like to discuss with you in private.'

The men slipped through a side door and across the grand entrance hall. They emerged into the cool night air, at the top of a long flight of stone steps.

The square below was deserted, save for a few strolling couples gazing into the illuminated shop displays. A solitary policeman idled beneath a street lamp.

'So,' said Redwood crisply. 'How can I help you, Mr Conrad?'

'I think it's rather more a question of what I can do for you.'

Redwood's eyes blazed with sudden anger.

'Your newspaper has done more than enough as it is. You have no respect for anything. You just want to tear things down because you have the power to do it.'

Conrad intervened smoothly: 'Look Arthur, I haven't come here to make excuses for the Herald. Take your grievances up with Rex Thorneycroft. I want to make you a proposition.'

'I hardly think I would be interested.'

Conrad's voice hardened: 'You would be a damn fool not to be.'

Redwood paused. He walked to the very edge of the town hall steps and gazed out across the Bradcaster skyline, beyond the shopping arcade to the distant lights of the industrial estates on the outskirts of the city.

Still with his back to Conrad, he said quietly: 'Let's hear it.'

'Arthur, you know I was born in Bradcaster. This is still the only place I feel at home. I want to help you save the football club because I know what it means to the people here.'

Conrad's voice was resonant with emotion and sincerity.

55

Redwood turned to look at him, regarded his open countenance and was almost convinced.

'You are not generally known as a football fan.'

'I stood on your terraces more than once. There are a lot of things about me that are not common knowledge.'

Redwood said warily: 'I can imagine.'

But he was beginning to believe that perhaps he had misjudged Conrad after all. Sometimes images are constructed of public men which are mere caricatures of their true selves.

Aware that Redwood was wavering, Conrad continued: 'The team isn't scoring goals, you need a striker. But you can't afford anyone who is good enough. Am I right?'

'In a nutshell, yes.'

'Am I also right in thinking that Gus Simmons is a young man with a very big future?'

'You have been reading the tabloids again, Mr Conrad,' said Redwood, becoming intrigued despite himself. 'They've built the boy up and I hope he can handle it. He is a fine player but he is raw and by all accounts he has a wild streak. He might burn out.'

'Not with someone like you to look after him.'

Redwood shot Conrad a look of surprise.

'What precisely are you trying to say?'

'That I would be willing to finance his transfer to Bradcaster City, whatever it took,' replied Conrad steadily. 'At zero interest with repayments frozen for the first 12 months.'

Redwood laughed bitterly.

'I should have known. You can't buy a piece of Bradcaster City just like that. It's not for sale to you or anybody else.'

'You misunderstand,' said Conrad, holding up a defensive palm. 'My media interests are quite enough to keep me occupied, I promise you. Let's just call this a philanthropic gesture by a friend of Bradcaster.'

Redwood found a sneaking liking for Conrad beginning to stir inside him. They both understood they were playing a game, a verbal fencing match, where the object was to keep the opponent guessing.

He gave Conrad an ironical smile. 'But there is a catch.'

'Naturally.'

'And what might it be?'

Conrad looked hard at Redwood, gauging if the moment was right.

He spoke slowly, weighing every word: 'It is, I think, well known that I run Spacelink, the satellite television company.'

Redwood simply nodded.

'You will also know that the Super League will be negotiating its first ever TV contract in the spring. A contract that will be worth a great deal of money to all concerned.'

'It hasn't escaped my attention.'

'I'm quite sure about that,' said Conrad with emphasis. 'Spacelink intends to win the Super League broadcast rights, Arthur. It is very important to us. So important, in fact, that we would like all the help we can get in securing the deal.'

Now Redwood understood: 'You want me to be your mouthpiece.'

'Bradcaster City is a big club. You are one of the most respected men in football. Your voice carries a lot of weight.'

Redwood shook his head sadly.

'I'm sorry, Mr Conrad. But I am getting a bit long in the tooth to be running around as your messenger.'

'All I am asking is that you speak to a few club chairmen, one or two of the Super League executives. Tell them how you see it. That's all.'

'Oh, come on!' snorted Redwood. 'You're willing to

stump up several million pounds just for that? Mr Conrad, you must think me very naive.'

Conrad took hold of Redwood's upper arm and gave it a friendly squeeze.

'Arthur, that's all, I promise you. It could make all the difference.'

Still suspicious, Redwood drew his arm away. He cast a glance back inside towards the council chamber, where the hum of voices was growing to an animated chatter.

'I think dinner is being served,' he said. 'We should go back inside.'

'Arthur, for God's sake!' cried Conrad in frustration. 'Have you listened to any of this?'

Redwood was already moving across the floor of the great entrance hall. Over his shoulder, he said: 'I will never do anything that is not in the best interests of Bradcaster City. No amount of money will change that.'

'Gus Simmons would be very much in the interests of your precious club, Arthur,' Conrad called after him.

Redwood paused at the chamber door, long enough for Conrad to join him. He seemed deep in thought.

Then he subjected Conrad to a scouring look, his blue eyes cold and unblinking.

'You are a very persistent man. I will put your proposal to the board. But I must stress I can't promise anything.'

Redwood strode into the chamber to join the buzzing throng. As he did so, Michael Conrad was unable to suppress a slow smile of triumph.

CITY TO CRASH?

Cash crisis for Bradcaster

WORLD EXCLUSIVE
by Colin Gregory

BRADCASTER CITY, one of the country's biggest football clubs, is on the verge of collapse.

The big-spending club is saddled with a crippling wage bill while recent transfer deals have left the coffers empty.

But the collection of expensive misfits has left Bradcaster firmly anchored to the foot of the First Division, while average home attendances are down by almost 10,000 a game and still falling.

A well-placed source revealed exclusively to the Daily World that Bradcaster City is struggling with debts of nearly £15 million and could fold before the end of the season.

The club also faces a further £10 million bill to redevelop its stadium in line with the all-seater recommendations of the Taylor Report.

Beleaguered Bradcaster owe construction companies a fortune for the ill-fated office complex on the club's city centre training ground.

The largely empty building stands as a monument to the financial folly of Arthur Redwood and his team of directors.

Already fans have called for their resignation because of poor performances on the field. These latest disclosures can only increase the pressure on Redwood, now nearing 70.

Said a top-level insider at the club: 'Make no mistake, this club could fold in a matter of weeks if something isn't done.

'Unfortunately, Arthur Redwood doesn't seem to grasp the enormity of the situation. I really don't think he can cope any more with controlling a First Division football team.

'In the interests of Bradcaster City, he should resign and let a younger man take the helm before it is too late.'

Simmons was taking a long, luxurious shower. The jet of water was hissing and steaming and splashing off his dark skin.

As he turned beneath the hot stream, bathing every part of his body, the muscles in his arms and chest flickered with quiet power.

Then he thrust his face into the water and felt an exhilarating warm rush. He passed a hand through his soaking tightly cropped hair.

Simmons switched off the shower and stepped forward into what seemed to be a changing room, floored with pale stone tiles and flanked by wooden benches. Discarded sports kit lay in an artful heap.

He wrapped a huge snow white towel around the lower half of his body, still dripping wet. Leaning forward, he picked up a small glass object full of pale yellow liquid.

Unscrewing the gold-coloured top, he dashed a few droplets into his palm and sniffed it with sensual approval.

He rubbed the fragrance into both hands and applied it to his face and neck with a few quick slaps. His skin tingled and grew taut.

Looking straight ahead, his gaze focused on some vague middle distance, he said: 'After a hard session in the gym, I like to enjoy myself a little. I want an aftershave that makes me feel good. That's why I use Workout by Calvin Angelo. Because it's for men who play hard.'

He paused for a few moments and blinked. His expression loosened.

'How was that?' he inquired, a little embarrassed.

'Just lovely, Gus. Absolutely lovely. Take five everybody.'

A florid man in early middle age moved towards Simmons and took hold of his naked arm. He was wearing an enormous linen shirt, the first few buttons undone to reveal a chunky gold neck chain and a deep brown tan.

'Lovely,' he repeated softly, squeezing the hard bicep.

Previously silent, the room erupted with a dozen voices. A lighting technician barked instructions. The cameraman cracked a filthy joke with a young and pretty stylist, who smiled wanly.

Juniors were sent scurrying for plastic cups of coffee.

The sound engineer signalled for his assistant to lower the boom that was swinging above the head of Simmons.

The perfect replica of a gymnasium shower room occupied one small corner of a big studio. Above it was a gantry clustered with dozens of spotlights.

Just out of camera shot, the fake stone tiles gave way to a tangle of thick electric cables and all the other paraphernalia of filming: light meters, shooting scripts, continuity clipboards, assorted hardware.

'Gus, love, can I have a word?' whispered the director, tugging Simmons towards a quiet corner of the set.

The footballer was unpleasantly conscious of his nakedness beneath the towel, which had been insisted on for the realism of the shot.

He had not imagined that quite so many people attended the filming of TV advertisements. He felt like a piece of beef being paraded on the hoof.

As well as the film crew, there was a fluttering account executive from the advertising agency and a chain-smoking, pony-tailed art director, who peered occasionally at the set through a rectangle of his own fingers.

There was also a tall, swarthy character in a double-breasted Italian suit who stood silently in the background, making notes in a pocket handbook. This was the man from Calvin Angelo, referred to in hushed tones as 'the client'.

And finally, flashing a broad smile of encouragement, there was Steve Wilde.

'This is a real bloody coup,' he had told Simmons. 'A million-pound campaign. Press advertising, 48-sheet posters and saturation TV coverage. This will make you famous, my boy.'

For a few days, the thought of it had been unbelievably seductive. But then the fantasy was ousted by this tawdry reality: a cynical act of deception, the stumbling repetition of words he would never really have spoken in a thousand years.

The director was still hissing in Simmons' ear: 'Just try to relax. You're doing awfully well for a first-timer, I promise. But Gus, baby, you are so-oo tense. You sound like you're reading the back of a soup tin. Just let the camera love you. Think macho.'

He made a ridiculous show of flexing his flabby arms in a parody of a bodybuilder. He stepped back from Simmons and opened his palms wide, his expression archly quizzical.

'OK?'

Simmons nodded dully.

'Right everybody,' called the director, clapping his hands. 'Back to your places. We're going to try it one more time.'

He plucked playfully at the towel around Simmons' lower torso.

'Hop into the shower Gus, there's a good lad.'

As he shuffled, humiliated, across the studio floor, Simmons caught a glimpse of Steve Wilde still grinning cheerily, making a thumbs-up gesture.

Eyes burning, Simmons speared him with a look of pure hatred.

Sid Graveney was puffing nervously on a fat cigar, clogging the air in a dark corner of a Bradcaster bar.

'I'm sure he knows it was me,' he was saying for the umpteenth time. 'I'm absolutely bloody convinced. He looks at me as if I've just crawled out from under a stone.'

Colin Gregory sucked in a deep drag from the dock end of a Marlboro and stubbed it into an overflowing ashtray. He took a slug of Scotch.

'Why should Redwood think you leaked the story? Every

63

single member of the board must have known the finances were crumbling.'

Graveney shook his head almost frantically.

'No, it had to be me. Redwood thinks that if he's forced out, I'll buy his shares and get controlling power. God knows, it's what the club needs but he'll never forgive me for this.'

'Then you might as well just brazen it out,' said Gregory, his eyes narrowing. 'Come on, Sid. You didn't ask me here just to listen to this sob story. What have you got for me?'

'You're a ruthless bastard,' muttered Graveney darkly.

Gregory laughed. He fished out a dog-eared notepad from his jacket pocket and placed it pointedly on the table in front of him.

'So are you, Sid. Let's stop playing silly buggers.'

Graveney's eyes darted around the dingy interior of the bar. Two old men were clinking dominoes in the far corner, supping gingerly on half pints of mild. A bored barman was drying glasses.

The place stank of stale beer and cigarette smoke. Beyond a yellowing frosted glass window, late afternoon light was dimming. Bradcaster traffic hummed in the distance.

'All right,' said Graveney. 'But this is strictly off the record, got it? Redwood called a special board meeting last night. He says he has four million pounds available to inject into the club.'

Gregory whistled softly through his teeth.

'Where the hell has that come from? The banks won't touch Bradcaster with a barge pole.'

'You won't bloody believe this.'

Graveney paused for emphasis: 'Michael Conrad has practically given him a blank cheque.'

It was rare for Gregory to betray surprise. He had been

a newspaperman for upwards of 20 years and he reckoned he had seen and heard just about everything.

But this time incredulity rendered him dumb. He gaped at Graveney, who nodded his head in confirmation.

'It's true,' said the big man urgently. 'God knows what he's up to. But the bastard knows we're desperate.'

Gregory was still trying to gather his thoughts.

He grasped at the questions that were flitting through his brain: 'Is he buying into the club? What the hell would he want with a lame duck like Bradcaster?'

'According to Redwood, there's no ulterior motive,' said Graveney, voice heavy with sarcasm. 'He's offering an interest-free loan as a gesture to the football club he supported as a boy.'

He added bitterly: 'What a load of bollocks.'

'But this isn't going to change things, is it?' asked Gregory, still puzzled. 'Four million quid is just a drop in the ocean. It will only buy a bit of breathing space.'

Graveney cut in impatiently: 'No, no. The money won't get anywhere near the creditors. It's for spending on a player, somebody who can score goals.'

'Anyone in mind?'

'Oh yes, Conrad has it all mapped out. Gus Simmons. A bloody playboy, it's all we need.'

Gregory's shrewd mind was beginning to whirr. Slowly he was slotting the pieces of the jigsaw together.

'Where is the money coming from, Sid? It can't be through Spacelink, Conrad's shareholders would have a fit.'

Graveney shook his head and drained his whisky glass. The bar was beginning to fill with sullen-looking labourers from a nearby building site.

'No, it's his own money all right,' said Graveney, suddenly anxious to end the conversation. 'It's being loaned to Redwood via a private company called Conrad

Reprographics. They do the film separations for his newspapers' colour supplements.'

The big man stood up abruptly and added: 'Look, I really have to go. Break the story but for God's sake keep me out of it.'

'Hang on a minute,' said Gregory sharply, blocking Graveney's path with his legs. 'Is that it? I have a very nervous editor and so far this is just hearsay. Haven't you got something in writing? Letters, the minutes of the meeting?'

Graveney looked at the reporter in anguish.

'You don't understand,' he said, almost plaintively. 'It was a secret meeting, no records were kept. Conrad is insisting on absolute secrecy.'

Gregory sank back into his chair in frustration.

Conrad used the laws of libel ruthlessly to silence critics and ruin his enemies. Every single newspaper in the country, even his own, ran scared of him.

Gregory knew the World would never take him on unless it was backed by documentary evidence or an affidavit from Graveney. There was absolutely no chance of either.

And if he approached Conrad directly, he would simply get a flat denial for his trouble.

'Leave it with me, Sid,' he said grimly as Graveney made for the door. 'I'll see what I can do.'

At least he had the Gus Simmons transfer story in the bag. No one could stop him writing that, as long as he didn't point the finger at Conrad.

But one day, he promised himself, he would get right to the rotten heart of Bradcaster City.

Even the urbane Steve Wilde felt a little intimidated by Spacelink's headquarters, with its deep-pile carpets in corporate blue and burgundy, its endless corridors, the sheer energy and bustle and scale of the place.

Now, in the cavernous interior of Michael Conrad's office, he felt a nervous spasm clutch his guts.

Conrad was striding across the floor towards him, right hand outstretched, smiling broadly.

'Steve!' he cried in greeting. 'Glad you could make it.'

He wrung Wilde's hand with a grip that was cold and powerful.

Wilde remembered Conrad from the early days of Spacelink, a time of huge uncertainty but also of strange optimism and excitement.

Wilde had been the producer of an expensive but ill-fated soap opera. As the ratings plunged, and quick to sense he was on a sinking ship, he had resigned to form his own public relations company.

His few dealings with Conrad had been tense and difficult and their parting had worsened relations still further. It had been an acrimonious departure.

Now, nearly five years later, Conrad had asked to see him. Why?

'Sit down,' said Conrad expansively, gesturing towards an enormous black leather sofa.

Wilde sank into it but immediately felt exposed as Conrad loomed over him. He hunched awkwardly forward, elbows on his knees.

'Coffee?' asked Conrad and then glanced at the slender Patek Philippe on his wrist. 'Or how about a real drink? I recall you were a Scotch man.'

Not for the first time, Wilde was reminded of Conrad's unerring attention to detail. Nothing, no matter how apparently trivial, was forgotten or wasted; rather it was filed away in Conrad's capacious memory for future use.

Many powerful, visionary men dealt only in concepts, abstractions, the grand picture. They left subordinates to flesh out the bones of their strategies.

But for Conrad that merely spelled vulnerability. He

made sure that no one ever carried more ammunition than he did.

'I'm partial to Laphroaig myself,' said Conrad easily as Wilde crouched in some discomfort. 'Will you join me?'

Without waiting for a reply, he strode across to a vast glass-fronted cabinet and took out a crystal decanter filled with golden liquid.

He splashed a generous measure into two glasses and handed one to Wilde.

'Cheers,' said Conrad.

Wilde smiled woodenly. Conrad was leaning against his desk, deliberately making the PR man crane his head upwards to look at him.

On top of the huge, highly polished desk were perched three telephones, a fax machine and a computer terminal showing the fluctuations of the Tokyo stock market.

Incongruously, there was also a framed photograph of Alexandra Conrad. Taken during her career as a top fashion model, it showed her strutting arrogantly down a catwalk in a Gaultier basque.

This was the allure of constriction. The shiny black plastic top forced her breasts into aggressive conical points.

Her legs, which seemed to stretch for ever, were caressed by the sheerest of sheer stockings. The tops of her bare thighs were broad and muscled like an athlete's.

'How is business, Steve?' asked Conrad. 'I keep hearing good things. Nice new riverside offices in Fulham, I believe.'

Momentarily distracted by the photograph of Alexandra, Wilde quickly regained his balance and flashed Conrad a smile.

'We're holding our own,' he said. 'Not that another big account wouldn't be very welcome. These are hard times, as you very well know.'

With just an infinitesimal pause, he ventured the intimacy: 'Michael.'

Conrad stiffened for a second. When he spoke there was a cool undercurrent in his voice.

'It's possible I may have some good news for Wilde Communications. But first of all, I'd like to talk about your relationship with Augustus Simmons.'

'Simmons? What about him?'

'I hear you poached him. Now his face is all over our television screens. You seem to be doing a good job.'

Wilde was annoyed; Conrad had the gift of getting under people's skin, no matter how smooth their exterior.

'I don't poach clients. His agent was a small time shyster and there was no contract. Simmons is better off with me.'

Tired of maintaining his poise, Wilde had slumped back into the enfolding cushions of the sofa. He took a defiant gulp of whisky, which burned as hot as his anger.

He knew Conrad was rubbishing him. It was the one thing he couldn't handle.

Conrad simply ignored his outburst.

'How much influence do you have with Simmons?'

'Enough,' said Wilde sullenly. 'For a footballer, he has a pretty high opinion of himself. But he likes money and at the end of the day, he'll do what I tell him.'

'Good,' mused Conrad, tilting his glass so that the whisky caught the light and glowed softly. 'Steve, I want to do a deal with you. You might call it a gentlemen's agreement.'

A crafty look crept into Wilde's eyes.

'Spacelink is about to shift its entire marketing strategy,' continued Conrad. 'We are adopting a strictly pay-per-view system. Selling that idea to the great British public won't come cheap.'

Wilde was scenting something big.

'I imagine not,' he said noncommittally, desperate to keep Conrad talking.

'We are looking for a public relations consultancy to help us in our efforts,' said Conrad casually. 'The contract for the first 12 months is worth a little over £1 million.'

He nailed Wilde with a piercing look: 'I think Wilde Communications can do the job. But there is a condition.'

'Name it.'

Conrad moved away from his desk to stand at a window overlooking the Thames. Gazing out across the water, he drained the last drop of Laphroaig from his glass.

Steve Wilde was in an ecstasy of anticipation. The Spacelink contract would double the billings of his agency; it would take him into a different league.

He was so tired of being a small fish in a big pond. He despised Conrad for treating him with contempt. But the ruthless, successful media baron was everything that Wilde himself wanted to be.

Conrad stood at the window for what seemed an eternity. Then, still with his back to Wilde, he said quietly: 'In the next few weeks, Augustus Simmons will be transferred away from Bristol United. A number of First Division clubs will offer a large amount of money for him. In the end, it will be down to the player himself to decide.

'I want you to make sure he chooses the correct club. For everybody's sake.'

Before Wilde could reply, Conrad spun around and stared at him, his eyes intense. Involuntarily, Wilde shrank back into his seat.

'That club is Bradcaster City,' said Conrad.

Wilde shook his head, stammering: 'I . . . I'm afraid I don't understand.'

'You don't have to. Just point Simmons in the right direction when the time comes. It will make you a rich man.'

Conrad strode over to Wilde and looked down at him, stretching out his right fist.

'Do we have a deal, Steve?'

Wilde rose uncertainly to his feet and clasped Conrad's hand in his, squeezing as hard as he could. He was conscious that his palm with soaked with sweat.

'Yes. Yes, I suppose we do. Simmons will sign for Bradcaster if that's what you want.'

'Excellent,' said Conrad dismissively, already turning away. 'Please keep me informed. Goodbye Steve.'

But just as Wilde reached the door, his brain in turmoil, at once humiliated and euphoric, he heard Conrad's clear voice calling out.

'By the way,' he was saying. 'This conversation never happened. You take my meaning, I'm sure.'

And Wilde felt Conrad's merciless eyes burning into his back.

Gus Simmons awoke gradually to a sick, insistent drumming in his head. It was like crawling out of a deep and dark pit.

As consciousness returned, his memory was piecing together fragments of the night before. There was no coherent pattern yet, just an ugly heap of unrelated images.

He remembered the beginning of the evening with perfect clarity. He had worn a slate grey double-breasted suit by Yves St Laurent, priding himself on not dressing like a footballer.

The bar of the Holiday Inn had been cluttered with the usual hotel flotsam: anonymous businessmen on expense accounts, good time girls wearing too many sequins, scrubbed young men making one bottle of imported premium lager last an hour.

But then there was a gaping emptiness in his recollection.

Trying to assemble the chronology of the night, he captured a moment of sudden panic.

His brain was numb with alcohol. There was music so loud he thought his head would burst.

The throbbing cadence of the bass was pummelling his senses into submission. A myriad of revolving lights, intense blues and vibrant reds, made his eyes ache.

All around him swirled intricate patterns of dry ice, collecting and refracting the light, shimmering and glowing.

He felt like he was suffocating in a cloud of gas. He was falling forward into space, utterly unbalanced and unable to save himself.

As he lay dozing in and out of sleep, Simmons felt the throbbing in his temples intensify until he was almost whimpering with pain.

He remembered a strange room. Two giggling women, their faces blurred, were offering him a straw and pointing to a line of fine white powder on a horizontal mirror. As he swayed over the glass, his own face leered at him, vacant and distorted.

Fingers were tugging at him, caressing and exposing him. They seemed to be touching every part of his body at once.

He was powerless to resist, even though he was striving hard to pull away, frightened because he was quite beyond his own control.

As the two pairs of hands explored him, he felt a great warmth spreading outwards from the centre of his body. It seeped into every part of him, growing hotter and hotter until finally something burst and darkness swallowed him.

By now Simmons was completely awake. He lay in a clammy sweat, his heart pounding with dread, its pulse vibrating in his head.

He thanked God that, at least, he was back home in the

Clifton town house he shared with Melanie. He had half expected to wake to some new nightmare of unfamiliarity.

His suit was folded over the back of a chair, his tie draped across it. Underneath, his shoes were neatly paired.

The vice that was crushing his forehead prevented him from looking over his shoulder. Instead he inched his arm backwards towards the other side of the big double bed.

He was hoping to touch living flesh but his fingers roamed fruitlessly over cool sheets. He thrashed about more urgently but it was no good. Melanie was not there.

Simmons groaned in pain and disappointment.

He levered his legs gingerly out of bed and raised himself up. Through watering eyes, he saw his alarm clock was showing nearly midday.

It was a Wednesday morning and he should have been at Bristol United's training ground at ten o'clock sharp.

An overpowering sense of futility was stirring inside him.

He heard a scuffling sound from the kitchen and, without bothering to cover himself with a dressing gown, he stumbled slowly downstairs.

At the open door of the kitchen, he paused. Melanie was at the sink with her back to him, her hands plunged in hot water.

She was wearing jeans and a plain white T-shirt. Her blonde hair was pulled off the nape of her neck into a ponytail, a few wispy strands still falling across the soft skin.

To Simmons, his mouth still foul with alcohol and his brain polluted with bad memories, she looked astonishingly lovely.

Because of the clattering of crockery in the bowl, she had not heard him appear. One arm was rubbing vigorously at a tenacious stain on the lid of a casserole dish.

But then, somehow, she sensed him and the muscles in

her neck grew rigid. She let her arms grow still.

'Bastard,' she said almost matter-of-factly, without turning around. 'You bastard.'

'I'm sorry,' said Simmons dully. 'I don't remember.'

He stayed in the doorway, unable to move. He wanted to rush over to her and clasp her in his arms and explain everything, all the bad dreams. But he couldn't find the words.

She turned, her hands dripping, and saw his nakedness and the pain in his eyes.

'Oh Gus,' she said softly.

Suddenly her eyes were burning. She wanted to retrieve the past, when Simmons was an unknown reserve team player and she was working in bars, nightclubs, anywhere to make ends meet.

But everything remained untouchable, like an old photograph propped on a mantelpiece. Those times had gone forever.

'Where did you sleep?' he was asking. 'I missed you.'

'On the sofa. You were in such a state.'

She shook her head in anger and compassion and added: 'Why do you do it? Why?'

This time he stepped forward and took her in his arms. He bent his head into the crook of her shoulder, wanting to be comforted.

'I don't know,' he mumbled, his breath warm on her breast. 'I don't know anything anymore.'

Her brain was humming with a thousand thoughts, none of which she could articulate. She wanted to know where he had been and with whom.

Above all, she wondered what could possibly happen to them now. Only partially disarmed, she remained stiff in his embrace.

'You're going to miss training again,' she said.

'Who cares?'

He moved back his head and looked into her eyes but she refused to meet his gaze. His breath stank of stale alcohol.

'I won't ever do this again,' he implored her. 'Mel, please.'

There was a tight knot at the pit of her stomach, as familiar a sensation as a recurring dream. She loved him more painfully than ever before.

But she no longer believed a word he said.

BRADCASTER TO SWOOP FOR SIMMO

Ailing giant finds mystery backer

ANOTHER STUNNING SPORTS EXCLUSIVE

by Colin Gregory

PLAYBOY soccer star Gus Simmons could be on his way to struggling Bradcaster City in a £4 million deal.

So far Bristol United boss Bill Waddell has rejected all approaches from top clubs keen to poach Britain's most lethal young striker.

But bottom-placed Bradcaster, without a win in nearly two months, are ready to gamble on the black ace. Their offer could create a new record for a transfer between English clubs.

This last-gasp move by debt-laden Bradcaster will shock the football world.

As revealed exclusively by the Daily World, the club was on the brink of oblivion but chairman Arthur Redwood has secured the backing of a mystery benefactor.

The club was remaining tight-lipped about the affair last night. But Bradcaster's tough Glaswegian manager Dougie McNally is reported to oppose the transfer.

Simmo is fast developing a reputation as a lover of the high life. And the star of the sexy Calvin Angelo aftershave campaign is already a household name.

McNally has always prized discipline above flair and is said to regard Simmo as a prima donna who could flounder at the highest level.

If the deal goes through, it could create yet more strife in a Bradcaster dressing room where morale is already dangerously low.

Alexandra Conrad was panting and squealing with delight.

Her luscious mane of raven hair was tied back and soaked with sweat. She was a tangle of limbs in a short

white skirt beneath which her panties peeped tantalisingly.

'No, no, Alex,' a man's voice was saying. 'Don't swat at
it like that. Keep your arm moving in a long slow arc.'

Still giggling, she replied: 'I'll never get the hang of this.
How did you get to be so good?'

'Just practice.'

'I'll bet.'

The young blond Australian laughed, showing a set of
perfect white teeth. He had the tan and muscular build of
a Bondi beach bum.

'Let's try again, OK?'

He flicked up a bright yellow tennis ball with his instep and volleyed it down towards the baseline, where
Alexandra was hopping from one foot to the other, balancing herself.

He couldn't help noticing the soft motion of her breasts
inside the sports shirt. He was finding it hard to concentrate on the flight of the ball, his eyes lingering on her
body as she swung her racquet.

She met the ball with a satisfying crunch on her fore-
hand, spearing it in at his feet as he approached the net.

Grunting, he dug out a half-volley which spooned up
into the middle of the court and bounced invitingly at
shoulder height.

She rushed in, steadied herself for a moment and then
hammered a topspin backhand down the line.

He lunged desperately at the ball but it whistled past the
edge of his racquet as he tumbled to the floor. It hit the
court six inches inside the baseline and span on viciously
into the netting.

'Wow,' exclaimed the coach, picking himself up. 'I think
we'd better call it a day. You're getting too good for me.'

There were a dozen courts in the cavernous interior of
the tennis club but all the others were deserted. Alexandra

insisted on playing at seven in the morning, even though the courts didn't officially open for another two hours.

As the wife of Michael Conrad, she expected to get what she wanted. She was rarely disappointed.

They strolled off the court together, both glistening with perspiration and breathing heavily.

As they reached the changing rooms, Alexandra dug the coach playfully in the ribs and said: 'You're sweating, I must be getting better.'

Then her voice changed and she murmured: 'Why don't you take a shower with me?'

His face registered amazement, swiftly overtaken by lust.

'Yeah, sure,' he said thickly.

Entering the ladies' changing room, Alexandra tossed her racquet into a corner and strode over to the first of a row of cubicles. She reached inside and twisted a tap, disgorging a steaming cascade of water.

Then she turned to look at him standing awkwardly in the centre of the room and, with a sleepy half-smile on her face, she began to undress.

First she reached both hands behind her neck to free her hair. She shook her head and the jet-black locks spilled over her shoulders.

Alexandra kicked off her tennis shoes and with long, silky movements, she peeled off her ankle-length white socks.

Still fixing him with her gaze, she wriggled out of her top and then unclasped her bra and let it fall. Her full breasts bobbed seductively, the dark brown nipples hardening.

She stepped out of her skirt and smoothed her briefs down over her thighs, caressing herself. Her dark bush was luxuriant and intoxicating. He felt the breath catch in his throat.

She danced into the shower, spreading out her arms to

let the hot water run in torrents all over her body.

'I thought you were joining me!' she called out.

Suddenly he was tearing at his own clothes, his fingers clumsy, quivering with desire.

Alexandra felt him grasp her from behind, his rearing erection rubbing into the small of her back. He reached beneath her raised arms to cup and squeeze her breasts, pinching the nipples between thumb and forefinger.

She gasped, and then let out a low, sensual moan of pleasure.

Turning to face him, Alexandra reached down and took his penis in both hands. It felt unbelievably long and hard, as though it was about to burst.

She began to rub him with infinitely slow strokes, grasping the head of his cock and easing her hands right down to the base until his foreskin tightened.

He grunted, eyes closed, his open Australian countenance a mixture of ecstasy and bewilderment.

Both were soaking wet as the water tingled against their skin, steam clogging the air. A spreading pool by the open cubicle door was nosing its way across the tiles.

He grabbed her by the waist and lifted her up, biceps straining. She leaned back against the shower wall, taking some of the weight, and wrapped her long legs around his back.

Then he simply lowered her onto the tip of his penis, searching out her warm opening.

Finding it, he let her fall a few inches and she engulfed him.

He came almost at once, great heaving spurts that seemed to be torn from deep inside him, pumping his semen right into her innermost reaches.

Alexandra was screaming and writhing in his lap as he slumped forward, keeping him clamped inside her and milking him of every last drop.

She was insistently demanding her own pleasure and he gritted his teeth and held on, softening, as she threw back her head and screamed again with all the breath in her lungs.

At the very peak of her pleasure, her body became so compressed and still she felt like a corpse. Then she exploded into an agonising orgasm that seemed to last for ever until finally she whimpered and went limp in his arms.

Gently, he laid her down on the floor of the cubicle, water spilling over her face.

After a few seconds, she opened her eyes and squinted up at him as he stood panting over her.

Alexandra gestured weakly with her hand.

'I've got things to do,' she said without a flicker of emotion. 'Run away and play now, there's a good boy.'

Bill Waddell was a bluff Yorkshireman who always wore a tracksuit, even on the rare occasions he appeared in the Bristol United boardroom.

He was most at home on the training field, where he coaxed, cajoled and lambasted his team into a well-oiled footballing machine.

The game was his life. A tough, hard-working right half during the Fifties, he had graduated into management by the hardest route, starting as youth team coach for a bunch of Fourth Division no-hopers.

Now, 30 years and nearly a dozen clubs later, his team was on the brink of the ultimate prize – a place in the money-spinning Super League.

He knew that Gus Simmons had transformed an ordinary Bristol United side into title contenders. He could hardly afford to lose him with half the season left and a hatful of points still to be secured.

But above all else, Bill Waddell was an honest man.

That was why Simmons had been summoned into his

presence. And why Steve Wilde had also been invited, even though Waddell regarded all agents as the lowest form of human life.

'Look Gus,' Waddell was saying earnestly. 'I'm not going to mess you about. Somebody is offering a lot of money for you and I think you've got a right to know.'

Characteristically, Waddell had arranged to meet in the Bristol United boot room, his place of sanctuary. This was where he huddled with his coaching staff, discussing tactics, making team selection, complaining about boardroom interference.

He had just taken a long, hard training session. Unusually, he had bullied the players, punishing them, singling out individuals for vicious criticism. Even Simmons has felt the weight of his tongue.

Both Waddell, in his ubiquitous tracksuit, and Simmons were still bathed in sweat. They lolled as only athletes do, their muscles loose.

By contrast, Steve Wilde was perched on a bench, looking hopelessly incongruous in a sharply-tailored Italian suit. Aware that he was outside his normal territory, he was more silent and watchful than usual.

He knew by now there was no point in trying to soft-soap Waddell. He simply bided his time, half an eye continually on Simmons as he gauged his reactions.

'Is it Bradcaster?' asked the striker simply. 'I read the papers like everyone else.'

Waddell just nodded.

'Do you want me to go?'

'You know I don't. Even the board want you to stay and you know what a money-grabbing bunch of bastards they are.'

'So why are you telling me this?'

Waddell frowned. He liked Simmons, despite his touch

82

of arrogance and his sometimes cavalier approach to the game.

'Because I don't want to stand in your way,' he said heavily. 'I won't pretend other clubs haven't made me offers.'

Simmons' eyes widened in surprise and he opened his mouth to speak.

Waddell held up a defensive hand and continued quickly: 'They were so piss-poor, I rejected them out of hand. They didn't reflect what you were worth. This is different.'

'Why?'

'The offer is three million pounds cash.'

Simmons looked stunned. He shook his head slowly in wonderment and disbelief.

'Mr Waddell,' cut in Wilde, his tone both nonchalant and slyly acidic. 'I think my client would be rather more interested in his own terms.'

The United manager shot him a withering look and, turning back to Simmons, said quietly: 'The signing-on fee is a million quid.'

He looked deep into the amazed eyes of Simmons.

'Gus, I had to tell you, didn't I?'

Simmons was looking down at his own legs, stretching out the dark lean limbs and wobbling the calf muscles. For a long time, he did not speak.

Finally, he muttered: 'I don't know, boss. They're bottom of the league. What happens if we go up and they go down? I'd be better off staying here.'

'Hardly,' interjected Wilde sardonically, sweeping his arm across the boot room. 'This is just a little club with small ideas. Bradcaster might have fallen on hard times but they're a big-time outfit.'

Looking straight at Simmons, he added passionately: 'Think about the money. You'd be made for life before you even kick a ball. Leave it to me. If Bradcaster are so interested in you, I can negotiate an unbelievable deal.'

A red glow of anger was spreading from the base of Waddell's neck across his weather-beaten features.

'Gus, that's the full story,' he said tightly. 'Redwood wants an answer by the end of the week.'

Then his voice softened and he added: 'Just think about it properly, that's all. And next time, leave the pet snake at home.'

Simmons smiled, for what seemed the first time in many weeks.

'Maybe I'll do that,' he said.

But then he thought about the money again and the rare smile turned to stone on his face.

Melanie Simmons was crying. It was not a raw, passionate weeping, rather a mute sorrow that had lasted for hours.

Her eyes were scalded with tears that ran unhindered down her candid, almost beautiful face. She refused to wipe them away because they were the emblem of her hurt.

She had spent the whole day packing her belongings and those of her husband into big wooden crates. Almost every object she picked up and stowed away had cut her to the quick, as if she were ransacking and defiling her own past.

Records they had bought for each other, trophies from his days as an apprentice footballer when things had been simpler. Letters from his uncle in Jamaica, a country he had never seen. A delicate gold necklace he had bought for her 18th birthday and insisted on fastening himself with clumsy fingers.

Worst of all, old photographs: the pair of them on their first holiday, giggly with love; her with the rest of the barmaids at the Copacabana Club, all pie-eyed and grinning cheekily. Her sweet and sensible father, arm wrapped protectively around his wife as they frolicked in the surf at a Cornish beach.

More than anything, those pictures captured the world she was leaving behind.

She was heading for a strange city almost 200 miles distant, away from family and friends and the life she had known since childhood. With her on this journey into the unknown was a man she still loved but whom she hardly knew or could call her own anymore.

That was why she was crying, as she stuffed these fragments into boxes. Because she knew they could not just be reassembled in some other place. Everything was about to change and she was sad and scared.

When Simmons came home from his wistful farewell at Bristol United, he found Melanie crouched cross-legged in the bare living room.

She was still sobbing silently, her face quite blank. Already the removal men had taken almost everything, leaving only a few fragile items. The room was filled with a great absence and she was still and small in the centre of it. Every sound was magnified by its emptiness and when Simmons spoke, the sound echoed in his head.

'Why are you crying?' he asked stupidly, arms lolling at his sides.

He was unable quite to approach and touch her. She made no reply but her sobbing stopped. She stared ahead vacantly, her eyes inflamed.

He felt a sudden ache in the pit of his stomach. He knelt down beside her and took her hand in his. It was limp and cold.

'Don't you want to go?' he said softly and a little helplessly.

She murmured low, her voice clogged with tears: 'You know I don't. Why do we have to? This is our home, where we belong.'

'Mel, don't,' he pleaded. 'We've been through this a hundred times. This is my big chance, everything I've ever wanted. Don't spoil it for me.'

Angrily, she pulled her hand away from his grip. Her eyes suddenly flashed with passion.

'What about me, you bastard? You don't care what I think. All you're interested in is money.'

'So why are you coming with me?'

'Because you're my husband,' she said, as though it was an accusation. 'And because you're not fit to be on your own.'

Simmons did not reply. Instead he remaining squatting on the floor of his denuded home, staring at the blank walls and empty shelves.

Although they were only a few inches apart, a great gulf was yawning between them. He had not expected this.

He had begun to hate the sound of her voice, which to him grew increasingly coarse and parochial as his own West Country burr evaporated.

He found her naive to the point of stupidity. She had refused to even discuss the intricacies of the financial package Wilde had negotiated.

He was beginning to find her a burden and a public embarrassment. Just as he felt himself reaching for the sky, there she was wrapped around his ankles, dragging him back down.

Yet she was still the bedrock of his being, safely anchoring him when all around seemed volatile and alien. Simmons knew that he needed her now more than ever.

'Come on,' he said, patting her shoulder. 'Let's get out of here. It will all look different in Bradcaster tomorrow, I promise.'

She made no sign that she had heard. Even to him, the words had an unbearably hollow ring.

'I'm warning you, Dougie,' hissed Arthur Redwood. 'I want you to behave yourself. Keep the sarcastic comments to yourself, understand?'

McNally scowled and looked thunderous behind his beetling eyebrows. For once, the Bradcaster manager was smartly dressed in a suit and tie.

Tugging irritably at his collar, he muttered: 'Oh aye, boss. I'll keep my mouth shut all right. But don't expect me to lick his black arse.'

The directors' box at Bradcaster City was packed and humming with noise. Redwood and McNally were seated behind a mahogany desk, bare except for a pitcher of water, three glasses and a paper document with a gold fountain pen laid across it.

The room was still filling with journalists: several dozen press reporters brandishing notebooks or dictaphones, a loud posse of photographers encamped in the front row of seats, a scattering of radio sportscasters with microphones.

There were also two television crews squabbling over the best position and erecting big spotlights. An engineer flicked a switch and bathed the desk in white, intense light. Redwood grimaced and shielded his eyes with a hand.

'For goodness' sake,' he snapped, betraying his tension. 'Point that thing somewhere else.'

Outside the Bradcaster stadium, a crowd of fans had been swelling for over an hour. They were gathered around the main entrance gates, spilling out into the road.

A pair of constables looked on but there was no sign of trouble. Rather the mood was celebratory, the crowd laughing and chanting songs. There was an overwhelming sense of expectancy.

Then someone shouted: 'There he is!'

Pandemonium broke out, hundreds of fans scuffling for a better view as a chauffeur-driven Bentley turned sedately into the sidestreet where they were waiting.

The car drew up at the gates and was immediately mobbed by the cheering crowd. Fists drummed on the roof and banged on the windows. Faces peered inside.

The mood was joyous but inside the Bentley, Gus Simmons felt trapped and nervous. Instinctively, he was flinching from the fusillade of hands and the curious stares.

He felt a pressure on his upper arm.

'Don't worry, Gus,' coaxed Steve Wilde, squeezing him. 'They love you. You'll soon get used to this.'

'Just drive,' said Simmons sharply to the chauffeur, who answered with a helpless shrug of his shoulders. The car was becalmed in a sea of people.

It was at least 20 minutes before a path could be cleared, by which time the reporters at the press conference were becoming decidedly agitated.

The footballer was met by a red-faced steward, who dashed off up a flight of stairs with the footballer in his wake. Sweating, Simmons finally burst into the directors' box and the whole press contingent swivelled to catch a glimpse of him.

'Ah,' exclaimed Arthur Redwood with audible relief. 'Here is the most valuable player in the history of Bradcaster City. Ladies and gentlemen, Augustus Simmons.'

He gestured across the room as Simmons squeezed past the seated journalists, flash bulbs already exploding. Behind him, Steve Wilde stood in a discreet corner at the back of the room, a self-satisfied smile spread across his face.

Settling down behind the desk, Simmons proferred his hand to Redwood and McNally in turn. The Glaswegian manager clasped it brusquely, as if it were contaminated.

'We have asked you here today to see Gus officially become our property,' Redwood announced. 'The fee is three million pounds, a club record. We have absolutely no doubt that he will prove a sound investment.'

Scrawling his signature on the bottom of the contract, he thrust the pen at Simmons. The clicking and flashing of the cameras intensified as the black star wrote his name and underlined it with a flourish.

He had the uncomfortable feeling that he was signing his life away, rendering himself open for public inspection.

Then the questions started to fly.

'Gus, why are you joining a club that is bottom of the First Division?' asked a tabloid reporter. 'It doesn't seem much of a career move.'

'Isn't it true that Dougie McNally opposed your transfer?' demanded another.

'What makes you think you can make it at this level?'

'How do you feel about being Bradcaster's first black player?'

'Do you care more about being a TV star than playing football?'

'Are you worth the money?'

Simmons dealt with the barrage of questions politely and with good grace. But inside him there was a tight knot of dread and panic. Is this what it would be like from now on?

He had been rattled enough by the heaving crowd at the gates. Now the media wanted to lift the lid on his deepest thoughts and desires, consuming him in their vast machine.

Already he was shrinking away, erecting a tough carapace to deflect those interminable questions and all that prying.

Gradually, after half an hour or so, the mob of reporters grew silent. Then Colin Gregory of the Daily World got to his feet, notebook still jammed inside his creased jacket.

'Just a point for you, Arthur,' he said casually, scratching an ear with his pen. 'We all know Bradcaster City are skint. Where exactly is this money coming from?'

Redwood shook his head firmly. He had been expecting that line of interrogation.

'I have absolutely no comment to make,' he said flatly. 'That is entirely a matter for the Bradcaster board.'

But Gregory was not about to let him off the hook so easily: 'Doesn't the source of the cash create a serious conflict of interest for Bradcaster City?'

For a moment, Redwood's eyes widened in surprise. Then he composed himself and forced a thin smile.

'You have been listening to idle gossip, Mr Gregory.'

With an air of finality, he stood up and leaned his palms on the table, adding: 'Thank you all for coming. That is the end of these proceedings.'

A murmur of conversation ran through the room and the TV crews started to pack away their gear. Photographers pointed their cameras at Simmons and finished off their rolls of film.

Redwood made a beeline for Gregory, who was exchanging coarse jokes with reporters from rival papers. He grabbed his arm.

'Come with me,' he said tersely.

With a cynical smile, Gregory followed the Bradcaster chairman. Redwood strode along a corridor and into one of the corporate boxes, beckoning Gregory inside.

'Now,' he said, closing the door behind them. 'What the hell do you know?'

'All about Michael Conrad. Are you going to admit that he's involved?'

Redwood moved away to the window, staring down at the familiar stud-marked turf. His brain was racing.

'Who told you?' he asked finally.

'You know I can't say. Is it true?'

It wasn't part of Redwood's character to tell lies, so he simply stayed silent. Gregory understood. But that wouldn't be enough to satisfy his editor.

'I know what's happening,' he said. 'Conrad is trying to buy Bradcaster's support for his TV deal. Don't you think you're compromising yourself a wee bit?'

Redwood answered softly: 'I'm just trying to save my club. But I shan't admit to any of this and you have no proof.'

Gregory knew he was right and he was angry.

'All right Arthur, have it your own way,' he said, his voice vibrating with passion. 'But one day I'm going to blow this story wide open. And when I do, you're for the bloody high jump.'

'What a waste of money!'

The jeer grew louder from the opposition terrace: 'What a waste of money!'

For a moment there was a desultory silence. And then, in answer, a vast chant rolled down from the Southside of Bradcaster City's packed stadium.

'Simmo!'

Thousands of fans clapped their hands in time and then bellowed out the single word: 'Simmo!'

Soon the song was picked up by the entire ground, which was full for the first time in months. They had all come to see Gus Simmons make his debut in a Bradcaster shirt, praying for their dreams to be rekindled.

And for the first half an hour, their new hero – the man carrying all their awakened hopes – had hardly touched the ball.

They were waiting for the flashes of brilliance, the searing pace, the cool and cocksure finishing. They were waiting for Simmo to live up to his hype. So far they were disappointed.

There had been many false dawns during the last 30 years at Bradcaster City and they wanted desperately for him to sweep away the rubbish of the past. They were tired of being a joke.

So they cloaked their fears in the only way they knew, by singing their hearts out.

'Simmo!' they called out, urging him on. 'Simmo!'

Down on the pitch, Simmons heard them and felt sick. The weight of their expectation was crushing him; his legs felt like jelly.

Already he had been battered almost into submission by the opposition defence. Dougie McNally was playing him as a lone target man. It was his job to lead the line, holding the ball up and waiting for support.

He was neither big enough nor strong enough. Under McNally's primitive Route One tactics, the ball was simply hoofed hopefully forward from defence.

His back was always to goal, rendering his devastating burst of acceleration useless. He was either making futile leaps against much taller defenders or struggling to control a bouncing ball.

Simmons had taken more punishment in 30 minutes of this game than in the rest of the season put together.

Time and again, he had suffered a knee in the back or elbow in the face. He had begun to lose his appetite for this unequal battle.

When he heard the away supporters taunting him as he chased impotently around the pitch, it had stiffened his resolve. But then the answering chant of the Bradcaster fans, their tangible sense of desperation, had cowed him totally.

So the glaring chance came at just the wrong time.

Bradcaster's keeper gathered a back pass at the edge of his area and immediately punted it forward into the opposition half. It landed beyond the primary line of defence, Simmons chasing it without conviction. The ball bounced up over the head of the sweeper and he turned nonchalantly to usher it back to his goalkeeper.

Then he glimpsed Simmons in the corner of his eye and accelerated, still untroubled. He was chasing backwards, head craning over his shoulder, when the collision happened.

Fatally, his goalkeeper had made no call. The two of them clattered into each other just inside the penalty area.

The sweeper grunted and went down, the air smashed from his lungs. Shaping to catch the ball, the keeper was knocked sideways and the ball spun off his fingertips.

It landed right in the path of the onrushing Simmons, who had sensed what was about to happen. He was arriving at pace with the whole goal gaping in front of him. But by now his composure was shot to pieces.

Instead of steadying himself, he lunged at the ball, looking to bulge the net.

The crowd was on its feet, screaming in anticipation of a certain goal. But the ball sliced horribly off the outside of Simmons' boot.

It skewed across the face of the goal, Bradcaster fans wide-eyed in disbelief, and ran out of play for a throw-in at the far touchline.

Simmons sank to the ground in horror. A terrible and heavy silence settled on the stadium.

Then he heard a lone, angry voice shouting out from the Southside: 'You useless black bastard!'

It grew into a chorus of disapproval. Simmons was used to racist abuse from away fans but he had never experienced anything like this from his own supporters.

He seemed to be marooned in a nightmare from which he could not awake, where everything was strange and hostile.

He left the field at half-time in a daze, pointedly ignored

by his team mates. By now the Bradcaster fans were mournfully incanting 'what a load of rubbish!'. A shower of seat cushions was raining down from the west stand.

Simmons hardly noticed. But when he reached the dressing room, his raw nerves were exposed again by a glowering Dougie McNally.

'Fucking hell!' he yelled. 'Three million quid for that pile of shit? My fucking granny could have stuck that one away. You're a disgrace.'

Simmons didn't say a word. The entire Bradcaster team was staring at him with eyes of hatred. He stood alone in the centre of the dressing room, quivering with shame and incipient rage.

'Get yourself back on that field and stop poncing around,' shouted McNally, his face red and contorted. 'Or by God, you'll be out on your black arse.'

But in the second half, the story was just the same. His spirit almost broken, he was completely dominated by the opposition's muscular defence.

On the stroke of the hour, Bradcaster went a goal down. They were now being completely outplayed and their fans were streaming off the terraces in disgust.

A few minutes from the end, Gus Simmons was put out of his misery. As the ball rolled out for a goal kick, a sign bearing the number ten was brandished from the Bradcaster dugout.

Seeing it, Simmons felt only an overwhelming sense of relief. He dragged his heavy limbs off the field to a cacophony of whistles and catcalls.

As he reached the touchline, McNally stood up to meet him.

'Get showered,' he ordered. 'Just get out of my fucking sight.'

Sick at heart, Simmons made the long walk down the player's tunnel alone.

One man had watched Simmons' dispirited exit with compassion and understanding.

To the footballing world, Rod Lyons was an enigma, a player of mercurial brilliance who had never achieved the greatness he promised. He had the sweetest left foot in the First Division, capable of thundering power and exquisite delicacy.

Where lesser players saw only chaos and heaving bodies, Lyons saw space and its possibilities.

Unlike other prodigiously gifted talents, he never shirked a challenge. He had a reputation for being hard, sometimes even brutal, at once a devastating ball winner and a creative magician.

But while Lyons had risen to the very fringes of the England team, he had always remained a mistrusted outsider. It was said he was too inconsistent, that he faded unaccountably from games. His critics claimed his temperament was suspect, that he lacked discipline.

The truth was rather different. For three years at the very peak of his ability, Rod Lyons had been an alcoholic.

At first his addiction went unnoticed. Then he started to show up for training shaking so badly that he couldn't undress himself.

On the pitch, Lyons was transforming himself from a strolling craftsman into a lumbering buffoon. Finally he was caught swigging from a whisky bottle during the interval of a big match.

Then Bradcaster City knew they had a problem on their hands. Pretty soon his sad secret became common knowledge in dressing rooms up and down the country.

Inevitably, the tabloids were alerted. Delving into their ragbag of cliches, they labelled him a flawed genius with an appetite for self-destruction.

Seeing everything he had worked for slipping from him, and with massive force of will, Lyons ditched the drink.

But by then it was too late. The image had stuck to him like a second skin. He was discarded from the England squad; a mob of big clubs scrambling for his signature simply melted away. He struggled on at Bradcaster but somehow the heart had left him, the gift that had made him special.

His career was dwindling into nothing. Then Dougie McNally arrived and oblivion descended sooner even than Lyons had expected. He was banished to the replacements' bench.

It was from there that he had watched the agony of Simmons. He recognised the shame and humiliation, shuddered at the barracking of the crowd, who had been merciless during his own dark days.

And he saw – even as Simmons was being crushed on the field – something unique and, in its way, almost beautiful. His sinewy grace and blistering speed, the geometric precision of his foraging runs.

He sensed the isolation of the truly gifted man. So the following Monday at training, when Simmons was being cold-shouldered by the rest of the Bradcaster team, Lyons extended the hand of friendship.

As the players changed, grinning, hurling foul-mouthed banter, Simmons seemed to occupy a still space of his own. He was being comprehensively ignored, unable to break into their tight coterie or even wanting to.

Lyons sat down on the bench next to him and clapped his knee.

'Don't worry son,' he whispered. 'They can be miserable bastards but they're not so bad really. You'll get used to them.'

Simmons glanced sideways at him with the light of gratitude in his eyes. He shook his head, bewildered.

'Why do they hate me?'

Over in a corner of the changing room, Dave Stewart,

the Bradcaster captain, was telling an obscene story about a girl he'd picked up on Saturday night. He was surrounded by a gang of players, all laughing coarsely.

'So I'd shafted her twice in the car, right? Shagged her brains out. Then do you know what she did?'

A dozen voices were urging him on. He paused for emphasis, with a cruel wolf's smile.

'She only asked for my fucking autograph!'

There was an explosion of laughter and whooping. Lyons looked at Simmons and shrugged.

'They hate you because you're better than they are,' he said. 'They can handle me because I was a pisshead. But you're different class. And you're being paid a fortune. They can't cope with that.'

Bradcaster's drab training ground was covered with a ghostly patina of frost. As the players trotted out, wreaths of breath hung above them in the cold winter air.

Dougie McNally himself had arrived to take the morning's session. It began with a few loosening up exercises and a gentle run around the perimeter of the pitches.

Then the players were split into fours for a game of head tennis, followed by a brisk five-a-side workout designed to hone their ball skills.

Simmons began to lose himself in the game, shimmying and feinting, flicking deft and accurate passes with the outside of his boot.

'Come on!' roared McNally at the toiling defenders in his wake. 'Get under him! He's taking the piss!'

But still Simmons danced unscathed among the flying studs and elbows. Members of his own team grew animated, shouting for the ball, encouraging him.

'Yes, Gus. Yes!'

'Man on! Turn, turn!'

'Do him for pace! Go on, Simmo lad!'

Stony-faced, McNally watched Simmons growing in

confidence. Just as the black striker was bearing down on goal again, he gave a sharp blast on the tin whistle hanging round his neck.

'All right, that'll do!' shouted the Scotsman. 'A quick breather and then some 11-a-side, the real thing. I want to see those tackles going in hard, got it?'

The players stood around gasping, hands on hips. A cloud of steam from their hot bodies settled in the crisp atmosphere. Simmons was swinging his pelvis in a slow arc, trying to keep loose, smiling with satisfaction.

McNally clapped his hands and yelled: 'OK, move yourselves! First team against the reserves, 20 minutes each way. And I want 100 per cent commitment, no coasting.'

The players began to jog across to the main pitch. One or two slapped Simmons playfully as they passed. For the first time since his arrival at Bradcaster City, he was enjoying himself.

But as he strode off with the rest of the first-choice 11, McNally called after him, his voice heavy with sarcasm: 'Oi, Simmons! Where the fuck are you going?'

Simmons turned with a puzzled expression.

'I took you off on Saturday, remember?' shouted the manager viciously. 'Get with the reserves.'

Several of the other players looked up in astonishment. McNally had a reputation for being a bad man to cross but no one could recall him conducting such a vendetta before.

For a moment Simmons was rooted to the spot. Then a white-hot anger began to spread through his body like a flame. Biting his tongue, he sprinted across the field to join the reserves and replacements.

Many of them were raw apprentices, with a sprinkling of cynical old lags like Rod Lyons, who grinned ruefully as Simmons approached.

'Jesus, he's really got it in for you, hasn't he?' he said.

Simmons' face was a mask of rage. He was on the brink of losing control completely.

'Bastard!' he spat. 'No one talks to me like that. I'll have his balls if it's the last thing I do.'

Lyons placed a restraining hand on his shoulder.

'Look Gus,' he said in a low voice, glancing over at McNally. 'Don't let him see he's winding you up. Just do your talking on the pitch, OK?'

Simmons nodded sullenly.

'Frank Miller will be marking you,' continued Lyons. 'Good player but a bit slow. Look for the ball behind him when I go wide. Let's rub McNally's nose in it, all right?'

'Love to,' said Simmons grimly and sprinted over to the centre circle.

The game started at a frenetic pace, McNally driving the players on with his whiplash tongue, cursing them if they let up even for an instant.

The first team was crashing the ball forward at every opportunity, bypassing the midfield. But in the heart of the reserve defence was a veteran centre back who remained dominant in the air despite his failing legs.

He was the rock on which all the first team attacks were foundering. And in the middle of the park, Rod Lyons was winning the ball with crunching tackles, feeding a flying 17-year-old winger who was roasting his opposing full back.

McNally was driven almost to distraction as the reserves gradually established their supremacy. He was roaring instructions and muttering exasperated oaths under his breath, hardly able to believe what was happening.

Throughout the breathtaking speed and shuddering physical collisions of the game, Simmons was making his quicksilver runs. He was darting right across the face of the defence, creating holes, searching for an opening.

Then it happened. Lyons skipped past a tackle in mid-field and burst towards the right-hand touchline. Instinctively the defence funnelled towards him and a yawning gap appeared in the centre of the penalty area.

Simmons had pulled Frank Miller way out of position near the far touchline. Now he turned and surged past him on a diagonal run into the box.

Lyons looked up and, just as the full back slid into him, he curled the ball tantalisingly behind the stretched defence. The keeper was scrambling to claim the cross, flapping at thin air.

Simmons arrived with sweet timing, Miller labouring behind him. He rose like a stag and with a powerful flick of his neck, buried the header right in the top corner.

'Oh, you beauty!' Rod Lyons was shouting. 'You bloody beauty!'

Simmons brandished his arm in triumph, savouring the moment. He jogged over to where McNally was standing dumbstruck and, with an insolent wink, said: 'Pick the bones out of that, you Scotch bastard.'

He turned away, his fists clenched. Deep in McNally's eyes, thoughts of vengeance burned with a fierce and consuming heat.

KING'S RANSOM FOR CLOWN SIMMO

Massive wage deal angers fans

Exclusive by Colin Gregory

SUPERFLOP striker Gus Simmons made himself a millionaire overnight when he signed for struggling Bradcaster City, the World can exclusively reveal.

That was the staggering signing-on fee negotiated by his sharp-suited agent Steve Wilde.

And the former Bristol United marksman stands to rake in another ONE MILLION POUNDS over the next three years, making him Britain's highest-paid football star.

Many of Bradcaster's fans from the Southside terraces are on the dole or working on the factory floor.

They will be amazed to learn that Simmo, substituted during a disastrous home debut, picks up a £6,000 pay cheque EVERY WEEK.

The club had drawn a veil of secrecy over the exact details of the striker's contract. And they are still refusing to reveal the identity of the shadowy figure who is stumping up the cash.

These revelations, confirmed by a well-placed insider, are sure to anger fans and throw the Bradcaster dressing room into turmoil.

Welcomed like a new Messiah, the club's first-ever black player has already been the target of racist abuse from a section of the supporters.

At the moment, Simmons looks as though he is carrying the world on his shoulders – or maybe it's just the weight of his £3 million price tag.

Michael Conrad scratched his name lazily with a gold Mont Blanc pen.

The vast shape of the M was like a looming viaduct, all massy strength and solidity; the C, equally big, was an elongated creative curve.

In between, the letters were as crabbed and correct as soldiers standing to attention, the index of an ordered mind. He underlined his signature with a single stroke, as straight and true as a gun barrel.

'There,' he said slowly. 'I hope you can handle this.'

For a moment, Steve Wilde looked pained then replied: 'We'll do a good job for you, Michael.'

'You'd better.'

They were sitting on opposite sides of an ornate table in an office at Conrad's merchant bank. The room, used only for ceremonial occasions, was a riot of Victorian chandeliers and elaborate architraving.

Hovering in the background were two expressionless men in blue pinstripe suits. Once Wilde had also signed the contract, they leaned forward like giant lugubrious flamingoes to witness it.

Then they withdrew. Wilde was conscious of how Conrad managed to fill even this airy, high-ceilinged room with his presence.

'You did well with Gus Simmons,' Conrad conceded. 'But this is altogether different. I won't hesitate to invoke the three months probationary clause if you make a balls-up.'

'I understand that.'

Emboldened by Conrad's signature at last on the Spacelink public relations contract, Wilde added: 'But there is still something bothering me.'

Conrad leaned back into his cracked leather armchair and said dismissively: 'Forgive me Steve, but I'm not sure I care about your discomfort.'

'Satisfy my curiosity at least.'

Conrad smiled briefly, without abandoning for a moment his predator's wariness. Over in a corner of the room, a grandfather clock was ticking like a death watch beetle. He glanced pointedly at his own wristwatch.

'Go ahead.'

'What is your interest in Gus Simmons?'

Conrad shrugged and said casually: 'He's a bloody good

footballer and Bradcaster is my home town. I wanted to help give the club a lift, that's all.'

A crafty smile flickered at the edge of Wilde's mouth.

'Did that include putting up the money for his transfer?'

Conrad's face hardened.

'Pure speculation,' he said between his teeth. 'Now, if you'll excuse me.'

He made to stand up but Wilde held out a conciliatory hand.

'Michael, please,' he said. 'I don't mean to pry but you chose to involve me in this. You can't blame me for wanting the full picture.'

Conrad snatched the contract from the table and waved it in Wilde's face, the blood rising in his cheeks.

'This is all you need to know, you bloody leech,' he snarled. 'I don't have to explain anything to you. Just keep your nose out of my affairs.'

On his feet, towering over Wilde, Conrad was on the brink of losing control. Then with a tremendous effort, he recovered his composure, his tightened face grew still.

'I believe that curiosity killed the cat, Mr Wilde,' he said coldly. 'I should hate to think that anything similar would happen to you.'

Redwood reflected it was difficult to get excited about a football match played in silence behind glass.

Looking down from the lofty perch of a hospitality box, soothed by champagne and canapes, it all looked rather ridiculous – grown men in short trousers chasing a bouncing ball.

Even the reverberation of the crowd was a mere subliminal hum. At this distance there was no passion, no sense of confrontation or conflict.

Too often these days, Redwood found himself watching

the game with half an eye, making small talk with a dull accountant or someone's overweight wife.

But this time his conversation had a definite if unpalatable purpose. He had taken Conrad's shilling and this was the pay-off.

Bradcaster were playing away at the West London home of high-flying Gunnersbury Park Rangers, a fashionable club that prided itself on playing classical football. They were on a winning streak and already, midway through the first half, were a goal up and dominating play.

Redwood was watching the game with his opposite number, millionaire property developer Gerald Waterstone, an Old Etonian with a taste for flashy gestures. He had been Redwood's biggest rival in the battle to sign Gus Simmons.

'Bloody glad you beat us to it, Arthur,' he said cheerfully as the pair peered down at the pitch. 'He's having an absolute nightmare.'

Redwood grimaced and forced a smile.

'He's not settled in yet. Don't worry, he'll be worth the money in the end.'

Waterstone was enjoying taunting the older man.

'Maybe,' he said with a broad grin. 'But he looks like a lost soul to me.'

The observation was painfully accurate. Once again a lone figure up front, Simmons was making endless runs for passes that never came. He seemed somehow dislocated from the rest of the team.

Redwood guided Waterstone away from the window towards a quiet corner of the room, taking a gulp from his glass of champagne.

'What's your view on the television rights for the Super League, Gerry?' he asked, as casually as he could manage.

Waterstone looked mildly startled. This was not the sort of gambit he associated with Arthur Redwood.

'Who should get them, you mean? I think ITV have done pretty well, don't you? Better the devil you know.'

'But what if Spacelink bid higher?' said Redwood earnestly. 'Everyone is having to rebuild their grounds and that's damned expensive. We've got to make sure we get the best deal.'

Waterstone looked doubtful for a moment and then beckoned a waitress to replenish his drink. She was young and pretty. He regarded her with interest as she tipped the foaming Moet et Chandon into his glass.

'Thank you, my dear,' he purred. 'You really did that terribly well. Top-up, Arthur?'

Redwood shook his head, which was already becoming fuddled with the unaccustomed alcohol.

'I don't know,' continued Waterstone, turning reluctantly from the waitress. 'Nobody watches that satellite stuff, do they? Could be shooting ourselves in the foot, old boy.'

'A lot of people will buy dishes if Spacelink win. I'm sick of armchair fans getting something for nothing.'

Waterstone's eyes narrowed with suspicion.

'My dear fellow, what's come over you? I thought it was all love of the game with you and bugger the cash.'

Redwood shrugged and replied: 'I just think the pools companies and the TV stations and everybody else have been ripping us off for long enough. It's time for a change.'

Waterstone gave a short, cynical bark of laughter.

'Oh, things would change all right. Like playing games on a Monday night in deserted stadiums, all for the benefit of television. Is that really what you want, Arthur?'

In his heart of hearts, Redwood knew that he was right. But he had made a promise and it was going to be fulfilled to the best of his ability. He stuck out a defiant jaw.

'If Spacelink bid higher, then we should vote them in. That's all I'm saying. We owe it to ourselves.'

'Oh well, let's just wait and see, shall we?' said Waterstone with supreme indifference. He was becoming bored with this conversation.

Turning back towards the window, he added in a different voice: 'Christ, look at that.'

Down on the terraces at the Bradcaster end, a great white banner had been unfurled. In black letters a yard high, it bore the cruel message: SIMMONS GO HOME.

The footballer himself was simply standing and gaping at it, as play carried on around him. Then, remembering himself, he struggled to rejoin the action but his legs seemed to be made of lead.

Redwood gazed down at the scene, weighing his own inner turmoil with the public humiliation of Simmons. For the first time in his football career, he asked himself if it was all worth it.

'The boy's not happy, Dougie. Anyone can see that.'

Arthur Redwood had called the Bradcaster manager into his office on Monday morning, just as he was about to lead a training session. It was unusual for Redwood to pull rank so publicly.

'I'm not exactly over the moon myself,' said the Scotsman irritably. 'He's just not doing the business, is he?'

'Perhaps you could be more helpful.'

McNally scowled impatiently.

'You talk about him as if he's a child. He should be big enough to stand on his own feet by now.'

Redwood fixed him with a fierce glare, his eyes cold and unyielding. There was a edge of barely suppressed anger and frustration in his voice.

'Look Dougie,' he said. 'We spent a lot of money on Simmons and you're not making the most of the investment. That's the bottom line.'

McNally grew defensive, muttering: 'I never wanted

him in the first place. He's a bloody prima donna and he can't hack it at this level. I warned you but you insisted.'

'The way you're playing doesn't suit him.'

'So you want me to change everything just for him?'

Redwood paused and sighed heavily. He had always tried to give his managers plenty of rope, even if it was only to hang themselves with in the end. But this time he felt he had no option but to intervene.

'No, I want you to change for the sake of everyone involved with this club,' he said steadily. 'No one likes what you're doing, least of all the fans. And they pay all our wages, in case you had forgotten.'

McNally exploded with resentment: 'Don't lecture me about the fans, Arthur. They don't give a toss about pretty football. They just want to see us win.'

'We haven't been doing too much of that recently,' observed Redwood with devastating acidity.

McNally lapsed into a sullen silence, a crimson flush suffusing his face. Staring at the floor, he was clasping and unclasping his hands, not quite daring to speak his mind.

'We're thumping too many high balls in at Simmons,' persisted Redwood. 'We need someone in the side who can thread it through to him on the deck, exploit his pace. What about Rod Lyons?'

McNally could no longer control himself.

'Jesus Christ! That bloody pisspot?'

Then a little of his anger receded and a stealthy look crept into his eyes.

'Simmons has been bending your ear, hasn't he?' he demanded. 'I might have known, the sneaky bastard. He hadn't got the bottle to come to me.'

Now it was Redwood's turn to look uncomfortable.

'He called me at home on Sunday,' he admitted. 'But he's every right to do that if you won't listen. He thinks you've got it in for him.'

'He's bloody right there,' snapped McNally. 'He's nothing but a waste of money.'

'Maybe Lyons can help him out.'

McNally shook his head violently.

'That drunk can't even help himself. He's just a shirker with a bad attitude.'

Redwood's voice was icy: 'He's off the bottle now, Dougie, And he's got talent, just like Gus Simmons. God knows we haven't got enough of that to be able to waste it.'

'So what are you saying?'

'I want you to pick Rod Lyons.'

'No.'

Redwood felt he was being backed into a corner. He had not expected the Scotsman to be so intractable.

Slowly, he said: 'You are making it very difficult for me. I have to safeguard the interests of this club as I see them.'

McNally glared at him, spitting out the bitter rejoinder: 'You mean sack me.'

'That is an option, yes.'

McNally was rising to his feet, already so far past the point of no return that he no longer bothered to conceal his contempt.

'Listen Redwood,' he snarled. 'I'm still the manager of Bradcaster City and I pick the team. If you don't like that, then get rid of me.'

With a thunderous slam of Redwood's office door, he was gone.

Gus Simmons was rubbing liniment into his legs, caressing the loose calf muscles.

Crouched on a dressing room bench, he was becoming hypnotised by the motion of his own hands as they smoothed the oil into his flesh. He was exorcising all the pain and tumult from his mind, which was drifting into blankness.

He eased on his elasticated shin pads and over them his blue Bradcaster stockings, tying them behind his knee. Then the ritual of his boots. He bent each in turn, testing the supplenesss of the leather, and checked the studs for any traces of mud.

Satisfied, he pulled them on and laced them carefully, passing the laces once beneath his instep before knotting them.

By the time he accomplished this, he was tightly focused within himself, oblivious to the raucous laughter or the shouts of motivation from the other players in the dressing room.

It was ten minutes before kick-off at another Bradcaster City home game. They were playing host to their bitter rivals from across the Pennines, Wakefield Town.

The turnstiles had been thronged for over an hour, as carefully segregated fans streamed through the city's backstreets. This was going to be Bradcaster's first capacity crowd for months.

Even inside the dressing room, deep beneath the west stand, the roar of the filling stadium was clearly audible. The atmosphere was growing tenser by the minute, every chant sending a wave of anticipation through the players.

Dougie McNally was bent over a defender, gripping his shoulders and hammering home some tactic in a low, intense voice.

'You got that?' he kept demanding, over and over again. The player was nodding mutely.

Dave Stewart, the Bradcaster captain, was pacing up and down the dressing room like a caged beast, his studs clattering on the floor. He caught sight of Simmons, who was leaning back with his eyes closed and sucking in deep lungfuls of air.

Stewart strode over and cuffed Simmons about the head, hard enough to hurt. Startled, the black striker's eyes widened in surprise and then in anger.

'You gonna pull your finger out today, black boy?' taunted Stewart. 'Start earning all that money?'

'Fuck off,' hissed Simmons, his body tensing like cat's.

Stewart was standing aggressively over him, fists bunched.

'What did you say?'

Simmons' voice was dripping with acid: 'I told you to fuck off, you carthorse.'

Enraged, Stewart swung back his fist, which was level with Simmons' face. But before he could deliver the blow, Simmons arched his back and swung his knee up viciously between his captain's legs.

Stewart let out a groan of agony and in an instant Simmons leapt at him, clutching at his throat. Under the weight of the onslaught, Stewart toppled backwards and landed heavily with the weight of the striker on him.

He screamed, an awful high-pitched noise. As he fell, his knee had twisted beneath him and been wrenched sideways.

Now he lay writhing in a heap, his face contorted.

'Jesus, oh Jesus,' he was whimpering.

The dressing room was in uproar. Dougie McNally was cursing and yelling at the physio, players were gathering around the supine shape of Stewart, trying to comfort him.

Simmons was staring at the pain-wracked face of his captain. All the frustration of the last few weeks had come spilling out. His face was still set in a mask of anger but gradually a sense of horror was seeping through.

The physio was placing cool fingers on the forehead of Stewart, exploring his damaged knee with the other hand.

He looked up at the anxious face of McNally, grimaced and said briskly: 'He's ripped his ligaments. Get a stretcher down here and get him to hospital fast.'

McNally gestured one of his players away down the corridor for help. He looked stunned.

'How bad is it?' he asked, not wanting to know the answer.

'Bad enough. He could be out for the rest of the season.'

'Oh God.'

He shook his head and looked bewildered. Then he turned to Simmons, who was rising slowly to his feet.

'You stupid black bastard,' he snapped. 'What the fuck was all that about?'

'He started it. Ask him.'

'I'm asking you.'

Simmons met McNally's glare with iron resolve.

'He was having a go,' he said. 'All of you have been on my back since I got here. I've had enough.'

Just then two ambulancemen burst into the room with a stretcher. They lifted Stewart gingerly off the floor, the Bradcaster physio barking instructions.

Their entrance burst the swelling tension between Simmons and his manager. McNally turned to watch the captain being carried away, still groaning, his forearm draped across his face.

The Scotsman glanced at his watch and cursed. It was just five minutes to kick-off and his team were due on the pitch.

'Right,' he shouted, clapping his hands for attention. 'We've got a football match to play. Put this out of your minds and concentrate on what I told you. Get your arses out there.'

The players filed towards the door, still looking shell-shocked. McNally looked across at the replacements, who were bringing up the rear of the shuffling, muttering group.

'You, Lyons!' he barked. 'Get stripped off, for Christ's sake. You're playing in the middle of the park.'

Rod Lyons swivelled around in amazement and McNally thrust a gnarled finger in his face.

'Just don't let me down,' he warned. 'Or you'll never play football for this club again.'

The midfielder discarded his tracksuit with feverish speed and dashed after the rest of the team. He caught them just as they emerged into daylight at the end of the tunnel.

They hit a wall of sound, which seemed to knock the breath out of Lyons' body. This was the first game he had started for over a year.

The opposing ranks of Bradcaster and Wakefield fans were tossing chants across the pitch to each other, thrusting their arms in unison, making obscene gestures. It was an almost gladiatorial atmosphere, pregnant with hatred and the lust for conquest.

Lyons felt the give of the turf beneath his studs. This time, he vowed to himself, it was going to be different.

Then the Bradcaster fans, realising he was on the pitch, began a chant which thrilled him to the core.

'There's only one Rod Lyons!' they sang. 'Only one Rod Lyons!'

It was like a homecoming. Lyons sprinted to the centre circle, where Gus Simmons was standing with a broad smile spread all over his face. The two men raised their arms high and cracked their palms together in a high-fives.

'All-right!' shouted Simmons above the roar of the crowd. 'Let's show these bastards what we can do.'

The game started at a breakneck pace with wild tackles coming in from all directions. Two yellow cards were brandished in the first five minutes before the pattern of the match began to emerge.

The midfield became the battleground, where Wakefield had a robust and destructive unit. But gradually Lyons started to boss the game, foraging for the ball and creating intricate triangles around the centre circle.

Simmons was pulling deep to link with him, flicking the ball wide and looking for the return behind defenders. With deft passes from Lyons delivered to his feet and into space, Simmons looked a different player, purposeful and inventive.

After half an hour, Bradcaster were firmly in control and the passionate Wakefield fans had grown quiet.

Then Simmons picked up another slide-rule pass from Lyons, turning out of a clumsy challenge. Looking up, he saw a gap and his pace took him clear but he was caught at the edge of the box by a scything late tackle, just as he was shaping to shoot.

The referee's whistle shrilled. A direct free kick just 20 yards out and almost straight in front of goal.

Simmons picked himself up, gingerly feeling his Achilles, and tossed the ball to Rod Lyons.

'Bend it,' he said simply.

Lyons placed the ball in front of him, faced by a wall of five Wakefield players clutching their groins. The keeper was anxiously bouncing from one goalpost to the other, screaming instructions.

Elsewhere in the penalty box, Bradcaster players were jostling for position, making dummy runs in a bid to tear holes in the defence. The referee gave another blast on his whistle.

Lyons took half a dozen almost casual strides and clipped the ball with his right instep. It curled beyond the wall towards the top corner.

Stranded on the other side of the goal, the keeper could

only watch leaden-footed. The Bradcaster fans were already shouting in triumph as the ball continued its arc.

But they let out a deep universal groan as it thudded against the angle of post and crossbar and rebounded back into play.

It bounced high into the air, the players underneath seeming to watch in slow motion. Simmons was bursting through the crowded penalty area and the Wakefield defence saw the danger too late.

He was already in the air by the time the defenders turned. In a split-second his header was bulging the back of an empty net.

Simmons clenched both fists in a salute to the crowd, a gesture of defiance as much as celebration. They were delirious. Suddenly everything was forgiven.

The first Bradcaster player to reach Simmons was Rod Lyons, who caught him in a joyous bear hug.

'You bastard!' he was shouting. 'You lucky, lucky bastard!'

Over on the touchline, amid the tumult of the crowd, even Dougie McNally wore a wry smile.

'Oh my God, listen to this,' said Simmons with an ironic laugh. 'All of a sudden, I'm a star.'

Scattered across his breakfast table were the Sunday tabloid newspapers. His plate of scrambled eggs and smoked Scottish salmon lay untouched, his cup of milky tea was stone cold.

' "Super Simmo In Goal Blitz",' he read aloud from a back page banner headline. 'This time yesterday, I was just some kind of rubbish. Look at this.'

He brandished another newspaper, which carried a photograph of him gesturing to the Bradcaster crowd, fingers aloft. The headline read: Three Of The Best From Dark Destroyer.

In his voice was a mixture of loathing and triumph: 'Hypocrites!'

He tossed the papers aside. Outside, the lawns were touched with frost, the trees bare and spectral. Melanie was staring at them through the French windows, her chin cupped in one palm.

'Mmm,' she mumbled absently.

The lone cawing of a crow was carried to them on the wind like the echo of a bad dream. The sky was black and thunderous, pregnant with rain.

'You're not even listening,' he said, hurt.

Stirring from her reverie, she replied: 'What? I'm sorry, I was just thinking, that's all.'

'The papers. They're all over me because I scored a hat trick.'

'Oh.'

He looked searchingly at his wife but her gaze had returned to the frost-shrouded garden.

'You don't care, do you?' he said angrily. 'I finally prove them all wrong and you don't give a shit. You weren't even at the match.'

'You know why,' she whispered softly, turning to look at him.

'Just because of something they shouted that day? I've had that since I could walk. It's like water off a duck's back.'

She shook her head sadly.

'Not from your own people, calling you names like that. How do you think it made me feel?'

'If it doesn't bother me, why should it bother you?'

Tears had started into her eyes. He looked away, not wanting to see, tired of her anguish.

'I felt ashamed,' she said, her voice unsteady.

He didn't trust himself to reply and they lapsed into an edgy silence. After a minute or two, his impatience swelled to the surface and he thrust his plate of cold eggs away noisily.

'What the hell is the matter with you anyway?' he demanded. 'Look at this place.'

He gestured around the airy room and towards the gardens, inviting her to collude in the pride of his possession.

'This is what I've given you. And all you do is complain.'

She replied dully: 'I didn't want to come here.'

Enraged, Simmons snatched up his tea and dashed it in her face. It drenched her and ran away in brown rivulets, all over her pale silk dressing gown. She stared at him in silent shock and amazement.

'Ungrateful bitch!' he screamed.

But already he was appalled by what he had done, angry words were dying in his throat. He grasped a linen napkin and jabbed it at her, almost tenderly.

Wordlessly, she took it from him and wiped her eyes. Fresh mascara clung to the material in great black smudges.

'What's gone wrong, Gus?' she asked with a child's simplicity, still dabbing at her cheeks.

He didn't reply for a moment. He had noticed the shape of her bare collarbone, the valley between her breasts. He was stung by reawakened desire.

Simmons reached out a tentative hand across the breakfast table and grasped her hand. Unwillingly at first, Melanie squeezed his fingers in reply. Even now, she could not find it in her heart to reject him.

'Why don't you hate me?' he asked softly. 'God knows you should.'

'Perhaps I do.'

'Don't say that.'

She looked at him with raw eyes, her expression full of longing and uncertainty.

'It's not you I hate,' she said. 'It's this place. It's so lonely, Gus. We're such a long way from home.'

Now he was imploring her: 'Look Mel, there's no going back. Now I'm scoring goals, things will be easier.'

She looked pained and withdrew her hand from his grasp.

'Only for you, can't you see that?'

Simmons let out a bitter sigh of exasperation and bewilderment. All she wanted was a fantasy of their life together, before the corrosive influence of fame had set in.

But Gus Simmons wasn't about to abandon the chase for glory just yet. Nostalgia was for has-beens and he was going places fast.

SEND ROUND THE BEGGING DISH!

Spacelink hits fans where it hurts

SOCCER fans will have to buy a satellite dish to watch televised live matches in next season's Super League.

Gone will be the days when the only cost of a Sunday afternoon goal feast was a packet of fags and a four-pack.

Under the terms of yesterday's £300 million deal, Michael Conrad's Spacelink will have exclusive broadcast rights to Super League games for the next five years.

But England's army of armchair fans is likely to have to fork out more than just £200 for a dish.

Spacelink has promised that next season's games will be free to subscribers of its sports channel.

But they seem certain to introduce so-called 'pay-to-view' in future years. That will see fans charged extra to watch the really big games.

The sheer size of the Spacelink bid has created a cash windfall for the breakaway Super League clubs. Each is guaranteed well over £1 million a year and, for regularly televised clubs, there could be a bonanza.

The Spacelink bid was accepted by a two-thirds majority after being recommended by Super League executives. It leaves ITV, who bid £200 million, out in the cold.

Supporters and MPs alike have reacted with fury to the news.

Labour's home affairs spokesman, Barry Driscoll, fumed: 'The greed of a handful of top clubs means our national game will be priced beyond the reach of most supporters. Many will have to choose between the cost of a season ticket or a satellite dish.'

The nationwide Football Fans Association labelled the deal 'a shabby sell-out which leaves supporters worse off than ever before'.

Even the players themselves are unhappy. The Union of Professional Footballers has yet to reach agreement with Super League officials over the size of their share-out.

They have also warned that playing games on Monday nights for the benefit of TV cameras could change the face of the game for ever.

Unless their demands are heeded by the new regime, the prospect of a crippling players' strike is very real.

But none of this opposition was enough to dampen the optimism of Tom Haslam, managing director of Spacelink.

'This is the beginning of a new era in sports broadcasting,' he claimed. 'It is a good deal for football and a good deal for the fans.

'We confidently expect that the quality of our coverage will persuade many millions more households to invest in satellite technology.'

Michael Conrad was floating lazily on his back, lulled by the blood-warm water in his indoor swimming pool.

Above him was a great glass dome that magnified the spring sunlight pouring through, creating a soft glow on his skin. The pool was tiled with an interlocking pattern of mosaics in vibrant aquamarines.

The effect was disconcerting; at once an echo from the Mediterranean and something indefinable and strange, a curious translucent fantasy world.

With a flick of his legs and turn of his body, Conrad dived to the bottom in a graceful curving descent. He touched the tiles with both hands, running his fingers over the raised edges.

Still submerged, he kicked his legs behind him like a frog and moved towards the far end of the pool, the light casting dappled and sinuous shapes across his body.

Reaching the wall, he burst upwards and broke the surface gasping, water streaming from his body. He hoisted himself onto the side of the pool and sat with his legs still dangling in the warm liquid, which was scented with chlorine and Scandinavian pines.

He was entirely naked.

A flash of white at the far end of the room caught his eye. Glancing up, he saw his wife Alexandra in a towelling bath robe and his heart clenched like a fist.

'Morning, darling!' she called out.

Her mane of hair was swept off her face in a pony tail. There were 20 years between them and it made her look younger still. She paused at the pool's edge and let the robe drop to the floor.

Her body was still perfect, Conrad thought. She raised her arms, tensed her legs and plunged into the water, diving deep. Surfacing, she set out in a slow front crawl, her elbows angular in the water.

In a few moments she reached him and thrust her face upwards between his knees, smiling and clasping his legs. With her face tilted towards him, she looked girlish and vulnerable.

He knew that was horribly deceptive but still he felt a pulse starting to thump in the base of his neck.

'Congratulations on the football deal,' she was saying in a singsong voice, kicking her legs to stay afloat. 'I'm sorry I wasn't here when you got in last night.'

'Where were you?'

'Oh, nowhere,' she replied maddeningly, pushing herself off into the water again.

He watched her perform a few sedate lengths of the pool with a rising sense of helplessness. She hauled herself out of the opposite end of the pool, bending for a towel to wipe her dripping body.

She rubbed vigorously and her breasts swayed in time to the motion. Reaching between her legs, she mopped at the soft, damp mound. Then she collapsed onto a sun lounger and stretched herself languorously, still naked.

As if drawn by some invisible force, Conrad rose to his feet and moved across the room towards her. She lay with her eyes closed but he knew she was aware of his presence. He stood awkwardly for a moment, marvelling: the delicate curve of her neck, the fine dark hairs below her navel, the swelling curves of her hips.

Abruptly, he knelt and bent his head towards the centre of her body. She shivered. With his tongue he parted the hair around her labia and lapped at her clitoris. Her body surged upwards to meet his flickering snake's tongue.

Conrad was tasting her, scenting her, burying his fingers deep into the flesh of her thighs. His mouth was filling with the juices of her arousal.

'Take me!' he heard her urging. 'For God's sake Michael, fuck me now!'

With a gnawing sense of unease, he clambered above her as she spread her legs for him hungrily. He stroked her moist opening with his fingers and she moaned out: 'Now, just do it, now!'

It felt like he was drowning.

'I . . . I'm sorry,' he stammered. 'I can't.'

Alexandra reached down between his legs, searching for him. But instead of grasping hardness, her fingers closed around something soft and flaccid. She threw her arm down, letting out a sigh of anger and disappointment.

'Jesus, not again!'

'I'm sorry,' Conrad repeated dully. 'It's not you, I promise.'

Alexandra was pushing him off with her legs.

'I know bloody well it's not me.'

Stumbling to his feet, Conrad went tense. In an instant, his expression of humiliation was replaced by a glowering mask of rage.

'What the hell do you mean by that?' he demanded, his voice thick with passion.

Suddenly Alexandra looked slightly frightened. She grabbed the towel to cover her nakedness.

'Nothing, Michael. Honestly.'

He was looming over her threateningly.

'Listen to me, you bitch,' he snarled. 'If I ever find out you've been with another man, I'll kill you both. Do you understand?'

Alexandra nodded dumbly. She knew he meant it and it chilled her to the bone.

Gregory sighed and swung his legs up onto his desk. It had been a long day. He fished for a Marlboro, lit it with his Zippo and sucked in a great lungful of smoke.

He closed his eyes and tilted back his head, blowing the smoke through his nostrils. It was just after nine o'clock in the evening and he had been hammering out his copy until the deadline for the last issue.

In the Daily World's Bradcaster office there were only a dozen or so journalists, a great fall from grace since the halcyon days when the city was a major media centre. Now just about everything was controlled from London, by people who got a nose bleed if they went further north than Watford.

Gregory leaned to switch off his computer screen. Idly, he began to leaf through his morning's mail, which had sat untouched all day.

It was the usual diet of feverishly over-written press releases about nothing in particular. Cursing under his breath, Gregory was tearing open envelopes, scanning the first couple of paragraphs of copy and then tossing the screwed-up paper into an overflowing waste bin.

'Bloody rubbish,' he was muttering to himself. 'Why do they send me this shit?'

Then something caught his eye: the royal blue and burgundy of the Spacelink logo on a sheet of headed paper.

The release was titled 'Spacelink Wins Super League Rights For £300 million'. Gregory smiled cynically. It was just a rehash of the previous day's announcement, with a quote from Conrad.

'We're on the march,' he was alleged to have said. 'Only Spacelink can broadcast the very best sporting action at home and from around the world. We are becoming a vital part of the British way of life.'

'Oh bollocks,' said Gregory aloud.

He took another deep drag from his cigarette and was about to discard the document. But then the very last paragraph leapt out at him.

'For more information,' it read. 'Please contact Steve Wilde at Wilde Communications.'

Another piece of the jigsaw.

'Jesus,' mused Gregory to himself. 'It's a stitch-up whichever way you look.'

From the corner of his eye, he glimpsed the portly shape of Harry Walters emerging from the editor's office, a set of bromides under his arm.

Gregory yelled out to him: 'Harry, got a minute?'

'No,' replied Walters but wandered over to Gregory's desk anyway. 'Make it quick.'

'Can you spare me tomorrow? There's something I want to check out down in the smoke. Well, Fulham anyhow.'

'West End poofters,' said Walters dismissively. 'Doesn't count. What's up?'

'It's this Bradcaster business. I'm getting close to breaking it right open and I need to speak to Steve Wilde. You know, that bloody shark that's looking after Simmons.'

Sitting at a nearby desk was Nick Forde, the World's northern show business editor. He pricked up his ears.

'Sorry to interrupt chaps,' he said. 'But is that the TV producer? Bit of a smarmy bastard?'

Gregory shook his head: 'Not to my knowledge, must be another bloke.'

But Forde persisted.

'No, I'm sure that's him. He used to run a soap opera on Spacelink, bloody terrible stuff. He jumped ship when the ratings went through the floor.'

Gregory grinned in triumph. Things were falling into place.

Harry Walters gave him a hard look and said: 'You'd better be off then. Just tread carefully, that's all.'

Then he smiled, adding: 'Have a pint of Fuller's for me.'

By the time Gregory got back to his flat, he felt shattered. Ignoring the days-old debris of unwashed plates and spilling ashtrays, he grabbed a whisky bottle from the kitchen table and poured himself a drink.

He collapsed on to a sofa and clicked on the television set. Impatiently, he skipped from channel to channel with the remote control, searching for something to hold his attention. It was the usual late-night diet of B-movies and music videos.

He squeezed the bridge of his nose, grimacing. Before he had taken even a single slug of Scotch, Gregory was fast asleep.

Just after nine o'clock the following morning, unshaven and still wearing the crumpled clothes he had slept in, he was hailing a cab outside Euston train station.

The journey across town seemed to take for ever. Gregory hated London: the thick pall of exhaust fumes from idle and angry traffic, the thrust and bustle of the streets, its rearing buildings, the whole impersonal machine.

The taxi crawled down the King's Road and into Fulham High Street, where oblivious pedestrians played chicken with the cars. Ahead of him, Gregory could make out Putney Bridge and then the car turned towards Fulham Palace Road.

A side street led down towards the river and the cab pulled up outside a converted brick boathouse.

'There you go, mate,' said the cabbie, turning over his left shoulder to squint at Gregory. 'That'll be nine pounds eighty.'

Gregory got out and jabbed a ten-pound note through the cab's front window.

'Keep the change,' he said.

The cabbie scowled: 'Oh, a bloody comedian.'

'Any chance of a receipt?'

'None at all, mate.'

The cab sped away, whining through its gears. Gregory stared up at the smoked glass windows of the boathouse, which were etched with two bold words: Wilde Communications.

Arrows pointed Gregory down a slipway to the rear of the building and then up an iron spiral staircase to the first floor. The reception area was fitted out in aggressive metropolitan chic, everything in black and white: angular lampstands and spindly minimalist chairs, pale leather sofas.

Gregory felt as though he had stepped into a monochrome movie. He also felt stubbly and unwashed.

The girl behind the desk was a glamorous West Indian, hair swept severely off her face and scraped into a bun, her full lips painted an iridescent scarlet. She wore saucer-shaped glasses which lent her a touch of arrogance.

'Can I help you?'

Her voice was clipped and precise. Gregory felt her eying him up and down.

'Colin Gregory, Daily World sports reporter. I'd like to see Steve Wilde.'

'Do you have an appointment?'

'No.'

She flashed him a frosty smile.

'Please take a seat. I'll see if Mr Wilde is available.'

'He'd better be, love. I've come a long way.'

Gregory sauntered over to one of the sofas and threw himself into it. Despite the total absence of ashtrays, he rummaged for his Marlboros and lit up.

The receptionist was glaring malevolently at him and whispering into the telephone. Finally, after a pantomime of shrugs and hand gestures, she replaced the receiver.

'Mr Wilde will be with you shortly.'

'Oh goody.'

Her luscious lips compressed into a thin red line of contempt. She resumed her typing, fingers clattering angrily on the computer keyboard.

In a few moments, Steve Wilde burst into the foyer with a wolfish grin. He bore down on Gregory with outstretched arm.

'Colin!' he said warmly. 'We haven't met but I know of you, naturally. What brings you to London?'

Rising, Gregory shook the proffered hand brusquely.

'You do.'

'I'm flattered. Come through.'

Wilde gestured towards his office, touching Gregory briefly in the small of his back as he passed.

'Make yourself at home.'

The room was dominated by a desk so large it could happily have accommodated a troupe of dancing elephants. Around the walls were hung garish original abstracts in oils. Through the window, Gregory could see the Thames sliding greasily by.

'Very nice,' he said sardonically.

'Thanks,' acknowledged Wilde, choosing to ignore the tone in Gregory's voice. 'Now, what can I do for you?'

He had settled in behind his enormous desk. Gregory wasn't getting caught like that. He stayed on his feet, pacing the room with his hands in his pockets.

'I believe you're handling the gin and tonic account for Spacelink these days.'

'If you mean the public relations contract, yes.'

'What's Michael Conrad like to work with?'

Wilde was getting a little testy.

'He's fine. Why do you ask?'

'You were one of his producers at Spacelink.'

It was not a question, merely a statement of fact. Wilde nodded.

Gregory gave Wilde a searching look.

'Very cosy,' he said.

'What the hell do you mean by that?' snapped Wilde, flustered.

'Michael Conrad wanted Gus Simmons to sign for Bradcaster City. You persuade the lad the move is in his best interests – and all of a sudden Conrad is throwing money at you.'

Wilde was on his feet.

'I don't know what you're suggesting . . . '

'I think you do,' interrupted Gregory, his voice steady. 'I think you're in it up to your neck. You've been bribed, you greedy bastard.'

Wilde had slumped back into his chair, shaking his head nervously.

'You can't prove any of this.'

'Oh come on. I know Conrad put up four million quid for the transfer. You were just a little bit of insurance. What the bloody hell is he up to?'

'I've no idea,' said Wilde weakly. 'Look, will you promise to keep me out of this?'

'What for? You haven't told me anything.'

There was a wheedling tone in Wilde's voice. He knew if Gregory's allegations hit the streets, his business would be ruined.

'I don't know anything,' he pleaded. 'I'm not even sure the money for Simmons was from him. Honestly, I'd tell you if I knew.'

Gregory snorted with impatience, turning for the door.

'I should have known that Conrad wouldn't trust a grasping shit like you. But I'm going to nail your balls to the mast along with his.'

As he left, Wilde was wearing a blank and stunned expression. Passing through the foyer, Gregory gave the receptionist a long, lascivious wink. She didn't even acknowledge his presence.

Day by day, Sid Graveney was growing ever more tense. His chain of butcher's shops was dipping into the red and devouring capital. Bradcaster City Football Club had become a source of pain and disillusionment.

Arthur Redwood, whom he had considered his friend, had grown distant and suspicious. Graveney bitterly regretted his secret conversations with the Daily World, his betrayal of Redwood.

But he still believed that any partnership with the ruthless Michael Conrad was a passport to destruction. Why couldn't Redwood see that?

Graveney was spending less and less time at the club because of the poisonous atmosphere of mistrust hanging over it. He was saddened that he was unable to share in Bradcaster's ripening success on the field.

So his life was turning sour. He felt crushed by isolation. He had no real friends in which to confide, only business acquaintances who would rejoice at his misfortune when his back was turned.

He had long since given up on his wife, a cold woman whose only interests were his bank balance and keeping up appearances. He was aching for a sense of human communion.

So he turned once again in the only direction he knew. With a pounding heart, he keyed in a familiar number on his car 'phone. A woman's voice answered, hard-edged, cautious.

'Hello love,' mumbled Graveney. 'It's Sid. Could you fit me in today? . . . Yeah, yeah . . . Sandra if she's around . . . OK . . . Nine o'clock? Fine.'

He replaced the receiver in its cradle and swung the BMW away out of town, gunning the powerful engine. He kept driving for several miles, threading his way through the moorland that lay north of Bradcaster.

Finally, he pulled up alongside an old stone wall topped with slates. He got out of the car and breathed the clean air. Far below him, hills of barren tundra tumbled almost to the edges of the city.

As he watched, the spring evening began slowly to darken; lights flickered in the distance, car headlamps were streaming away from Bradcaster. Graveney was conscious of a rising emptiness inside him.

He glanced at the luminous fingers of his watch in the

gloom. Almost half past eight. He climbed back into the car and pointed it towards the glowing city.

It was near the appointed time when he reached a dark backstreet on the east side of Bradcaster. The BMW secreted itself among shadows and overflowing sacks of refuse.

A pale light shone from behind blinds in a shabby shop front. Across the window, peeling plastic letters spelled out the words: Poppy's Health Club.

Glancing furtively up and down the deserted street, Graveney strode quickly to the doorway and disappeared inside. Just as he did so, another car nosed down the street.

It parked close by and extinguished its headlights. But no driver emerged.

Inside, a hard-faced blonde looked up as Graveney entered.

'Sign the book,' she said in a bored voice, pushing over a register of signatures.

Graveney scribbled the single word 'Sid'. He noticed with a momentary twinge of amusement that the previous punter had signed himself as Saddam Hussein.

'You know where to go,' said the blonde, jabbing her thumb towards a dingy staircase. 'She's waiting for you.'

Graveney mounted the stairs with a dry throat, pushed open a door and moved inside. It was a drab room with a bare light bulb; street lamps glinted through the thin, stained curtains.

Squatting on a chair in the centre of the room was a plain middle-aged woman in a white tunic. She was smoking a cigarette, its filter stained with her cheap lipstick.

There was a wedding ring on one of the plump fingers of her left hand. She looked up.

'Hello love,' she said wearily. 'Get yourself ready, I'll be with you in a minute.'

She continued dragging at the cigarette. In the room was

another chair, a sink and a leather couch with a plastic sheet laid across it. Graveney took several notes from his wallet and placed them on the chair.

Clumsily, he started to unbutton his clothes, discarding them in a pile on the floor. He stood there naked like a great pot-bellied schoolboy. He clambered onto the couch and lay face up, wordlessly staring at the ceiling.

'Usual is it, love?' said the woman.

Graveney grunted. Stubbing out her cigarette, the woman unzipped her tunic and stepped out of it. She unclasped her bra, freeing a pendulous and heavily veined pair of breasts, but retained her shapeless white knickers.

She advanced towards Graveney, rubbing oil into her palms. Swinging a clumsy leg across the couch, she straddled his waist. He stared at her swinging breasts as she began to massage the oil into his chest, tweaking the nipples between her long fingernails.

'Uugghh,' came a noise from Graveney's throat.

After a few minutes of this, she moved her weight to his thighs and started to stroke closer and closer to his groin. His penis was stiff and twitching to meet her teasing hands. Each time, the oily fingers brushed a little nearer and then withdrew.

Then, without warning, she grasped him hard with both hands and caressed the full length of his shaft. Graveney gave a loud, involuntary scream of ecstasy.

A split-second later, the door burst open and the whore screeched her surprise. Graveney struggled to rise but her dead weight across his thighs prevented him.

He saw the dark shape of a man and then his eyes were speared by the blinding light from a camera's flash bulb. Instinctively, he thrust out a palm towards the camera, protecting his face.

But by then the man was gone and it was too late.

* * *

'I thought you would like this,' said Conrad. 'It's a tape of the radio commentary for the 1959 cup final.'

Redwood was cradling the cassette in his hands, an expression of delight suffusing his face. He was shaking his head in disbelief.

'The television coverage had been wiped,' Conrad was continuing. 'But this was still locked away in a vault at the BBC. Fortunately, I was able to pull a few strings. Must bring back memories.'

Redwood smiled and said in a wistful voice: 'Oh yes. It was the greatest day of my life. We had a marvellous team in those days.'

'I remember.'

The two men were in Conrad's suite at the luxurious Bradcaster Hilton, whose Georgian facade reared above one of the city's main thoroughfares.

'Can I get you a drink, Arthur?' enquired Conrad, moving towards a huge refrigerator housed within a wooden cabinet.

He flipped it open to reveal an array of brightly-coloured bottles and cans.

'Why not?' said a suddenly garrulous Redwood. 'I'll have a brandy with you. Here's to Bradcaster City and the 1959 cup final.'

He grabbed the offered drink and clinked his glass expansively against Conrad's. His nostalgic smile held a warmth that had not been seen for many weeks.

'This was very good of you,' he said, tapping the cassette inside his breast pocket. 'What made you think of it?'

Conrad stared directly at Redwood with an expression of absolute sincerity.

'I wanted to thank you. Winning the Super League rights was a triumph for Spacelink. Your work behind the scenes helped persuade a few waverers that we were the best bet.'

Momentarily, Redwood looked uncomfortable.

'Oh, I don't know it made all that much difference,' he said quickly. 'The money will be very welcome, of course. But I hope Spacelink won't insist on too many games being played on a Monday evening.'

Conrad smiled and spread his fingers in a defensive gesture.

'It's not up to me, Arthur.'

There was a hint of suspicion in Redwood's face but he made no comment. Taking another swig of brandy, he deposited himself in an antique leather armchair.

Conrad remained standing, cupping his glass in the palm of his hand and gently swilling around the brandy to release its pungent fragrance.

His voice acquired a heavier and more serious tone: 'Arthur, I'm afraid I have some bad news for you.'

Redwood glanced up, startled.

'It relates to the loan I made to Bradcaster to fund the transfer of Gus Simmons.'

'What the hell do you mean?' snapped Redwood, panic-stricken. 'Is there a problem?'

'I'm afraid so. As you know, it was convenient for me to advance the money through one of my private companies. That company has now fallen on hard times.'

Conrad was calmly staring down into his brandy, still softly swirling it. Redwood had grown still and his voice was tight.

'What are you trying to say?'

'I have no option but to recall the loan.'

Redwood was out of his chair, eyes popping, his face masked with shock and rage.

'You can't do that! For God's sake, the money has already changed hands!'

'I am perfectly within my rights,' said Conrad steadily. 'You may recall the bankruptcy clause in our agreement. Conrad Reprographics faces liquidation and, in those circumstances, I have the power to recall the money.'

Redwood was running nervous fingers through his white-grey hair. He was fighting hard against hysteria.

'How can that be? Your own newspapers were its biggest customer.'

Conrad shrugged and bared his teeth in a malevolent smile.

'It was no longer competitive,' he said. 'We found a better deal elsewhere.'

Redwood had thrown himself back into the chair, holding his head in his hands as if it were about to burst.

'You just can't do this,' he intoned, almost to himself. 'You just can't.'

Then he looked up and bored into Conrad with his cold blue eyes.

'You're going to ruin Bradcaster City. Is that what you want, you bastard?'

Even Conrad was taken aback for a second by the ferocity of Redwood's stare. But he soon composed himself.

'Of course not,' he said soothingly and paused. 'Indeed it is possible that my newspapers will come back into the fold. But there is a condition.'

'I thought there might be,' muttered Redwood bitterly.

Conrad stepped out onto the balcony of the top-floor suite. Beneath him, traffic was roaring and honking in a rush-hour log jam. The whole of the west side of Bradcaster was spread out like a scale model.

'This is a big, vibrant city,' Conrad murmured with his back to Redwood. 'It's going places. But its football club is still trapped in the Fifties. It badly needs an injection of leadership.'

Conrad turned to face the silent, glowering Arthur Redwood.

'I want to buy your share of the club, Arthur. That's the condition.'

As the Bradcaster team coach threaded its way deeper into London, Simmons became quieter and more withdrawn.

Alongside him, Rod Lyons had long since given up making conversation and instead had a pair of stereo headphones clamped to his ears. His mouth was moving silently in time with the lyrics.

Bradcaster were on the crest of a wave, unbeaten for the last dozen matches and rising rapidly up the league. The rest of the coach was humming with confidence; players were laughing, swapping insults, talking tactics.

But Simmons himself remained aloof. He knew the supporters of this particular North London side had a reputation for virulent racism, he had been warned what to expect.

But he wasn't looking forward to it one little bit. Thank God Melanie wasn't going to be in the crowd.

Nearing the ground, hours before kick-off, there were already signs of fans gathering. Tight knots of youths were lounging outside pubs, clutching pints of ale. Desultory chanting came from somewhere in the distance.

As the coach turned towards the stadium car park, it came across a gang of 50 or so men, bedecked in the tribal colours of their team. Many also wore the skinhead uniform: jeans and braces, Doc Martens, swastikas.

Like a pack of wild animals they surrounded the coach, banging and kicking the sides, shouting obscenities. The players were used to this and simply stared straight ahead, ignoring the commotion.

But then one man reared up at Simmons' window, eyes wild. He was horribly gaunt, emphasised by the shaven head. There were tattoos around the base of his neck and a cross in the middle of his forehead.

He was yelling at the top of his voice, face contorted, the tendons in his neck tight as bow strings. Although dulled by glass, the sound still knifed through the coach's interior.

'Nigger!' he was shouting, banging on the window with his fist. 'You fucking nigger bastard!'

By the time the coach reached sanctuary inside the stadium, a terrible stillness and silence had descended. No other player wanted to look at Simmons. Even Rod Lyons was bowing his head in shame and embarrassment.

Simmons stayed on the coach for a long time after the other players had alighted. His face was still and expressionless but his mind was racing.

He remained in the same withdrawn state throughout the build-up to the match. Instinctively, everyone respected the barrier he had erected around himself. Even Dougie McNally left him alone.

Although thousands of Bradcaster fans had made the long journey south, they did nothing to assuage the violently partisan atmosphere that was gradually swelling inside the stadium. It became a furnace of hatred.

When Bradcaster took the field, the animal chorus of booing and jeering was literally deafening. Simmons was at the very end of the line. As soon as he felt his studs sink into the turf, a great weight was lifted from his shoulders. Now this was his arena.

He sprinted hard into the centre of the pitch, testing himself. He felt weightless. He was flicking a ball in the air from foot to foot and it felt like a part of him, attached by some invisible thread.

Over in the terrace at the far end of the ground, a forest of arms was thrusting in a Nazi salute. As Simmons juggled with the ball, the heaving mass of bodies began to make a throaty, insistent sound with rounded mouths.

It was aimed at Simmons and it was meant to be the noise of a monkey.

He heard it and absorbed it within himself. The game

started and, from the first whistle, Simmons was unstoppable, carving out space with his runs, skating past toiling defenders.

Bradcaster had the match in a stranglehold, the opposition pinned in their own half and under incessant pressure. Gradually the crowd grew still until the travelling fans began to make themselves heard.

'You only sing when you're winning!' they taunted. 'Only sing when you're win-ning!'

Bradcaster forced a throw-in near the corner flag and Simmons dashed over to take it, looking to keep play moving. It was near the end where the opposition supporters were most tightly packed.

Simmons grabbed the ball and brought it back over his shoulders, eyes swivelling, searching for space. Just then something flew from the terraces and landed at his feet. He couldn't help glancing down to look.

It was a banana. And the crowd began chanting their ugly animal noises again.

For a moment, a look of utter repulsion and hatred swept across the face of Simmons. Then he smiled, arrogantly. Tossing the ball aside, he bent to pick up the banana.

He stared into the crowd, scanning the faces. He began to peel the banana with his long and delicate fingers, caressing it. Then he popped it into his mouth and bit off a huge chunk.

In a pantomime of ecstasy, he chewed the fruit, still with the smile spread over his face, rubbing his belly. The crowd had stopped its chant and was staring at him in disbelief.

A uniformed policeman stepped forward towards the touchline and hissed at Simmons: 'Oi! For Christ's sake, pack it in. You'll start a riot.'

Simmons nodded, threw aside the banana and reached for the ball. He glanced up, looking for someone to make a run, but even the players were rooted to the spot.

Behind the opposition goal, the crowd seemed to have shrunk in on itself. The terracing was alive with a low and angry murmuring.

Simmons' mouth twisted in a bitterly satisfied smile. He had made his point.

Arthur Redwood had been wrestling with his conscience ever since the nightmarish meeting with Conrad.

He knew that if Conrad carried out his threat and re-called the loan, Bradcaster City would inevitably be destroyed. A club that once had been the finest in the land and where tradition and decency still held some meaning.

He could hardly stand by and let that happen. Yet something else was gnawing away at Redwood; something that he was fighting against and that he considered unworthy.

It was the sickening feeling that he had been fleeced. Every time he thought about it, he was overwhelmed with rage and humiliation. How could he have been so blind?

There was also the matter of his reputation. Redwood was a man who demanded and expected respect. Throughout the world of football and far beyond, it was known that his word was his irrevocable bond. He would never have been suspected of a cowardly or dishonest act.

Yet now he had been fatally compromised. As Spacelink's errand boy, he had poured poison into the ears of many of his friends and acquaintances in the game. His tongue had betrayed his heart.

Finally, there was his beloved Bradcaster City. How could he face selling his share in the club to a shark like Michael Conrad? It would be a betrayal of everything he believed in.

Yet still he kept returning to the inescapable truth: unless Conrad and his lust for power were appeased, Bradcaster City would simply cease to exist. Wasn't that the most damning betrayal of all?

For three long days and nights, these contradictory thoughts had paralysed Redwood's brain. He was incapable of performing even the most menial chore; his chin was stubbled, his stomach empty. Everything else was subjugated to the battle raging in his head.

He had no choice but to convene an extraordinary meeting of the Bradcaster board. But even as his Daimler approached the stadium, he had no clear idea of what he would say.

Redwood knew that he and Sid Graveney held the axis of power at the football club. Graveney's quarter share combined with his own 30 per cent spelled absolute executive authority.

Most of the other shares were dissipated in dribs and drabs among dozens of descendants of the original founders. They were represented by a couple of token board appointments, elderly gentlemen who kept their mouths shut and were content with the perks of their position.

Only the club secretary and finance director, Harold Robinson, had amassed a substantial holding, amounting to just under a tenth. Redwood was pretty sure both Graveney and Robinson would be antagonistic to Conrad's interference.

That meant it would be hard for the media mogul to forge a power base; maybe the club could take his money and still keep him at arm's length. Or maybe not. They were dealing with a resourceful and ruthless man.

Still the thoughts were whirring in his head, without conclusion. They were all waiting for him when he entered the boardroom and his heart missed a beat.

'Good morning, gentlemen,' he said briskly, making for the head of the long and highly polished mahogany table.

The other four men gaped in astonishment at his unkempt appearance. The normally dapper Redwood looked as if he had slept in his clothes, which in fact he had. His blazer was creased and crumpled, his regimental tie askew, his chin grizzled.

But the ice-blue eyes still glinted. Arthur Redwood wasn't about to lose control just yet.

'What the bloody hell is all this about?' blustered Graveney as Redwood eased himself into his seat. 'I've got a business to run.'

Harold Robinson raised his hand to silence Graveney. Already he was beginning to realise that something was very wrong.

'I felt I had no option but to call this meeting,' said Redwood in a steady voice. 'Something has occurred which throws the entire future of this football club into jeopardy.'

Everyone around the table registered their amazement. Redwood paused for a few moments to let the gravity of the situation sink in.

But before he could continue, Graveney cut in: 'Conrad! I might have known. That bastard has stitched us up somehow.'

'Michael Conrad is involved, yes.'

Graveney sank back into his chair, shaking his head. He seemed, as he often did these days, to be on the verge of a violent fit.

Robinson said softly: 'Perhaps you had better explain.'

Redwood took a deep breath, still unsure of how to play this particular hand. Then he set his jaw and plunged in.

'Mr Conrad has made me an offer of two million pounds for my share in Bradcaster City. I have given the matter a great deal of thought and, reluctantly, I have decided to accept. As you know, any sale of shares has to be sanctioned by the board and that is why I called this meeting.'

There was a shocked silence. Around the walls of the

142

boardroom, the players in a collection of team photographs seemed to gaze down ironically.

Then Robinson murmured in a voice cracking with emotion: 'Arthur, why? Why?'

'It is not something I have done lightly. I . . . '

But Graveney had risen to his feet, banging the table with his fists, drowning out the clear, calm voice of Redwood.

'You've sold out, you bastard!' he was screaming. 'You had this planned all along. You let Conrad get his foot in the door and now he's kicking it down. You bloody Judas!'

Redwood did not get angry; he merely shook his head sadly. He seemed to be divorced from what was happening, occupying a different dimension. He was the only man in the room in command of himself.

'Sit down, Sid,' he said wearily. 'Let's try and be civilised about this, shall we?'

But Graveney had stalked over to the far end of the room, deliberately turning his back on Redwood. He was angrily splashing coffee into his cup from a gurgling percolator.

'This is not what I would have chosen,' continued Redwood, fixing Robinson with his gaze. 'But I was issued with an ultimatum. Unless I sell out to Conrad, he will withdraw his loan. He can do it, I assure you.'

He cleared his throat and for a moment tears welled in his eyes and burned there fiercely.

'I don't need to spell it out,' he said in a voice that was suddenly too loud. 'Everything we have worked for all these years would be destroyed. I can't allow that to happen.'

Robinson gave him a compassionate look and said: 'Jesus, Arthur, I'm sorry. How the hell have we let this happen?'

'Because none of you old fools would listen!' shouted

Graveney, dashing down his coffee cup and turning to point an angry, accusing finger around the table.

'I warned you till I was blue in the face. For Christ's sake, climb down out of your ivory towers. You were all so bloody naive. People like Conrad don't do anybody favours.'

In a still and faraway voice, Redwood said: 'I thought he would be happy with the deal we struck. I had promised to canvass on Spacelink's behalf during the TV rights negotiations.'

Then suddenly his face crumpled into an image of abject humiliation.

'I never told you at the time. I was too ashamed.'

Robinson was staring at him in disbelief.

'But Arthur,' he said, his voice rising. 'This club voted against Spacelink.'

'That was the majority decision of the board. It didn't stop me trying to influence others in the opposite direction.'

'Good God.'

The room lapsed into an uneasy silence. Silently, Sid Graveney slumped back into his seat, his face still tight with suppressed rage. Robinson looked shellshocked, the two other board members shifted uncomfortably but said nothing.

'So can we put Conrad's offer to the vote?' blurted Redwood as the silence grew oppressive.

He had chosen his path and now he was stumbling blindly onwards, determined to reach his goal but struggling to quieten the voices of dissent inside his head. He had not been prepared for this; his abdication scene lacked nobility.

With an effort, Robinson stirred himself.

'Two million is well below what your share is worth,' he said. 'Simmons is a major asset and, since we put together our unbeaten run, attendances have gone through the roof. He's lifting your leg, Arthur.'

'I know that. But what choice do we have?'

'Oh, spare us your bleeding heart,' spat Graveney. 'You're coming out of this smelling of roses. What's the matter, was it all getting too much for you? Do you think you can just walk away with two million quid stuffed in your back pocket? You fucking fraud!'

Robinson's voice was stern and icy, slicing through the big man's bluster: 'Sid, you're right out of order. Get off his back. He's done more for this club than any man alive.'

Graveney subsided into a dark sulk, swatting his hand dismissively. A pensive look stole across Robinson's face as he adjusted to the situation, balancing the possible advantages of Conrad's intervention.

'Do I take it that you are asking us to endorse this offer, Arthur?'

'Yes, I am.'

'It would certainly help our liquidity,' mused Robinson. 'Conrad is a rich man and let's face it, we need all the cash we can get if we're going to comply with the Taylor Report. This could prove a useful windfall.'

Graveney could no longer hold his tongue and exploded: 'I just don't believe this! You're falling for it all over again! Can't you see what Conrad is trying to do? Do you think he'll be content with a minority stake?'

His face was crimson and his breathing came in long, laboured gasps. He looked as if he might suffer a stroke at any moment.

Robinson was calm in reply: 'If the remaining shareholders present a united front, what can he do? Besides, we have no choice.'

Again the room grew still. Harold Robinson and his accountant's brain had made an unanswerable case. When it came to the vote, four arms were raised in assent without the need for deliberation.

Only Graveney remained defiant. Despite the bluff and machismo, he retained his back-street toughness and he had reached the end of his tether. Now he was ready to fight.

CONRAD BUYS IN TO BRADCASTER

So it was him all along

By Colin Gregory

THE identity of the shadowy millionaire who is bankrolling ailing soccer giants Bradcaster City has been revealed.

He is none other than media tycoon Michael Conrad, owner of a chain of regional newspapers and boss of TV satellite company Spacelink.

In a sensational development last night, the club announced that Conrad has acquired the 30 per cent stake of Arthur Redwood, Bradcaster's last remaining link with a glorious past.

He is thought to have paid about £2 million, well below the market value. It is small change for a man who bid nearly £300 million for the Super League TV rights.

The football world has been astounded by the news that Redwood is to relinquish his share of a club which he managed to successive championship triumphs in the late Fifties.

Bradcaster have cited poor health as the reason for his decision, although he seems to have recovered fully from his illness of last year.

For the time being, he will remain as club chairman as Michael Conrad takes his seat on the board as the largest single shareholder.

The move has aroused speculation that Conrad is moving to take complete control of Bradcaster City.

From rock bottom, the team has put together a winning run to lift themselves into contention for a lucrative place in Europe.

Prime reason for this U-turn has been the £3 million purchase of super striker Gus Simmons. After a poor start, Simmo has scored 21 goals including two hat tricks.

It now seems certain that it was moneybags Michael Conrad who put up the cash for the deal. Clearly, his generosity was the prelude to this latest move.

Last night's announcement was met with dismay by Bradcaster supporters and violent opposition from within the club.

Director Sid Graveney has already labelled Redwood's sell-off as 'a betrayal of everything this club stands for'.

Although the board has approved the deal by a majority vote, Conrad will find it difficult to assume control of Bradcaster while Graveney remains in opposition.

He is actively canvassing the remaining shareholders to resist Conrad's influence.

Yet so far, no one has touched upon the most worrying aspect of this tangled affair.

If Conrad was funding Bradcaster City nearly six months ago, that means the club was fatally compromised when considering details of the rival ITV and Spacelink television bids.

And it raises the suspicion that Conrad was trying to buy the support of the influential club.

Watch this space. This whole deal is a can of worms which in time Bradcaster City might wish they had never opened.

'Jesus Christ, Harry. That's not the story I wrote.'

Colin Gregory had burst into the editor's office of the Daily World, brandishing a copy of that morning's paper.

Tossing it angrily towards Walters, he leaned across his desk and demanded: 'Who lost their bottle?'

The editor looked wearily at him and gestured to an empty chair.

'Sit down, Colin. It's too early in the morning for a scene. And shut the door.'

Gregory turned on his heel and slammed the door so hard it sounded like a rifle shot. In the newsroom, half a dozen reporters and a few startled subs raised their heads briefly.

'Now,' said Walters. 'What's your problem?'

'Somebody cut the balls off my story, Harry. Was it you?'

'As a matter of fact, it wasn't.'

Gregory sank into the vacant chair with a great sigh of exasperation.

'I might have known. Those fucking preening nancy boys in the London office, with their two-hour lunch breaks and their Gucci shoes. They wouldn't know a good story if one fell on them.'

Walters shook his head, his heavy jowls wobbling.

'What did you expect, Colin? Have you looked at the other papers today? Everyone else ran the Conrad story straight. The old man stuck his neck out to let you say as much as you did.'

Gregory snorted contemptuously.

'Oh, come on! We both know that whole deal was a stitch-up right from the start. Redwood was running around like Conrad's lap dog for weeks before Spacelink won the TV contract. Now he's a millionaire overnight. He was bought and he isn't the only one.'

'You've only got Sid Graveney's word for that.'

'Well, he's been right about everything else, hasn't he? And you wouldn't print that either.'

Walters regarded Gregory with an arrogant and condescending gaze that was quite maddening.

'Welcome to the real world, Colin,' he said. 'You know what Conrad and his shit-hot lawyers are like. These are basically unsupported allegations, you haven't got a fucking leg to stand on. We could just about claim fair comment for what we said. But any further and . . .'

He emitted a harsh sound between his teeth, miming a knife slashing his throat.

Gregory scowled and looked at the floor; what Walters was saying was unpalatable but undeniable. This year the World had already been stung for a million over an article about a pop star's bizarre sexual preferences.

The story had been true but they couldn't make it stand up. And when it comes to assessing damages, libel juries like to punish rich and sleazy tabloid newspapers.

Now caution was the watchword. The slightest hint of controversy was enough to send the editor into a huddle with his lawyers. There was no question of a head-on fight with someone as powerful as Michael Conrad.

'Look,' said Walters, more gently. 'I know you're disappointed but you're just pissing into the wind with this story. Just stick to the sports reporting and leave stuff like this to the news boys.'

'Anything for a quiet life, eh, Harry?'

Walters simply shrugged and smiled his cynical smile. Gregory could see that he was on his own.

It was the last game of an eventful season for Bradcaster City Football Club and there was a festival atmosphere in their packed stadium.

From the depths of despair in autumn, the team had hauled itself to its highest league position for years. If only we had made a better start, mused the faithful on the terraces, if only . . .

But one big prize remained within Bradcaster's grasp. Three points against today's visitors, Coventry Albion, and they would be assured of the runners-up spot – and a place in next season's UEFA Cup.

It was many years since Bradcaster had faced European opposition: now they were heading back into football's elite. The whole city was alive with anticipation.

But with Coventry teetering on the edge of relegation and elimination from the lifeblood of the Super League, this was a game in which no prisoners would be taken, no quarter offered.

The roar which greeted the Bradcaster players as they sprinted onto the pitch was enough to take the head from the shoulders. It split the air and seemed to echo for ever in the hazy sunshine of an early summer afternoon.

As the Coventry side fanned out towards their own supporters at the far end of the ground, Bradcaster lined up in the centre circle. At a given signal, they each raised an arm and saluted every corner of the stadium in turn.

The response was electrifying. Another tidal wave of sound swept through the stands and across the terraces, so deafening that no one could distinguish their own cry from the general mayhem.

The face of every player was a mask of tension, muscles twitching. The Indian file broke up in a dozen different directions as players dashed away, twisting and turning. Again the crowd exploded in anticipation.

The limbs of Gus Simmons were so tight he could hardly trap a ball or summon enough energy for a practice shot. This was the biggest match of his career and his nerves were shot to pieces.

He tried deep breathing exercises but they just seemed to intensify the thumping in his chest. Team mates were shouting at him, geeing him up, but their mouths seemed to flap soundlessly like those of goldfish.

The match started but Simmons was still in a different world. The ear-shattering noise of the crowd was lulling his other senses into a sort of trance. He drifted across the pitch, sick and giddy, hardly touching the ball.

Where he normally darted into vulnerable space, here he was running up blind alleys, colliding with defenders. When he did gain possession, his first touch let him down, the ball spinning out of his control.

'For Christ's sake!' Rod Lyons was screaming at him. 'What's the matter with you? Pull yourself together!'

Minutes later, a still-incensed Lyons was booked for a scything tackle which left an opponent writhing. The game was beginning to spiral out of the referee's command and degenerate into an ugly brawl.

There was simply too much at stake. After almost every challenge, players were pushing and jostling each other in angry recrimination. Soon the crowd absorbed the mood on the pitch and the chants grew increasingly threatening.

Then suddenly, after another skirmish in midfield, Rod Lyons emerged with the ball at his feet, glanced up and curved a long pass over the heads of the oncoming Coventry defence, who were playing the offside trap.

But the sweeper had been too slow advancing. Timing his run to perfection, Simmons had sneaked behind the defence and collected the pass at the edge of the area with just the goalkeeper to beat.

'Go on!' roared the Bradcaster fans behind the goal. 'Go on!'

His legs felt like lead. Every split-second seemed to take an age as he tried to steady himself, the keeper hurtling towards him. Painstakingly, striving for accuracy not power, he curled his shot beyond the keeper's flailing left hand.

The moment he struck the ball, he knew it was all

wrong. He threw his hands to his face in horror and for a moment the crowd went quiet.

The ball missed the far post by two yards and clattered into the advertising hoardings. It was the last chance of the first half.

All Simmons wanted to do was get as far away as possible from the noise and the frenetic pace and the pressure-cooker atmosphere of the match. Instead he was confronted in the Bradcaster dressing room by Dougie McNally.

'What are you trying to pull, Simmons?' yelled the Scotsman. 'You're like a fucking zombie out there! Get your shit together or you'll be off, top scorer or no bloody top scorer. Got it? Eh?'

Simmons nodded wearily. Although he was looking straight into his manager's face, his eyes were focused elsewhere.

'He's right, Gus,' said Rod Lyons under his breath as the players filed back for the second half. 'You've got to snap out of it or we'll lose this. Come on, it's just another game, no big deal.'

But the sound of the crowd as they reached the touchline told another story. For the next half-hour, Simmons was as ineffectual as he had been before.

The game developed into a midfield stalemate, neither side having the wit or invention to create an opening. Rod Lyons was toiling tirelessly to hold the Bradcaster unit together but everything broke down when the ball reached Simmons.

Time and again, he was shouldered off the ball with contemptuous ease or it simply cannoned off his shins as he struggled to control it.

From the corner of his eye, Simmons glimpsed McNally fingering the number ten sign in the dugout. He was about to be taken off: a season that had embraced both triumph and humiliation was ultimately to leave a bitter taste.

Then, with the final whistle just five minutes away and both sides needing a win, a Coventry defender suffered a horrendous rush of blood.

Simmons had picked up the ball just where the by-line and the edge of the penalty area coincided. He had his back to goal and none of his team mates was available. There was no danger.

But just as he was being shepherded harmlessly away by the full-back, the Coventry sweeper lunged in and took his legs away. Simmons crumpled to the ground and the referee's whistle shrilled.

He pointed to the spot and was immediately besieged by an enraged posse of Coventry players. He waved them away but they continued to jostle him and, ruffled, he began to brandish his yellow card.

They sloped sullenly off. The stadium was in uproar: Bradcaster fans cheering, euphoric; the Coventry end yelling abuse at the referee and the still-prone Simmons.

By the time Simmons hauled himself gingerly to his feet, Rod Lyons had the ball and was preparing to take the penalty.

Simmons grabbed it from him and hissed: 'I'll take it.'

'Don't be bloody stupid.'

'I want to take it.'

It had become a farce, both players tugging the ball in opposite directions. Lyons let go and turned towards the Bradcaster dugout, gesturing helplessly. Dougie McNally nodded his assent.

'All right,' said Lyons with passion. 'But don't fuck up.'

Simmons placed the ball precisely on the spot and retreated. The packed Coventry fans behind the goal were whistling and jeering insanely.

Suddenly he felt utterly alone. But he knew he had to do this, to prove something to himself. It was a test of nerve.

He tried to shut out everything but the football lying in

front of him: the dancing goalkeeper, the players ranged behind him hardly daring to watch, the cacophony behind the goal and the welling, nervous silence of the Bradcaster fans.

A whistle sounded. He began his run but his legs felt as if they would give way beneath him. Just as he struck the ball, the goalkeeper committed himself and dived to his left.

Simmons had out-thought him, driving his shot hard into the centre of the goal, a foot above the ground. But the keeper twisted in desperation and stuck out a leg.

Slicing off his boot, the ball thumped against the inside of a post and trickled agonisingly back across the face of the goal. Suddenly pandemonium broke loose.

Players from both sides were sprinting into the goal-mouth, the keeper was scrambling to his feet. But Gus Simmons had a head start and blinding pace.

He slid in feet first, flicked at the ball and a moment later was engulfed in a tangled mass of bodies. Confusion reigned, the referee struggling to get a clear view.

Then he gave a long blast on his whistle and pointed back upfield. For there was the ball, deflected by the boot of Simmons, nuzzling against the back of the net.

It was the body blow that finally finished Coventry. Their heads drooped and their spirits sank. Just a few minutes later, Bradcaster City were back in Europe to the vociferous and unbounded joy of their fans.

High up in the directors' box, a lone figure permitted himself a satisfied smile. He took a circumspect sip from a glass of champagne.

Michael Conrad's investment was already beginning to pay off.

For the time being, Graveney had stopped visiting prostitutes.

He could not push from his mind the scene in the massage parlour. The weight of the whore across his thighs, her terrible screaming, the shadowy figure and a sudden flash of light exploding onto his retina.

It had lodged in his brain as a single image, a single experience, just as a camera shutter captures an instant for ever more. It lay in wait for him in his quieter moods, catching him off guard.

Then the full force of the moment would come rushing in on him, his heart would start thumping and he would blush in fearfulness and shame.

All sorts of explanations were spinning through his mind. He first thought that it was some sad crank out for kicks. After all, he knew more than most about the sick appetites of the mind.

He wondered if his wife had put a tail on him. But why? Sexual jealousy had long since died in her; the indifference she felt towards him was absolute. As long as he was discreet, he could have indulged the most base desires.

So Graveney was forced to seek a more sinister motive. For days on end, he waited for his startled face to appear beneath a lurid tabloid headline. But nothing happened.

To keep his anxiety from gnawing away at him, he threw himself into his work.

He masterminded a refinancing package for his butchery chain to give him breathing space with the banks. He commissioned a design company to give his shops a radical face-lift, aiming to strike back at the supermarkets who were leeching his custom.

And he moved to thwart Michael Conrad from taking control of Bradcaster City.

Graveney tracked down dozens and dozens of shareholders in the club. Each held a mere handful of shares, passed on from previous generations, lost in attics or yellowing in dusty drawers.

After days of toil, he had identified a further 20 per cent of the club's equity. The rest had simply disappeared: addresses that no longer existed, names that could not be traced, a natural erosion across several generations.

But what he found was enough. He visited every shareholder in turn, many of whom were bewildered by his sudden materialisation on their doorsteps. Then he made them a deal.

He secured first refusal on their shares, at a price to match any other offer they received. Now there was no way Conrad could secure the extra equity he needed.

Not unless he paid many times above the market rate, because Graveney was prepared to bankrupt himself to protect Bradcaster. In a way it was a test of his virility, for this had ceased to be mere business and become a kind of combat.

To succeed, Conrad had to want Bradcaster City every bit as much as Graveney desired to shut him out.

Surely Conrad would simply walk away when he realised the odds were stacked against him. He was playing games, indulging himself, flexing his muscles a little.

But he was too shrewd an operator to get embroiled in a bloody and expensive conflict, he had too many distractions elsewhere. This was a confrontation Graveney genuinely thought he could win.

It didn't occur to him that Michael Conrad might not be using the same set of rules.

Simmons was dressed in the royal blue and white of Bradcaster City, a football wedged in the crook of his arm.

Beneath him a young blonde girl was prostrate on the ground, arms clasped around his legs. She was raking her long scarlet nails across the dark flesh of his thigh.

She wore the shortest of ra-ra skirts and a skimpy vest

beneath which her unfettered breasts swelled and rubbed against him.

'Look,' Simmons exclaimed in exasperation. 'Is this really necessary?'

Steve Wilde stepped forward into the glare of an arc light.

'Gus please, trust me,' he murmured soothingly. 'It's ironic. She's meant to be a cheerleader. You knew all about this.'

'I didn't expect her to be draped all over me.'

The blonde squirmed free and sat cross-legged on the floor.

'Will you just make your minds up?' she complained in a broad Cockney accent, scowling. 'I don't like it any more than he does. But I'm a professional, I do what I'm told.'

'So shut up,' snapped Wilde.

The blonde pouted but said nothing.

Wilde whispered into Simmons' ear: 'Come on Gus, loosen up. We're wasting studio time and it doesn't come cheap. Just do it as we planned and if you don't like the rushes, we'll think of something else. I promise.' –

'Oh, all right. But I should never have let you talk me into this.'

Wilde stepped back and nodded to an intense-looking young director with a ponytail, who clapped his hands to alert the rest of the crew.

'Right,' said the director briskly. 'Positions everyone. Sharon, get hold of Gus. No, no . . . like you had him before, that's better.'

He smiled encouragingly and a little wearily at Simmons, adding: 'Just look straight into this camera with the red light on. Remember it's four beats and then in, OK? And just relax.'

He snapped his fingers and from somewhere a pumping, hypnotic groove bounced around the tiny studio and echoed off the hardware.

A deep bass voice boomed out: 'I got pace on the turn and the tricks of the trade. I got money to burn and the chicks to parade. So let's rap! Huh! Do the Simmo Rap!'

Simmons' mouth was flapping helplessly as the quick-fire lyrics tumbled on. He had missed his cue completely and, with rising panic, he was struggling to catch up.

His wild eyes were staring straight into the lens of the camera, where he glimpsed his own pitiful reflection. Gamely, the blonde was continuing to caress him.

'No, no!' the director screamed. 'Turn the bloody music off!'

There was a sudden heavy silence as the rap groove expired. Sighing, the blonde disengaged herself again.

'How many more times, Gus?'

The director banged his fingers rhythmically into his palm for emphasis.

'Four beats and then you start. Got it?'

'Oh, fuck off,' snapped Simmons, tossing the football away into a corner of the studio with his eyes blazing.

'Charming.'

Once again, Steve Wilde dashed over to intervene. He cradled Simmons' shoulders with a protective arm.

'Come on, Gus. Just concentrate and everything will be fine. I know it's a little hard to get used to but . . .'

Angrily, Simmons jerked away from Wilde's embrace.

'This is just shit!' he blurted. 'Who wrote those words? I'm married, for Christ's sake.'

Wilde flashed his practised smile. His voice was loaded with lofty compassion, as if he were addressing a pre-cocious but wayward child.

'Gus, I told you. It's just a joke, no one will take it seriously. But it means we can get some glamour into the video.'

'You call that glamour?'

The blonde had popped a strip of chewing gum into her mouth and was munching away like a cow in a field. Wordlessly, she raised the middle finger of her right hand in Simmons' direction.

'The punters will go for it. Football fans have simple tastes.'

'So what makes you think they'll get the joke?'

Wilde sighed. Gus Simmons was proving a most difficult client. But he was also making bags of money – and 15 per cent of a stack is worth having.

'Let's try it once again, shall we?' said Wilde, patience just beginning to fray at the edges, trying to guide Simmons back into the spotlight.

The player stood still as a rock.

'It's not even my voice. It's a fucking fiasco.'

'No one will ever suspect. You know what you were like on that sound check.'

'But it isn't anything like me!'

This time Wilde had suffered enough. His diplomacy was shredded.

'We didn't use you because you were crap!' he shouted. 'You can't even get this right. I make you the richest footballer in the country and all you do is complain.

'If this record goes in at number one, we're talking big bucks and mega exposure. If you want to walk away from that, go ahead. Otherwise, for once in your life, do as you're told.'

For a moment, a horribly pregnant silence descended and Wilde wondered if he had gone too far. Then a broad grin split the face of Simmons.

He scratched his head, still smiling ruefully.

'I don't know, the things I do for you,' he said, casting his eyes around the studio and the lolling crew, the still-masticating model.

Steve Wilde was smiling too but in relief. A looming

crisis had been averted, albeit temporarily; the gravy train was still rolling. Just.

At seven o'clock in the morning, the breakfast room of the Bradcaster Hilton was virtually deserted.

Michael Conrad has been ushered to a table in the recess of a great bay window. Thoughtfully, he gazed down on Bradcaster streets still shaking off their lethargy, although by now the summer sun was sharpening to a glare.

A refuse wagon rumbled down the main street, the workers tossing out oaths and banter. The wagon's steel teeth were grinding and crushing the debris of the night: fast-food wrappers and empty bottles, discarded packs of cigarettes, cans and cardboard boxes.

This town is dirtier than I remember it, thought Conrad. These drabs buildings and polluted streets, the crushing atmosphere of insularity and decay, the way people spoke and thought. None of this reached out to him anymore.

He wanted to believe Bradcaster was a rising power again, sweeping aside its industrial past, embracing high-technology and marketing's black arts.

He wanted Bradcaster to preserve his childhood and all its memories intact, to be the rock on which the present was based and the loadstone of his future.

But each time he returned, his empire and his influence expanding with every visit, he felt curiously isolated. As his world grew more and more immense, he craved some point of stillness and solidity that would hold everything together.

Somehow this grey provincial city was failing to deliver. But still he was driven on, pounded by memories and the need for connection.

Among the most powerful of his recollections was of standing among men, a forest of legs, struggling for a view of his team of demi-gods. The cold wind blowing across the stony Southside terrace at Bradcaster City FC. His father hoisting him onto his shoulders and pouring out hot sweet tea from a Thermos flask.

Then out of work and luck in the hard years after the war, Conrad's father finally found a place in chambers. He became one of the most brilliant barristers of his generation, the family decamped to London and Michael entered a world of wealth and privilege.

For many years, Conrad had unconsciously avoided Bradcaster. Instead he had created a kind of personal mythology around it, buttressing his sense of who he was.

Now he had come back, he was disturbed to discover the truth of a trite maxim: the past is another country. This Bradcaster was a stinking cesspit compared to the celestial visions in his mind.

But Conrad was a man who could not easily change course and who equated possession with control.

So despite an awakening sense of futility, he was reaching out to seize his past and absorb it within himself. That was why he wanted to buy Bradcaster City.

As he stared down on the empty streets, Conrad toyed absently with his breakfast. He sipped at the bitter dregs of a cup of black coffee.

Just then he became aware of a commotion at the other end of the room. Swivelling in his seat, he saw a man trying to force his way past a waiter, who was protesting vigorously.

'No, no,' the waiter was shouting, tugging at the interloper's sleeve. 'Mr Conrad is not to be disturbed.'

The man was wide-eyed and struggling; the scene was developing into a fracas.

'I want to talk to you,' the man called out to Conrad.

He was shabbily dressed in an old jacket and a shiny pair of corduroy trousers. From the corner of his hip pocket, the dog-eared pages of a notebook protruded. He hadn't shaved that morning.

It was Colin Gregory.

'I work for the Daily World,' he added.

Conrad gestured to the waiter to let him through. As the dishevelled Gregory approached his table, Conrad regarded him with frank distaste.

Panting from his exertions, the reporter demanded: 'Are you planning to take control of Bradcaster City, Mr Conrad?'

Without waiting to be invited, Gregory tugged out a heavy chair and sat down opposite Conrad. He produced his notebook with a theatrical flourish. His breath reeked of stale alcohol.

'How did you know I was here?' demanded Conrad in a tight voice.

'Friends in low places.'

'I do not normally conduct press interviews at this time of morning in hotel dining rooms. Perhaps you should leave.'

Gregory persisted: 'Did you put up the money for the transfer of Gus Simmons to Bradcaster?'

The hint of a smile flickered across Conrad's face.

'No comment.'

'Weren't you trying to buy Arthur Redwood's support in the television rights auction?'

'I don't think Arthur is a man who can be bought, do you?'

'Isn't it true that you bribed Steve Wilde to make sure Simmons chose Bradcaster?'

Conrad was beginning to tire of this particular game.

He beckoned the waiter over to his table and with a fixed expression said: 'Now we have a witness. If you continue to repeat these allegations, I shall sue you for slander.'

'Bastard,' hissed Gregory between his teeth. 'Your type

think they can do what the fuck they like. But sooner or later, you're going to come unstuck. I'll be watching out for you.'

With an angry thrust of his legs, he scraped the chair away from the table and stood up.

'And another thing,' he said as he moved towards the door. 'Your newspapers are full of shit.'

By the time he stumbled into the street, Gregory's head was pounding and his throat was parched. He felt giddy from lack of food and too much drink the night before. He had been dead to the world when roused by the early morning call from his contact on the Hilton's front desk.

Rubbing the gum from his eyes, he made for a seedy cafe in a backstreet. Inside, he ordered beans on toast and a mug of steaming tea was plonked down in front of him. He lit his habitual Marlboro, took a long drag and coughed abruptly.

His confrontation with Conrad had been on the spur of the moment, galvanised by frustration. Now he was asking himself exactly what he had hoped to achieve.

Conrad was never going to fold under direct pressure tactics and, now he was alerted to Gregory's suspicions, he would cover his tracks even more carefully.

'Bloody fool,' Gregory said aloud, stubbing out another cigarette in his saucer.

Feeling sick and squinting painfully into the sun, he arrived for work at the World. Almost as soon as he sank groaning into his chair, the editor's door burst open.

'Gregory, get your arse in here!' roared Walters.

The reporter winced.

'Jesus, Harry, keep your voice down.'

Walters' face was like thunder. With a deepening sense of apprehension, Gregory crossed the newsroom and disappeared into his office.

'I thought I told you to drop that Michael Conrad story,' snapped the editor.

Gregory gaped at him.

'What do you mean?'

'Don't fuck about, Colin. You just tackled him in his hotel, for Christ's sake.'

'So he's come bleating to you about it.'

'As a matter of fact, no. He took it up with our beloved proprietor, who gave the old man a bollocking, who passed it on to me. Now it's your turn.'

Gregory sounded bitter and incredulous: 'You mean he just picked up the 'phone to Lord Farnham? Just like that? I thought they were supposed to be rivals.'

Walters was working up a fine head of steam, clouting the table with both palms for emphasis.

'Fucking hell, Colin, why don't you grow up? Farnham was probably a mate of Conrad's daddy. You know how it works, it's a different fucking world. Once Conrad mentioned the word "libel", he'd have run a mile. None of these fucking bluebloods have got any guts.'

Gregory eyed Walters, who by now was quivering with rage, in loathing and contempt.

'But you've got them, eh Harry?' he sneered. 'If you sniffed a good story, you'd pass out.'

Eyes popping, Walters lurched across his desk to thrust his bloated face into Gregory's.

'Just get out of my fucking sight!' he screamed. 'Or so help me, you'll end up filing copy from Bradcaster reserves. Got it?'

Smiling sardonically, Gregory beat a retreat. By the time he reached his desk and clicked on the screen, he was feeling very much better. The row with Walters had invigorated him; he hummed gently to himself as he lit another Marlboro.

'I'll have that bastard Conrad yet,' he mused to himself. 'I just need to be a bit more subtle, that's all.'

Melanie Simmons was plucking frantically at her husband's elbow, pleading for attention.

'Gus? Do I look OK? Gus!'

Simmons grunted disinterestedly.

'You're not even looking!'

They were sitting in the back of a chauffeur-driven Rolls-Royce, which was gliding through West London. Melanie was wriggling against the pale cream leather upholstery, peering nervously into a compact mirror and dabbing at her make-up.

Simmons turned to look at her and winced inwardly.

'You look fine,' he said without conviction.

Melanie had a pretty if unremarkable face: her snub nose was perhaps a little too large, her pale blue eyes a touch too wide apart, for her to be truly beautiful. But dressed simply, with a splash of vibrant lipstick to animate her face, she could look like a million dollars.

Now she looked like a ten-quid tart. Her dress was a pink satin confection with fussy bows and a plunging neckline, which she regretted and was tugging at obsessively.

As she flopped back in despair into the car's cool leather, the dress was creasing and riding up her thighs. The tops of her suspenders were peeking out but somehow it was not an erotic sight.

Her brand-new stilettoes were already beginning to rub painfully. Her lovely golden hair, which normally spilled naturally over her shoulders, was crushed and crimped and teased. A seemingly impenetrable mask of foundation covered her face.

The Rolls-Royce crossed the Thames at Kew Bridge and swung right towards Richmond. After a few more turns down tree-lined streets, it nosed through a vast pair of ornate wrought iron gates in black and gold.

They guarded the gap in a 12-feet high brick wall, which was topped with barbed wire and mounted with security cameras. As the car passed, a helmeted security guard nodded at the chauffeur.

The gravel driveway wound through a green maze of towering shrubs and mature trees and then, suddenly, a mansion house swept into view.

'Bloody hell,' murmured Melanie.

With a soft rumbling, the car drew up at the base of an imposing flight of stone steps. They led to a huge pair of neo-classical marble pillars and seemed to rise for ever, like a stairway to heaven.

By now the chauffeur had flipped open Melanie's door and was gesturing expansively for her to alight. Gripping the hem of her dress, she swung her legs out and her heels sank into the damp gravel. There was trepidation etched into her face as she hauled herself awkwardly upright.

She smoothed the dress over her hips and glanced across to where Simmons was also being helped from the car. Their eyes met and, for what seemed the first time in many months, a mutual understanding flickered. What were they doing here?

'This way please,' said the chauffeur in an accent Melanie could not quite identify, ushering them away from the steps.

They followed him down a path of sandstone slabs which ran along the side of the house, past a burgeoning green jungle of trees and undergrowth where invisible birds sang sweetly. It was a beautifully mild summer night and, as the light slowly began to fade, the sky was suffused with crimson at the far horizon.

This was another world. Strains of music were wafting on the soft air as the chauffeur's shiny black boots squeaked incongruously ahead of them.

They turned a corner and a huge undulating lawn swept away to a far grove of beech trees. It was a flawless intense

168

green, reminding Simmons of a football pitch on the first day of the season.

At the end of the lawn, a big white marquee had been erected. By now the music had grown more distinct; it was a string quartet playing Shostakovich. Inside, voices and laughter could clearly be heard. The chauffeur bowed solemnly and pointed.

Before withdrawing, he said: 'Mr Conrad is expecting you. Have a pleasant evening.'

As Simmons strode purposefully towards the marquee, Melanie struggled in his wake, her heels sinking into the lush turf. She was beginning to lose the last vestiges of self-possession.

'Will you slow down!' she hissed, face reddening.

Sighing, he halted and turned to look at her. A knot of irritation was tightening in his stomach. She threaded her arm through the crook of his elbow and hung on grimly.

As they walked, a figure in an incandescent white tuxedo appeared at the mouth of the marquee. He paused to light a cigar and his shape grew hazy amid a swirling blue-grey cloud.

It was Michael Conrad. Urgently Melanie squeezed Simmons' arm.

'Is that him?' she whispered.

Simmons nodded silently.

'Jesus, he looks like Robert Redford in that film. What was it called? You know, "The Great Gatsby" or something.'

By now, Conrad had spotted them and was advancing across the lawn with his hand outstretched, beaming.

'Gus!' he cried. 'We'd nearly given you up.'

He wrung the hand of the footballer. He took in his superbly tailored dinner suit, the flamboyant cummerbund in crimson and white polka dot. He approved.

Then he turned to Melanie and subjected her to his

remorseless analytical eye. His smile lost none of its intensity.

'This must be your wife,' he murmured, gazing deep into her eyes.

She blushed furiously with shame and self-consciousness. Conrad took her fingers and pressed them to his dry lips.

'Delighted,' he said. 'You look very lovely.'

He beckoned them inside and as they appeared, the string quartet lapsed into silence. The eyes of several hundred guests, all in their finery, locked on to the trio. Melanie felt herself go giddy.

'Ladies and gentlemen,' boomed Conrad. 'As you know, this little party is to celebrate the entry of Bradcaster City, a football club in which I have more than a passing interest, into European competition next season.'

There was a ripple of polite laughter and some applause. As Simmons scanned the faces in the crowd, he noticed without surprise that both Arthur Redwood and Sid Graveney were absent. He wondered if they had even been invited.

'The man largely responsible for that success on the field has just arrived,' continued Conrad. 'I give you Augustus Simmons.'

He flung his arm out towards the footballer, milking applause like an emcee in a tacky nightclub. But the rush of clapping and cheering was warm and genuine enough. Simmons gave a slightly bemused smile.

At a signal from Conrad, the musicians began sawing away at their instruments again and the applause died down. Melanie heaved a huge sigh of relief as the guests turned back to their own coteries and conversations.

'Come and meet my wife,' said Conrad, playing the charming host, enjoying parading the star his millions had acquired. 'There she is now.'

Alexandra was throwing back her head and laughing uproariously. She held a glass of dry Martini delicately at the neck with thumb and forefinger.

Even in this glittering presence, she was a riot of colour. She was dressed from head to toe in Rifat Ozbek. Above a pair of vibrant pink stretch rayon trousers, she wore a lilac jacket whose cuffs and sleeves were worked with Indonesian embroidery.

Underneath, her soft green brocade waistcoat was left undone, revealing the olive skin of her belly and a plunging white shell lace bra. As she laughed, her breasts shook almost imperceptibly.

She was chatting to a young and handsome man with a wolfish smile, who melted away as Conrad approached.

For a moment, a frown darkened Conrad's face and then he called out: 'Alex! I want you to meet someone.'

As she shifted through a crowd of guests, balancing her glass precariously, Simmons watched in wonderment. He had never seen such a beautiful woman or one so utterly self-contained.

Gazing at her, he realised he was reaching out far beyond himself, to something new and strange. She smiled at him and his heart began pummelling at his ribs.

'This is my wife,' Conrad was saying in a voice that sounded many miles distant. 'Alex, this is Gus Simmons. And his wife.'

There was a flicker of a pause before he added: 'Melanie.'

Alexandra flashed a warm smile at Simmons and held his gaze. Something caught alight in her as well. She extended a delicate hand and, when he grasped it, squeezed his fingers for a second longer than was necessary.

'Your face seems familiar,' she said with playful irony. 'Should I know you?'

For a moment, as the rules of etiquette demanded, she inclined her head towards Melanie and smiled with the corners of her mouth. Then her eyes began devouring Simmons again.

'Only if you like football,' he said thickly, feeling foolish.

'Michael,' she said, regarding her husband with a mock pout. 'You didn't tell me the famous Simmo was going to enliven this dreary evening.'

She gave Simmons a sly look, adding: 'That is your nickname, isn't it?'

'I'm afraid so,' he replied. 'Football fans like to shorten things.'

Her voice dropped another octave: 'What a shame.'

The blood burned in his cheeks. He became conscious of Melanie shifting uncomfortably and glanced down at her, noticing first the tension in her jaw.

Then he saw the whole picture: her gaucheness and naivety, the ludicrous dress which was slipping to expose her breasts, her straggly hair and smudged lipstick.

And there was Alexandra Conrad, exquisite and effortless. There was a kind of hunger in her eyes as she stared at him; he was painfully conscious of his own body beneath the constricting dinner suit. Absently, he tugged at his bow tie.

'You would make a wonderful model,' she breathed. 'A good friend of mine edits one of the glossies. I'm sure I could swing it and it would make a hell of a front cover. You're very popular with the ladies, I hear.'

Simmons glanced awkwardly at Melanie and muttered: 'Oh, you know. It's all hype.'

'But darling, that's what makes the world go round. Are you game?'

Simmons could sense the atmosphere darkening as Conrad and Melanie exchanged glances in an unlikely alliance. But he was losing his head and hardly cared what happened next.

'Yes,' he said. 'I suppose I am.'

*   *   *

A stunned silence hung over the boardroom of Bradcaster City Football Club.

Around the table, worried men were exchanging glances. Arthur Redwood's face was impassive but his eyes were darting nervously. Sid Graveney was shaking his head angrily and opening his mouth to speak. Harold Robinson silenced him with an upraised palm.

They were all watching Conrad as he delivered a radical monologue in calmly measured tones.

'My accountants have looked over the figures and I can assure you there is no alternative except the bankruptcy courts,' he continued.

'To pay for the ground redevelopment, which is mandatory, we have to double both the cost of admission and the price of a season ticket. Starting this autumn. It's as simple as that.'

Graveney could no longer be restrained.

He burst in: 'Don't be bloody stupid, man. The work won't even be finished then. You're asking the fans to pay through the nose for the privilege of sitting in a building site.'

'That's precisely my point,' replied the unruffled Conrad. 'The stadium will be at severely reduced capacity for the whole of next season. But we've got to increase turnstile receipts and there is only one answer.'

'They just won't wear it!' exploded Graveney.

'I think they will. We're in Europe for the first time in decades, Simmons is rattling in goals. The fans like success, Sid, maybe because they're not used to it. They'll pay the extra to watch us winning.'

'What if they can't afford it? Not everybody is made of money like you, Conrad. We're talking about ordinary working people, who've been watching Bradcaster all their lives. We'd be pricing them out.'

Conrad flashed a cynical smile.

'Then perhaps they should buy a satellite dish and stay at home.'

There was uproar in the room; even Redwood joined in the chorus of protest. Still smiling, Conrad raised his hand in a mock apology.

'Look Sid,' he said in a more conciliatory tone. 'I hear what you're saying but you are living in the past. We've got to drag football out of the dark ages. Improve the facilities, inject some razzmatazz, get families into the stadium. We need people who don't mind paying to enjoy their leisure.'

'God help us,' snarled Graveney.

Determined to stop the argument spiralling out of control, Redwood intervened from the head of the table.

'Please,' he said sharply. 'Let's try to look at this objectively without squabbling like children. Harold, what's your view?'

The club secretary paused for a few moments and when he spoke, he measured every word.

'I can see the advantages of what Mr Conrad is proposing. With the club in form, the time could be right to jack up the prices. Doing it now will help cash flow enormously. I'm for it.'

Graveney cursed in a stage whisper. Even Redwood looked momentarily taken aback.

'Then I move we put it to the vote,' said Conrad, moving quickly to seize the advantage.

Now there was no escape. With Robinson's support and the obedience of the intimidated elderly directors, Conrad was unstoppable.

Graveney and, after a moment's deliberation, Redwood raised their arms in opposition but it was futile. The motion was carried and Bradcaster City had been changed for ever.

In a strangely deflated mood, the meeting broke up

and everyone began scurrying away from the table, like fugitives fleeing the scene of a crime.

Silent, head bowed, Redwood knew that he had witnessed the end of an era, the dawn of something harsh and unforgiving.

Graveney was still muttering oaths under his breath as he headed for the door. Conrad, fingers steepled in front of him, remained seated at the great boardroom table.

'Sid,' he called out. 'Have you got a minute?'

Startled, Graveney turned and asked: 'What for?'

Conrad beckoned to an empty chair.

'I want to talk to you.'

By now, everyone else had left. With a suspicious look, Graveney crossed the floor and sank into the seat opposite Conrad. His eyes were still blazing with anger.

'What?' he barked.

'Sid, I want to be your friend but you're not making it very easy.'

'Why the hell should I? You're pulling this club apart brick by brick. Everyone else wants to lick your arse but I'm buggered if I'm going to.'

Conrad smiled wanly.

'Who says I like arselickers?'

'Your type always does.'

Conrad sighed sorrowfully. He reached beneath the table and brought out a brown leather attache case. He flicked the combination locks, opened the case and fished out a large manila envelope, which he tossed across the table towards Graveney.

'I genuinely don't mean you any harm, Sid,' he said softly. 'But I think you should take a look at this.'

A sense of horror had settled in the pit of Sid Graveney's ample belly. His fingers quivered as he ripped open the envelope. Inside was a single black and white photograph.

It was a scene from a terrible and sordid nightmare. There was the whore, her mouth stretched in a silent screech, her breasts lined with bulging veins. In her hands she held Graveney's engorged penis, just as it had started to spurt.

There was his shocked face as he struggled to rise, the whore's crushing weight across his legs. And there, captured on film, was the sad fulfilment of all his threadbare fantasies.

Tears misted his eyes. Despite his bulk, he seemed suddenly shrunken as if something had collapsed inside.

'I'm sorry,' said Conrad. 'This places you in a very awkward position.'

There was a catch in Graveney's voice as he replied: 'You set me up, you bastard. You set me up.'

'Obviously I can't say how the photograph came into my possession,' continued Conrad. 'I shall do my best to protect you but there is always a chance the tabloids could pick up a story like this. That could be very embarrassing, even ruinous. I know you're well respected in this town. Your wife moves in exalted circles, too, I believe.'

'I might have known,' Graveney was saying mechanically, burying his face in his hands. 'I might have bloody known.'

For an instant, an expression of something like compassion swept across Conrad's face. Then his mouth tightened and the steely glint in his eyes returned.

'I'm thinking of Bradcaster,' he said. 'Things are at a delicate stage and we can't afford a scandal. I think it would be better for everyone if you considered resigning as a director.'

He paused for a few seconds to let his words sink in to Graveney's battered consciousness.

'I'd be willing to pay the market rate for your shares. But you have to go now.'

Graveney gave a bitter, defeated laugh.

'That's what you wanted all along, isn't it? Total control. A man like you can't stand to have equals. So you play dirty.'

'Business is a hard game, Sid. You've got to learn to take the knocks.'

Graveney looked weary and washed-out.

'Oh, fuck it,' he said. 'I'm sick of fighting for this bloody ungrateful club. But you don't know what you're doing. This place will ruin you, big as you are.'

'Maybe,' said Conrad.

He smiled complacently.

Simmons was surrounded by a white-hot bank of studio lights and their reflecting umbrellas. His forehead was beginning to bead with perspiration.

Three hours had passed and he was getting tetchy. He mopped at his brow with the sleeve of a ludicrously expensive suit by Gianni Versace.

'Look, I can't stand much more of this,' he exclaimed. 'Haven't you got what you want yet?'

The art director – a glamorous pencil-thin girl in a micro skirt – glanced at the photographer, who shrugged.

'OK, Gus,' she said brightly. 'Take a break. You're doing awfully well. Only a couple more outfits to go and that's the whole of his special collection.'

Simmons grimaced and started tugging off his jacket. Then he caught a glimpse of Alexandra Conrad tiptoeing past tripods and cables at the back of the studio. His expression changed.

Smiling, she waved at him. She was dressed simply in a cashmere sweater and leggings, her face almost un-touched by make-up. Expecting flamboyance and artifice, Simmons was quite disarmed.

'How's it going?' she called out, pausing to exchange air kisses with the art director.

'As a model, I make a great footballer.'

'Oh, don't be silly. The camera loves you, I can tell.'

By now she had reached him in the circle of white light. She clutched his shoulders, lifted herself up and kissed him fleetingly on the cheek.

For a moment, he felt the warmth and softness of her body. He breathed a musky draught of her perfume and was giddied by it.

She stepped back and said: 'You look fine.'

'Thanks.'

'Antonia tells me you're going on the front cover. It took me five long years to get my face there. Be grateful.'

'I am,' he said. 'Honestly.'

She pursed her mouth comically and he was charmed.

With a playful glint in her eye, she asked: 'Why did you refuse to pose with the girls they chose? Weren't they beautiful enough?'

Simmons looked uncomfortable.

'No, it wasn't that,' he mumbled. 'But I had enough trouble after the video I made. Melanie gets very jealous.'

Alexandra's voice was creamy and seductive as she caught his gaze: 'I can understand that. Does she have any need to be?'

Simmons laughed.

'I really couldn't say.'

The art director's voice cut in: 'Gus, when you're ready.'

Simmons turned to Alexandra and shrugged helplessly.

'Sorry,' he said, spreading his palms. 'These friends of yours are slave drivers.'

Before he knew what was happening, she had secretly pressed a small folded piece of paper into his hand. His eyes widened in surprise and he opened his mouth to speak but she was already disappearing.

'Come on, Gus,' the photographer chimed in. 'We want to get home tonight.'

'Yeah, yeah, just a minute,' replied Simmons absently.

He unfolded the note, smoothed out the creases and slowly his face registered a dawning astonishment.

In a sprawling hand, it read: 'Room 1011, Royal Gardens Hotel, Kensington. Tonight 8 pm.'

WHEN WILL THIS MAN STOP?

Conrad takes control at Bradcaster

by Colin Gregory

THE black shadow of Michael Conrad hovered ever more dominatingly over British football last night.

The media giant, whose Spacelink TV company has just paid £300 million to televise the Super League, has bought his way to power at Bradcaster City.

He has acquired the shares of meat magnate Sid Graveney for an undisclosed sum. Together with the 30 per cent stake he bought in a shock move earlier this year, the deal gives him a controlling interest in the club.

Graveney has resigned from the board and Arthur Redwood,

the most successful manager in City's history, has been replaced as chairman by Conrad himself. His consolation prize is the courtesy title of Vice President.

As boss of Spacelink, Conrad already held the purse strings of the fledgling Super League, due to kick off next month. Now he also controls one of the so-called 'Big Seven' Super League clubs, he is without question the most powerful man in British football.

Mystery surrounds Graveney's sell-out decision. He had been the Bradcaster board's most aggressive opponent of Conrad.

Yesterday, he issued a terse statement through his solicitor which read: 'It is with great reluctance that I have decided to sell my interest in Bradcaster City. I now plan to devote more time to my other business interests.'

As news of the Conrad takeover sunk in, the club seemed in a state of shock. But star striker Gus Simmons delivered a defiant 'business as usual' message.

'This sort of thing can be very unsettling but the team is professional enough to cope,' he said. 'By the time the new season starts, we will be raring to go and confident of doing very well. We no longer fear anybody.'

But Dave Pearson, secretary of the Bradcaster Supporters' Club, expressed the fears of many ordinary fans.

'This is the end of an era,' he claimed. 'Good men like Redwood and Graveney seem to have been just tossed aside. What does Michael Conrad know or care about football?

'His newspapers and his television programmes are cheap and tacky and that's not what we're used to here. This has left a bitter taste in everyone's mouth.'

Among dark shadows and stony silhouettes, a man lay in a pool of white light.

He seemed deeply troubled and was murmuring to himself: 'If it were done when 'tis done, then 'twere well it were done quickly . . . '

His voice was deep and resonant, echoing in the vast silence. Almost choked with tears, it was the testament of a soul in torment.

Conrad shifted in his seat, leaning sideways.

His breath was warm against his companion's ear as he whispered: 'Bloody hell, Tom, this is the last time you bring me to the National. This is torture.'

'Ssshhh!'

Tom Haslam should have known better than to subject his Spacelink boss, who had a notoriously low boredom threshold, to three hours of Shakespeare.

It had been a lame excuse to get him out of the office. Haslam was beginning to detect unmistakable signs of tension in Conrad, unheard of even in the station's darkest days.

He hissed back: 'Don't be such a philistine. You need a dose of culture after all those game shows we dish up.'

He felt Conrad shake with laughter in the darkness.

Then came the whispered rejoinder: 'They pull bigger audiences than this bollocks, dear boy.'

A wild-eyed woman had stepped onto the stage and started berating the man, like a terrier worrying an ox.

'Was the hope drunk wherein you dressed yourself?' she was complaining, plucking contemptuously at his garments. 'Hath it slept since?'

By now Conrad had lost interest completely.

'So,' he said to Haslam, his voice getting more audible with each syllable. 'What do you make of this so-called players' strike? Have they get the bottle?'

Appalled, Haslam muttered: 'We can't talk about this now. For God's sake, Michael, shut up.'

'Have they got the stomach for a fight? Yes or no.'

Even in Conrad's low murmur, Haslam could detect a a steely determination. He sighed. This subject was not going to go away.

'Yes, I think they have. They want a much bigger slice of the cake. Five per cent of the TV receipts at an agreed minimum of two million a year.'

'Greedy bastards,' exclaimed Conrad loudly, drawing a barrage of reproving hisses. 'But that's not our problem, is it?'

Angered by the incessant nagging of his wife, the

man on stage had drawn himself up to his full height, a vast and impressive bulk. His face was stern and unyielding.

'Prithee peace,' he thundered. 'I dare do all that may become a man; who dares do more is none.'

'That's not all,' whispered Haslam. 'They say we want to screen too many matches. They're particularly unhappy about playing on Monday evenings.'

'What difference does that make?'

Haslam muttered: 'They say it will kill the game, no one will show up at the turnstiles.'

There was a long pause.

Then Conrad asked bluntly: 'What's your advice?'

'Compromise. We can't afford the embarrassment of cancelled games, not to mention the lost advertising revenue.'

Onstage, the woman's voice was building to a shrill crescendo as her husband wavered: 'We fail? But screw your courage to the sticking place, and we'll not fail.'

At some subliminal level, Conrad heard the words and they echoed in his brain.

'No,' he said firmly. 'We tough it out. Let's see if we can call their bluff.'

Haslam sank back into his seat in helpless frustration but made no reply. Conrad had sailed close to the wind so many times that sooner or later he was going to capsize. There was nothing to do but batten down the hatches and start praying.

Down on the stage, the two figures were disappearing into the gloom.

As they did so, a parting line floated to the back of the auditorium and seemed to hang there: 'False face must hide what the false heart doth know.'

But if Conrad heard, he made no sign. He dug Haslam in the ribs.

'Come on, Tom,' he urged. 'Let's get out of here. I'll buy you a drink to celebrate our impending victory.'

Face bathed in a cold sweat, heart thumping uncontrollably, Simmons rapped lightly on the hotel door.

He waited for what seemed an age, glancing nervously up and down the hotel corridor. He caught the hum of an approaching lift and for a second was tempted to just walk away.

But then he steeled himself and knocked again, loudly this time. The door opened almost immediately.

Alexandra Conrad smiled, a warm smile that nevertheless was tinged with triumph. She wore a silk kimono in pure white and her feet were bare.

Wordlessly, she stepped back and Simmons entered with a horrible emptiness gnawing at his guts. He hovered uncomfortably at the side of a huge double bed, which smelled subtly of her perfume. The covers were already tousled.

'You came,' she said.

'How could I refuse?'

Alexandra laughed and asked brightly: 'Drink?'

Without waiting for a reply, she bent to open a small refrigerator and plucked out a dewy bottle of vintage Bollinger. Expertly, she discarded the foil and wire and popped the cork, splashing the contents into a pair of champagne flutes.

Brandishing the drinks, she said: 'Let's go out onto the balcony, it's such a lovely evening.'

Simmons had the feeling that this episode was completely out of his control. He decided to let her momentum carry him along.

From the tenth floor of the Royal Gardens, the figures still scurrying in Kensington High Street seemed curiously insignificant. Away over Kensington Palace towards Hyde

Park, the trees were in their lush summer beauty. The sun was reddening above the horizon.

Simmons took a sip of champagne and coughed as the bubbles burst on the roof of his mouth. Alexandra giggled delightedly.

'Careful!' she cried. 'You're obviously not used to this stuff.'

'I've had my share. Maybe too much.'

'Naughty boy.'

Girlishly, she peered over the balcony rail, one shapely foot wagging excitedly in the air. Simmons gazed in anguish at the shape of her buttocks beneath the tightened white silk.

'London is beautiful from this height,' she was saying over her shoulder.

'So are you,' he replied thickly.

Without knowing quite what he was doing, he stood behind her and placed both hands just above her hips. She gasped.

His fingers crept beneath her arms to cup her breasts. His breathing became laboured. He peeled away the kimono and, as his hands touched her naked skin, the champagne glass slipped between her fingers.

Down and down it fell, shattering soundlessly on the pavement below. He squeezed her nipples between thumb and forefinger, teasing and provoking them until they were proud.

She could feel his hardness, like a warmth seeping into her.

'Do you want to fuck me?' she breathed.

'Of course I do.'

'Say it!' she demanded.

Maddened, he bellowed: 'I want to fuck you!'

She turned and wrapped her arms around him. Their lips met in an overwhelming, suffocating kiss, their bodies grinding together.

Still tasting her hot breath, Simmons dragged her backwards towards the bed and then tossed her down. Her mane of hair spread across the white sheets. With an indolent smile, she parted her legs and started stroking herself.

Simmons was tearing at his clothes, frantic to possess her. Then, naked and aroused, he fell onto her and buried his face between her thighs.

As his tongue found the spot, her whole body contracted. She let out a scream of pleasure. Suddenly she was tugging at his hair, dragging him upwards.

'Now!' she shouted. 'Take me now!'

She reached and her fingers closed around his cock, which was thick and powerful. Then she simply guided him into her, slowly, inch by inch.

Each movement of his hips brought a fresh moan from somewhere deep inside her. She was thrashing her head from side to side, her eyes were screwed tight.

As he thrust deeper, she opened to receive him. The friction was exquisite and unbearable.

By now Simmons was being engulfed by a shuddering wave of ecstasy. Sensing it, Alexandra shifted her hips and wrapped her legs around his back, matching his accelerating rhythm with urgent motions of her own.

'Oh,' he murmured involuntarily. 'Oh, no.'

Seeing his face contorted with the onset of his climax, Alexandra too was sent freefalling over the edge. She was sobbing out loud, her voice mingling with his own cries.

The orgasm seemed to tear out the roots of his body. He slumped onto her chest, gasping, spent.

She clung tightly to him and whispered: 'My darling.'

For a few moments a warm sense of tranquillity and repletion descended.

Then, mouth pressed against her neck, he said: 'I love you.'

He sensed her body grow still and realised his sickening mistake. She said nothing but her silence was more eloquent than words.

So there they lay, Simmons still inside her but now it felt nothing like possession. He had stormed the citadel only to be overpowered within.

'I'm sorry,' he said, kissing her ear lobe. 'Forget I said that.'

But both of them knew that he had meant it.

Graveney was getting very drunk. In a backstreet bar in a poor part of town, he was killing his sense of shame with Scotch.

He was slumped in a corner among dirty glasses and ancient cigarette butts. The paint was peeling off walls stained dark brown by decades of smoke.

A jukebox was playing tunes from long ago: Patsy Cline, Nat King Cole, Roy Orbison. All were ballads and, as Graveney's senses dimmed, they seemed to collapse into a morass of melancholia. It felt like he was drowning in treacle.

He took another gulp of whisky and banged his fist hard on the table.

'What's this?' he shouted, voice slurring. 'This music is no good. Get it off.'

A couple of fat men with tattoos glanced up incuriously.

'Keep your hair on, grandad,' said the slouching adolescent behind the bar. 'I think it's crap as well but it's all we got.'

Graveney lapsed into querulous muttering. Swigging again at the Scotch, he realised with panic that his throat was totally numb.

A great sadness swelled inside him, beating at his temples. Tears welled in his eyes and coursed down his face, which was contorting with grief. Heaving sobs began to seize his body.

He tried to fight his way back from the abyss, holding his breath to stop the sobbing. He plunged his face into his hands and felt the dampness of his own tears.

Gradually he grew still. Then he sensed a presence behind him and strong fingers clasped his shoulder.

'Sid?' came a slightly embarrassed voice. 'Are you all right?'

It was Colin Gregory.

The reporter sat down beside Graveney, who stared at him with bloodshot eyes. No hint of recognition flickered in his face.

But then he said tonelessly: 'What the bloody hell do you want?'

'Just to talk.'

Gregory rummaged for his cigarettes and offered one to Graveney, who declined. Every sound – the crumpling of the packet, the click and whoosh of the Zippo, Gregory's blissful inhalation – was unnaturally loud.

Graveney belched and his pungent, booze-soaked breath caught in the reporter's nostrils.

'How did you find me?' demanded Graveney in a thick voice.

'Oh, you know. Contacts.'

Graveney laughed bitterly.

'Spies, you mean.'

He regarded Gregory with narrowed eyes, trying hard to sharpen a dizzying lack of focus. He flapped an unco-ordinated hand, a sick parody of a child's marionette.

'Don't want to talk to you,' he declared, voice getting louder. 'Not to anyone. Just fuck off and leave me alone. You hear?'

Gregory could see pain and vulnerability etched into his face. As a shark can detect the minutest trace of blood in the sea, the reporter could smell a story.

'Come on, Sid, don't be silly,' he said slyly. 'Can I get you a drink?'

Graveney grunted his assent. Soon he was cradling another Scotch in his big coarse hands.

'Why did you do it?' asked the reporter gently.

Graveney looked up blankly and said: 'What?'

'Let Conrad buy you out. You just gave up, didn't you?'

For a few moments, Graveney's eyes misted over again. Hunched over the table, clutching his glass for comfort, he seemed the shapeless and empty husk of a man.

'You don't know,' he said sadly, shaking his head. 'I tried but it was no use.'

'What do you mean, Sid? Tell me.'

'So you can splash it all over your, your . . . '

He paused to compose himself and slurred triumphantly: 'Shit rag.'

Gregory could see that he was coming apart, growing ever more incoherent and confused. Now his coaxing had an edge of desperation.

'Just tell me why you sold out. I want to understand.'

Head lolling into his head, Graveney mumbled: 'No choice, I had no choice.'

Urgently Gregory tugged his arm and hissed: 'Did Conrad stitch you up somehow? Is that what happened?'

With a wordless noise of protest, Graveney struggled to pull away from his grip. His head swayed backwards and for a moment the whites of his eyes were visible.

Then his head came crashing down onto the table with a sickening thud, scattering glasses and upending the ashtray.

'Oi!' shouted the youth behind the bar. 'Get that drunk old git out of here!'

Gregory was on his feet cursing, slapping Graveney's face. But it was no good: he was out cold.

Disgusted, Gregory finally abandoned his frantic efforts at revival and said in a tight voice: 'Not my problem, sonny. You look after him.'

Once again the squalid story of the battle for Bradcaster City had eluded him.

With trembling fingers, Redwood was packing away decades of his memories into a small wooden tea chest.

He had stripped the photographs from the walls of his chairman's office. He had cleared his desk of clutter and contracts.

Now the room looked bare and desolate. The tea chest was spilling over as Redwood crammed it with relics, working mechanically, his face set.

When he was finished, he stared down mournfully at the collection of objects. He seemed bewildered and looked older than before, bowed as under a great weight. He passed a hand unsteadily across his eyes.

He was breathing heavily, struggling to contain his emotion.

'I can't believe it,' he said aloud. 'I just can't believe it.'

There was a thick vibration in his voice which threatened to break into a sob. He suddenly felt awkward and foolish just standing in the centre of the empty room, arms lolling uselessly at his sides.

He drew in a great lungful of air and bent to pick up the overflowing chest. His fingers squeezed beneath the base and he heaved it into the air, grunting with the effort.

He leaned back to take the weight against his breast but his legs were buckling. He was swaying from side to side as he struggled out of the room.

Just at that moment, Conrad appeared in the doorway, blocking his path. A look of hatred burned in the perspiring face of Redwood.

'Arthur, for goodness' sake, let me take that,' said Conrad quickly. 'You'll do yourself a mischief.'

He made a grab for the chest but Redwood backed away shaking his head insistently.

'I don't need your help,' he snapped. 'I can manage.'

Conrad was advancing towards him, smiling and reaching out his hands.

'Don't be silly,' he coaxed.

He clasped a corner of the chest but Redwood tugged it viciously from him. As he did so, a delicate engraved bowl in Waterford crystal was dislodged and dropped to the floor.

With a crash, it shattered into a thousand fragments, which glinted wickedly against the royal blue carpet.

There was an appalled silence as both men surveyed the damage.

Then Redwood dashed the tea chest to the ground and blurted: 'You . . . you evil man. You destroy everything you touch. Nothing is sacred to you, is it? You trample over other people's dreams but you have none yourself. You just want to smash everything to pieces.'

For once, Conrad was unsettled.

'Look, Arthur,' he mumbled. 'I'm sorry about the bowl. I'll get you another one.'

There was a savage, contemptuous glint in Redwood's eyes. His lips were curling into a rictus of fury.

'You think you can solve any problem by throwing money at it,' he shouted. 'But there are some things even you can't buy.'

Stung, Conrad snapped back: 'I bought your precious football club, Arthur. And I bought my way into this office. Think about that when you're unpacking your trash.'

Redwood glowered impotently. Everything – power, vocation, self-respect – had been usurped by this man.

By accepting the loan for Simmons, he had kick-started the inexorable machinery of Conrad's ambition. Now he was faced by the wreckage of all that underpinned his sense of who he was.

A red mist swam before his eyes. He grabbed at the tea chest and, with a violent lunge, turned it upside down.

With a tremendous smashing and clattering, everything spilled out onto the floor in a chaos of disintegration. Picture frames cracked and glass shattered. Silver trophies clanged and clashed.

'There,' screamed Redwood, his chest heaving. 'This is all yours now. I don't want it because it stinks of you and your money.'

In a furious passion, he swept from the room. For a few moments, Conrad stared after him in stupefaction and disbelief.

Then he began to laugh.

·

PLAYERS' STRIKE LOOMS AGAIN

Stars could pull the plug on Spacelink

SOCCER'S new Super League was heading for disaster last night.

Talks between Spacelink bosses and the players' union broke down amid angry accusations from both sides. Now the prospect of an all-out strike is looming.

The satellite company is refusing to climb down from its pledge to screen 50 matches every season.

'We are paying £300 million for the exclusive Super League rights,' said an angry Tom Haslam, managing director of Spacelink. 'We want value for money for ourselves and our subscribers. It's as simple as that.'

But the players are digging in their heels, claiming saturation coverage will lead to empty stadia and public apathy.

Fresh from his successful battle with the Super League over the TV cash share-out, UPF chief executive Graham Wright was quietly confident before last night's meeting.

But he found Spacelink head Michael Conrad a harder nut to crack. Emerging ashen-faced, he told waiting reporters: 'Spacelink are not prepared to budge an inch and we must now consider the possibility of industrial action.

'That is not a decision we would take lightly. But we will not hesitate to act to protect the interests of the fans and of the game itself.'

Yesterday's last-ditch negotiations were arranged by Super League bosses, desperate to achieve stability before the new season opens next month.

'We wanted to meet the players half way but our hands were tied by the terms of the TV contract,' said one insider.

'We hoped that, given the genuine strength of feeling among the players, Spacelink would make some concessions. It is a matter of some regret that they have proved so obstinate.'

With the first games scheduled for less than three weeks

hence, the rift is threatening to turn into a trial of strength.

Everyone knows that Michael Conrad is unlikely to back down. Less certain is the commitment of football's elite players, who would be risking their six-figure salaries and flash cars if they heed the strike call.

Melanie Simmons was getting ready for her husband. In the bathroom she was applying the finishing touches to her make-up, inking in the mascara around her eyelashes.

Her mouth was pursed in a tight O of concentration; her lips were a vibrant red. She wore great swathes of blue eye shadow which almost, but not quite, matched the iridescence of her pupils.

With a sigh, she screwed the tiny mascara brush back into its bottle and surveyed herself in the mirror above the sink. The artificial face of a stranger stared back at her.

Her glance flitted anxiously to her wristwatch: ten minutes to midnight. Just at that moment, she heard the crunch of gravel as Simmons' Mercedes pulled up outside the front door and her heart leapt. He was early.

Suddenly she was consumed by nerves; she felt sick to the pit of her stomach. Downstairs there was the rattle of a key turning in the lock and then the door slammed.

Melanie stayed rooted to the spot. There was a seemingly interminable clattering in the hallway and then she heard his light athletic tread on the stairs.

She emerged into their bedroom just as he appeared in the doorway, looking weary and troubled.

'Oh, hullo love,' he said dully. 'What a bloody journey.'

Already he was discarding his jacket and tugging at his shirt. He yawned expansively.

Melanie advanced a nervous yard towards him.

'How was London?' she ventured.

'Hectic.'

'I missed you.'

Her voice was full of a girlish yearning. Simmons stopped unbuckling his trousers to look at her, seeing her properly for the first time since he had entered the room.

The first thing he noticed was her painted face, and the blonde hair swept up from the nape of her neck. Then his gaze moved away from her frightened eyes and he realised she was wearing fishnet stockings and steep high heels beneath her dressing gown.

Embarrassed, she blurted: 'What are you looking at?'

With abrupt, stiff movements, she unknotted the belt of her gown and tossed it to the floor. Simmons gaped.

She was wearing a black basque edged with red lace, which compressed her waist and forced her breasts outwards in offering. Beneath the basque, her navel was visible and at the crease of her thighs he saw a tiny black silk G-string.

Melanie smiled uncertainly.

'What do you think?' she asked shyly.

Simmons spluttered: 'I . . . you look nice. Very nice.'

He was beginning to feel he was trapped in some bizarre dream. Then he caught the desperation in her face and knew this was for real. He could only guess at what had driven her to this last-ditch seduction.

She moved towards him and reached out a hand towards his bare chest. With infinite gentleness, she caressed him, her fingers quivering slightly. Her touch seemed to burn raw tracks across his skin.

He grabbed her wrist and muttered: 'Stop it. Please.'

She was staring up at him but he could not meet her gaze.

'Why won't you make love to me?' she whispered. 'Are you ashamed?'

There was a fierce stinging behind his eyes and he blinked back tears. He shook his head, his eyes still fixed on the floor.

'I don't know, I just can't.'

In a voice that was suddenly calm and even, she asked: 'There's someone else, isn't there?'

He felt giddy and couldn't help glancing at her. Her eyes were wide and unblinking and full of intensity.

Somehow this wasn't the moment for honesty.

'No,' he lied. 'Of course not.'

Involuntarily, he clasped her to him and kissed her hungrily, tasting her salt tongue. Her mouth was soft and warm and comforting. Gasping, he bit the base of her neck.

'Oh Gus,' she said, holding him tight.

With sheer physical strength, he bent her across his thigh and dragged her roughly to the floor. His whole body was aflame with longing, as if something had been awaken after deep slumber.

But as he loomed over her, his hand cradling her head, he saw her eyes were full of a kind of terror; a dread that this act would solve nothing and there would be nothing left to try.

Her whole body was racked with tension and her eyes seemed to be leeching the life from him. His aroused blood grew still and cold.

With limp arms, he let her go and stumbled to his feet.

'I'm sorry,' he murmured. 'I'm really sorry.'

His nerve gone, he dashed from the room. Melanie lay quite motionless, beyond tears, staring blankly at the ceiling.

She had never felt so alone.

The following day at training, Simmons ran himself ragged, striving to exhaust himself so utterly that last night's memories would stop burning in his brain.

Normally languid and elegant, he chased every ball with ferocity, delivering crunching tackles and spewing out foul-mouthed exhortations to the other players.

'Simmons, for Christ's sake!' bellowed Dougie McNally from the touchline. 'This is only a practice match. Save it for the start of the season.'

But still he continued in his frantic pursuit of the ball, diving in with aggressive high tackles, shouldering players aside ruthlessly. In the end, a bemused McNally had no option but to blow his whistle early before Simmons did himself or someone else an injury.

In the changing room, Simmons sat drenched in sweat. He was always slightly taciturn but today even his friend Rod Lyons was afraid to venture a word.

While showering, he scrubbed at his body so vigorously that he seemed to be trying to wash away some invisible stain beneath his skin. The other players huddled together and stared furtively at him, a little afraid of his intensity.

There was no horse play, no filthy jokes, no banter. With his brooding presence, Simmons had choked the normal atmosphere of easy friendship.

He was the last to leave the barbed wire encampment of Bradcaster's training ground. Incongruously, an August sun was blazing away overhead; the air was warm and still, the horizons hazy.

There was the usual posse of young autograph hunters surrounding his Mercedes in the car park. They began to babble excitedly as he appeared and rushed towards him brandishing pens and programmes.

It was the last thing he wanted. But they had waited a

long time and it wasn't so long ago that he had kept similar vigils. Sighing, he allowed himself to be engulfed by the shrill-voiced tide.

As the last child dashed away, satisfied and chattering, a figure detached itself from a car a dozen yards away.

'Gus?' a voice called out. 'Could you spare a minute?'

Squinting into the sun, Simmons could see only a vague silhouette advancing towards him. Gradually the figure resolved itself into the shape of Graham Wright, boss of the Union of Professional Footballers.

Wright had been a tough, no-nonsense full back and he brought the same direct approach to his union work. He was respected and well-liked in the game.

Smiling but slightly bemused, Simmons extended his hand in greeting.

'Hello, Graham,' he said. 'What are you doing skulking around this dump?'

Clasping his hand firmly and nodding towards the Mercedes, Wright replied: 'I wanted a private word. Why don't we drive for a while?'

'OK.'

As Simmons drove away, huge decaying tenements loomed overhead, unredeemed by sunlight. Dirty children squabbled in the gutters, packs of dogs marauded through a desert of dust and rubble and broken glass.

'Nice round here, isn't it?' said Wright, gazing through the window.

Simmons glanced at him in sudden irritation and snapped: 'Look Graham, get to the bloody point. You haven't come all this way for a guided tour of the shitholes of Bradcaster.'

Wright laughed.

'They said you were a prickly bastard.'

'Only when I'm being pissed about.'

'All right,' said Wright heavily, as a gang of loitering youths followed the Mercedes with dull eyes. 'It's about the possibility of industrial action by the players. I wanted to sound you out.'

'Why?' asked Simmons, gunning the car up a long straight road, a cloud of white dust settling slowly behind them.

'Because you're the flavour of the month. You could set an example.'

'What for?'

Now it was Wright's turn to betray his anger.

Glaring at Simmons, he said tightly: 'Doesn't it matter to you what they're doing to the game with their greed? Or are you just interested in your fancy car and your posh clothes?'

Simmons screeched to a halt at a red light, dipping the clutch and revving the engine viciously.

'Get off my back, will you?' he muttered. 'Why does everyone want a piece of me? Get someone else to play the martyr, I'm not interested.'

Wright sensed he had touched a raw nerve.

'Look Gus,' he said in a more conciliatory tone. 'Football used to be the working man's game. You grew up near the Bristol docks, so can understand what I'm saying.'

Simmons' voice was sullen: 'So what?'

'With Conrad running the game, people like that are just being frozen out. They can't pay turnstile prices and they certainly don't have the price of a dish. Somebody has got to make a stand.'

His anger gone, Simmons eased the Mercedes away from the traffic lights but a streak of stubbornness remained embedded inside him.

'But it doesn't have to be me,' he said evenly.

Wright had swivelled round in the passenger seat and was staring earnestly at Simmons, who deliberately kept his eyes on the road.

'You won't be on your own,' he was urging. 'If you're

solid, everyone else will fall in behind. You're the key to our strategy.'

Simmons grinned sardonically.

'And what strategy might that be?'

'We don't want an all-out strike,' said Wright. 'That could destroy the game altogether. We're going to concentrate on a single big match, just to show we mean business. And that's where you come in.'

'Oh, is it?'

By now Wright's enthusiasm was running away with him. He had grabbed Simmons' arm just below the shoulder and was squeezing it hard.

'The first Monday evening fixture is Bradcaster versus Sheffield City,' he said, flexing his fingers for extra emphasis. 'It's the only game that night. So even if Spacelink get wind of the plan, they can't take their cameras to another stadium. It would be a major embarrassment.'

He chuckled to himself and added: 'Just to make it more satisfying, Michael Conrad's own team would be shitting on him from a great height.'

Simmons slammed on the brakes, so hard the nose of the Mercedes dipped towards the broken tarmac.

'You're fucking mad,' he said, looking at Wright and his blankly committed countenance for the first time. 'Our players just won't do it. They're all scared to death of the sack.'

Wright gave Simmons a strange look.

'Just like you, eh, Gus?' he asked softly.

In a moment, he had tugged open the catch of the passenger door and stepped outside. Slamming it without further words, he strolled away up the road towards the tenements.

Simmons watched his shape slowly receding in the driving mirror.

With a sudden snort of amusement, he let out the

clutch and propelled the Mercedes, wheels squealing in the dirt, towards the far horizon.

For the last two days, Alexandra Conrad had been in a state of anxiety bordering on hysteria.

She was a passionate and impulsive woman who had embarked on many sexual adventures both before and during her marriage. But none had left her feeling quite like this.

Almost implausibly beautiful, Alexandra found it easy to tease and dominate her lovers. She never gave herself during the act of love; rather her pleasure was essentially solitary, masturbatory.

Sex leeched her lovers of their virility, even when they seemed to be broaching her innermost defences. Yet the night with Simmons in her hotel room was quite different.

At the time, it had not seemed so. His mumbled protestations of love as he crumpled at her breast were merely worrying and embarrassing, a complication she could have done without.

But as the hours wore on, Alexandra began to feel sick and empty. She recalled the touch of his fingers on her body, making her senses flare with desire.

She remembered the urgency of his kiss, the sharp nick of his teeth at the nape of her neck, his lean and muscular body.

Above all, she rehearsed over and again the moment of penetration, his infinite care as he eased into her, filling her completely. The sense of completeness as he moved inside her, not like an invading power but prompting instead a swelling internal sweetness.

She became frantic at this loss of control. But although she tried to force him from her mind, her awakened longing was simply too powerful.

Her husband's voice cut through her reverie: 'What the hell is the matter with you?'

She jumped and muttered distantly: 'Uh?'

'You've been mooning about the house all day,' said Conrad. 'You haven't even got dressed.'

It was true; she wore the same silk kimono that Simmons had torn from her in his passion. She was sitting absently at the grand piano in the drawing room, one finger unconsciously plinking at the keys.

Conrad had swept into the room with a worried frown and now stood at the French windows, gazing pensively across the lawns.

'I'm sorry,' said Alexandra, recovering herself. 'I just feel lazy today.'

She uncoiled from the piano stool and moved across towards him, laying a hand lightly on his shoulders. He shivered slightly, as if surprised by the warmth of the gesture.

'Something the matter?' asked Alexandra.

'Yes,' he said slowly, turning to face her.

Not for the first time, she noticed the onset of age and fatigue in the lines around his eyes.

Abruptly, he added: 'You got on pretty well with Gus Simmons, didn't you?'

Her eyes widened and for a terrifying moment, she thought it was an accusation. But then she saw he had another motive.

'He was quite nice for a footballer,' she said, heart pounding, trying to keep her voice steady.

Conrad laughed and for a moment his face cleared.

'Oh, come on, Alex. He was smitten with you, anyone could see that. His wife was so bloody gauche, I'm not surprised.'

'Yes, she was a funny little thing, wasn't she? Not what I expected at all.'

As she spoke, Alexandra imagined Simmons coupling urgently with Melanie, limbs flailing. The thought was indescribable agony to her. Now she understood something of Conrad's own possessiveness towards her.

'I'd like you to speak to Simmons,' he said.

Again Alexandra was startled. She flushed guiltily.

'What on earth for?' she asked, eyes downcast.

'I hear he is considering strike action. That could create serious complications for me.'

Conrad turned away from the windows, face troubled, and stared at Alexandra. She felt as if his cold grey eyes were scouring all her dark secrets.

'I think you might have some influence with him,' he said in a strange voice, tinged with suspicion.

It was almost as if he knew he was playing the pimp. But still he had to drive on with his compulsive, Machiavellian machinations.

Alexandra's eyes darted around the room, quite unable to meet his gaze. She was beginning to feel this was a situation where everyone was on the brink of chaos.

'What do you want me to do?' she said quietly.

'Butter him up a bit. Help him to see that a strike is in no one's best interests.'

'Why should he listen to me?'

Conrad regarded her with a curiously detached look: the lithe perfection beneath the kimono, her almost-too-full lips, the masses of raven hair. And the feckless, wilful streak captured in her eyes.

'He'll listen,' he said.

For days, Redwood had hidden himself from the scrutiny of the world in his lonely and desolate house.

Since the scene with Conrad, a sense of outraged humiliation was festering inside him like a cancer. Painfully, he remembered his own impotent rage as he dashed his belongings to the floor.

Worst of all, he could still hear the cruel laughter of Conrad as he dashed away down the corridor, tears scalding his eyes. It echoed in his head, insistent and threatening, growing in volume until his brain was full of it.

But he did not lose control of himself. Each morning, he rose early, washed and shaved with minute care. He dressed impeccably in blazer and regimental tie, knife-edge creases in his slacks, shoes buffed to an improbable sheen. A crimson handkerchief dangled raffishly from his top pocket.

But he didn't leave the house and, since he was untouched by appetite, he prepared no meals. He simply sat in the big armchair in his front room, staring away into the window's blue square of sky, into nothingness.

All the time, he was rehearsing his sense of wrong, honing his hatred to a fine point.

Bradcaster City had been the source of all his joy, the repository of all he had achieved. But it had been snatched from him, was itself changed into something alien and menacing.

Michael Conrad was an easy man to hate but it went beyond him. This was the collision between the new world and the old, the pursuit of cash and the love of honour.

As he saw it, Redwood was being carried away by barbarian forces but there was no one to hear or heed his screams.

Irritated by the continual jangling of the telephone, he finally left it off the hook, completing his isolation. But then, on the fourth morning of his retreat, Redwood was stirred by a knock at the front door.

Startled by this invasion of his silence, he sat still and waited for the caller to go away. But the knocking came again, louder this time.

For a few moments, things went quiet. Then Redwood heard the scuffling of feet on the path outside and a face appeared at the living room window.

It was Sid Graveney. He squinted inside, eyes adjusting to the relative darkness, and caught sight of Redwood shrinking back into his chair.

'For Christ's sake, Arthur,' he yelled, voice muffled by the glass. 'Are you deaf?'

He disappeared from sight and, sighing heavily, Redwood prised himself from the armchair and made for the door. Clicking the latch and revealing Graveney on the step, Redwood could not prevent a faint smile rising to his lips.

The big man was scowling and lifting up his right foot for inspection. To reach the window, he had been forced to clamber across a flower bed recently freshened by a late summer downpour. All over his shoes and the bottom of his trousers, black damp earth was clinging.

But then Redwood saw the dark circles around Graveney's eyes, his crumbling physical presence, and the incipient smile turned to stone.

'Come in, Sid,' he said gently.

As they passed into the living room, he added: 'Drink?'

Graveney grimaced and said: 'No thanks, I've been doing a bit too much of that recently.'

As the big man perched on the edge of Redwood's sofa, there was a terrific awkwardness, as if all their angry words of recent months lay between them in a great pile.

'Look Arthur,' blurted Graveney. 'I wanted to square things with you. I said some pretty tough things. But I know how wrong that was.'

For a few seconds, Redwood closed his eyes in contemplation and rubbed the bridge of his aquiline nose.

'Why did you do it?' he asked finally. 'After everything you said, you made me feel like a criminal. Then you sell out to Conrad just the same.'

Graveney sank back and, in a voice that was suddenly choked, whispered: 'I can't tell you that but believe me, I had no choice. Conrad has taken us both for bloody fools, hasn't he?'

'Yes, he has,' said Redwood in weariness and hatred.

'We can't let him get away with it.'

Redwood snorted cynically.

'He already has, Sid. He can do what he likes now.'

There was a note of urgent pleading in Graveney's voice as he replied: 'You can keep a check on him, Arthur, stop him from ruining the club completely. Everyone respects you, especially the fans. He can't afford to ignore that.'

Redwood was hit by a sudden surge of anger.

'For God's sake, you're as bad as he is. Do you really want me to sit on the board, nodding like a puppet, while he pulls the place apart? He thinks some Mickey Mouse title will keep me happy. But I showed him.'

Again he was enacting his ritual of demolition in Conrad's new office, mouth twisted into a furious and resentful sneer. Graveney stared at him helplessly.

'Arthur, please,' he cajoled. 'Think about it. Someone's got to be the voice of Bradcaster's conscience.'

Redwood glared at him but, as the words slowly sank in, the older man's face softened a little. A quizzical look supervened.

'Why does this matter to you now?' he asked quietly.

A dark look passed across Graveney's face.

As he replied, it was as though a curtain had parted to show his desolate and withered spirit: 'Let's just say I wanted to settle a few accounts.'

SIMMO TO STRIKE?

Star in tug-of-war drama

Exclusive by Colin Gregory

GUS SIMMONS is the intended secret weapon as football's war of words threatens to erupt into open conflict.

But in a bizarre twist, the Bradcaster marksman's loyalty is being claimed by both sides!

Boss of the Union of Professional Footballers, Graham Wright, has called for a one-off strike next Monday. Its target is the glamour fixture between Bradcaster and last season's champions Sheffield City.

It would be a double blow to Michael Conrad, chairman of both Bradcaster and TV satellite company Spacelink, which is hoping to screen the clash as its first live game of the season.

Players are furious that their demands for fewer Monday matches have not been heeded and are heading for a showdown with the Super League and its Spacelink paymasters.

Wright is confident Simmo will show solidarity and refuse to play. With his backing, the bargaining power of the UPF would receive a massive boost.

Yet rumours at Bradcaster suggest Conrad is moving fast to snuff out the strike threat.

He is sure to personally lobby Simmo to pull on the blue jersey on Monday night. Some players are said to have been offered cash incentives to turn out.

Meanwhile, the charismatic star was remaining tight-lipped yesterday. Looking tired and drawn after a training session, he brushed aside questions and sped away in his £30,000 Mercedes convertible.

Only time will tell if Simmo is prepared to risk his fast-lane lifestyle – and take on the wealthiest and most powerful man in British football.

Dusk was settling as Simmons turned into the appointed lane of a Bradcaster industrial estate, his car headlights illuminating row after row of modern brick-built factory units.

Right at the end of the cul-de-sac, in a glare of sodium, was the sign he was seeking: Flashlight Photography. He pulled up on the forecourt and killed the engine, peering through the windscreen for a sign of life.

Stepping out of the car, he saw the main reception area was cloaked in darkness. But a rectangle of pale light shone beneath the door of the fire exit around the side.

Conscious of the sound of his shoes on the concrete slabs, his pulse pumping in his throat, he moved towards the tiny beacon. He pushed at the door and with a creak, it gave inwards.

Uncertainly, he entered a big and echoing room. A faint glow came from a light bulb far away but his eyes were struggling to make sense of the humps and shadows around him.

'Hello?' he called out. 'Is there anybody in here?'

There was no reply. Simmons cursed in frustration and trepidation.

Suddenly, the room was bathed in intense white light. Retinas aching, Simmons screwed his eyelids tight and thrust out a palm for protection.

Then he heard the sound of musical laughter and a woman's voice called out: 'Oh sorry, did I frighten you?'

As his eyes adjusted to the brightness, a figure stepped in front of the spotlight, which cast it into silhouette. It glowed beatifically as in a religious painting.

Alexandra Conrad had always had a flair for the dramatic gesture.

'Turn the rest of the bloody lights on,' growled Simmons, angered by the charade.

She fumbled for a switch and several strip lights flickered into life overhead. Now he could see her face, he noticed a hint of vulnerability he had not seen before and his heart contracted.

She smiled, a little uncertainly.

'Hello,' she said.

They circled each other like two wary animals. Simmons saw they were in a huge photographic studio, divided into sets and flanked everywhere by lights and cameras and snaking electric cables.

This time he was determined to be cool. But she looked as preternaturally lovely as ever, and it was difficult for his voice not to betray his heart.

'What the hell is all this about?' he demanded.

Ignoring him, she murmured: 'I didn't think I would see you again.'

Her voice was full of longing and nostalgia for that first night. From somewhere her dark and dreadful eyes had found a new warmth and his sense of purpose caved in.

'Why here?' he asked, not really caring.

'Discretion. A friend of mine runs it.'

She moved away towards one of the sets, beckoning him to follow.

'Come and sit down,' she said. 'I need to talk to you.'

Unbelievably, an ornate four-poster bed squatted in a corner of the studio. It was enclosed by great swathes of red silk, tied back with golden tassels. The plump pillows were in heavily worked lace and the sheets a billowing and spotless white cotton.

Alexandra giggled again and said over her shoulder: 'I thought this would amuse you. It's just been used for a soft porn shoot.'

She threw herself onto the bed and cupped her face in her hands. But she was no longer playing the coquette and in her face there was a flickering nervousness.

Simmons kept his distance, one arm leaning against a heavy camera on a tripod. He regarded her with suspicious desire.

'I must have been mad to come here,' he muttered.

'But you came.'

Still prone on the bed, she flicked off her shoes and kicked her legs absently. She wore a simple summer dress based on a Matisse painting, all vibrant reds and oranges.

In the glare of the studio lights, her skin seemed pale, almost phosphorescent.

After a pause in which each could hear the other breathing, she said: 'My husband asked me to see you. Fortunately, it was what I wanted, too.'

Simmons merely stared in disbelief.

'He wants me to tell you not to strike on Monday. Now I've told you.'

Simmons' voice was icy: 'So you're whoring for him.'

'I came because I wanted to.'

The look of truth was in her eyes. His gaze raked her body, which was tense and expectant.

'Why?' he asked almost helplessly.

For a few moments, she didn't reply.

Then, in a strange voice, she said: 'Can you see me? In the camera, I mean. Have a look.'

She gestured towards the Canon on top of its tripod. Without knowing why, he obeyed, standing on tiptoe to peer through the viewfinder. There she was, captured within a green box of intersecting lines.

Staring up at the lens, she called out: 'Take a picture of me. Just press the button on the end of that lead.'

He did as he was told and, in an instant, half a dozen flashlights flared into life.

'Again,' she said, adopting a burning heavy-lidded gaze that stirred him even through the lens.

Soon he was clicking away ferociously as she shifted her position on the bed: creating angular patterns with her body, eyes locked on the camera. He knew that somehow she was giving herself as completely as she knew.

Her breathing grew laboured and he realised she was fumbling for the zip at the back of her dress. She freed her arms and her sweet breasts swung into view. His fingers squeezed compulsively at the shutter switch.

She arched her back and wriggled her hips and suddenly

she was naked. Shaking, he saw the dark secret cleft between her thighs as she rose to her knees among the crumpled sheets.

'Don't stop,' she gasped, lifting her mane of hair from the nape of her neck, tensing her breasts.

He could not tear himself from the camera, as with her fingers she parted the inner lips of her sex and offered herself to him. If he watched with his naked eyes, she would surely burn him to nothing like a leaf in a blowtorch flame.

But already his blood was on fire. In the end, he had no choice. He stumbled forward towards her, maddened by desire, and she opened her arms to receive him.

Everything – trust, honour, dignity, conscience – shrivelled and blackened as he entered the inferno.

For the umpteenth time, Gregory glanced impatiently at his watch. He cursed and lit another Marlboro.

It was almost nine o'clock in the evening and Giovanni's restaurant was beginning to fill and buzz. The habitually scruffy Gregory looked incongruous among the mock Baroque decor.

He was going to have a hell of a job getting the expenses for this little jaunt past a tightarse like Harry Walters.

Gregory crooked a forefinger in the direction of a waiter. As he approached the table, he performed an elaborate mime of ignorance – shrugging expansively, showing his palms, pouting his bottom lip.

'Bloody hell, Marco,' hissed Gregory as the waiter leaned towards him. 'What's going on? You said he booked a table at eight.'

'What can I say?' demanded the Italian. 'Maybe he has been delayed, yes?'

Gregory cursed again, so loudly several diners glared at him in outrage.

'Well if I'm going to be here all night, I'd better have

another Scotch,' he said. 'For Christ's sake, make it a large one.'

The waiter scurried away and, as as he neared the bar, almost collided with a customer fresh off the street.

'Ah!' beamed Marco. 'You are here at last.'

With a flourish, he indicated the only remaining empty table, slightly isolated in a dark corner.

Simmons had come to Giovanni's alone. He wanted time to think, to sift through all the conflicting motives and plans of action that were whirring in his brain. He wanted to calm his shattered emotions with a plate of pasta and a robust chianti.

Giovanni's was not a place for open-mouthed gaping at celebrities. Rather there was a decorous undercurrent of interest, a ripple of gossip, the odd surreptitious glance from behind a menu.

But one pair of eyes followed Simmons with frank curiosity as he took his place and ordered a dry Martini.

Almost before he had settled himself, the reporter appeared at his elbow with a terse: 'Mind if I join you?'

Without waiting for a reply from the startled footballer, Gregory sat down and introduced himself.

'I know who you are,' snapped Simmons. 'Now piss off.'

The reporter simply ignored him: 'Are you planning to strike on Monday, Gus? Everyone wants to know.'

Simmons' face was a potent mixture of anger and disbelief. For a second, it seemed he was about to strike Gregory, who was leering across the table and trying to unsettle him.

'I told you once,' he said tightly. 'Get away from me before I break your arm.'

Gregory tutted sardonically.

'Don't make threats, Gus. It won't look very good in the paper, will it?'

Enraged, Simmons was flagging at a waiter to remove the interloping reporter. Gregory glanced anxiously over his shoulder.

'Is Conrad putting any pressure on you?' he gabbled. 'Is there any money on the table? What's the mood of the other players?'

Simmons' face was still like thunder and his jaw was clamped shut.

In desperation, just as a sombre-looking head waiter arrived at the table, Gregory said: 'Did you know that Steve Wilde was bribed to bring you to Bradcaster?'

Simmons' expression changed; a seeping incredulity spread across his face. Briskly, he waved the waiter away and regarded Gregory with gimlet eyes.

'What did you say?'

'You were bought body and soul. Conrad put up the money for your transfer, that's how he got his foot in the door.'

'Tell me something I don't know.'

Gregory knew he was flying a kite, that none of this was substantiated. But he wanted to keep Simmons talking, whatever it took.

'Did you know that Wilde used to be a TV producer for Spacelink?' he asked, searching for an opening, a hint of soft underbelly.

Simmons shook his head slowly, a sickening anticipation stirring in his guts.

'Five minutes after you arrive at Bradcaster, his company was awarded the publicity contract for Spacelink,' persisted Gregory. 'What does that suggest to you?'

Simmons remained dumb but his brain was racing. He remembered how Wilde had countered every objection to the Bradcaster move, how insistent and persuasive he had been.

As if reading his mind, Gregory cut in: 'I don't think

Mr Wilde was offering very objective advice, do you?'

How could he not have seen it? Unwittingly, he had been the stepping stone for Conrad's rise to power and the price for Wilde's complicity.

To them he was no more than a senseless hunk of black flesh.

Still Gregory was prodding him: 'So, how about it, Gus? Are you going to strike?'

'Wait and see.'

With a sudden violent motion, Simmons levered himself from his chair. Before Gregory could prevent him, he had dashed across the floor and stumbled out into the street.

Already the desire for revenge was rising inside him like a poisonous fume.

For a long time, Graveney had sat and watched the sky darkening over distant Bradcaster.

There was something in these bleak and windswept hills that drew him in times of trouble. Something about their primeval permanence, their looming silence.

They lay all around him like great slumbering beasts as a blood-red sun slid below the horizon. A sudden violent gust of wind splattered raindrops across the windscreen of the BMW.

Graveney felt as if a huge weight was squatting on his chest. He peered down into the valley through a film of rain, squinting as the shape of the landscape grew indistinct.

Occasionally his car's interior was lit by the flare of headlights on the road nearby. Shadows flickered across his face but he remained quite motionless, eyes focused on the far distance.

He was running memories in his head, over and over again like a deranged projectionist in an empty picture house. He was trying to splice his life together into a coherent pattern but instead all the images lay in an obstinate, haphazard heap.

The BMW had cut four deep trenches into the moist earth before coming to rest 100 yards from the nearest dirt track.

Graveney had remained in the car for so long, its chassis was nuzzling the ground. He flicked absently at the windscreen wiper and instantly his view clarified: a few yards of turf tumbling away into nothing and, below, the translucent glow of Bradcaster.

He gave the ignition key an extra turn and the engine burst into life. In his brain, a blank and silent screen had descended.

He rammed the car into gear and kicked the gas pedal down to the boards. With the engine screaming in protest, he let out the clutch.

But the wheels were spinning in the trenches, disgorging showers of black clods. Cursing, Graveney kept gunning the engine but the car simply wouldn't budge.

His shoulders slumped and his head collapsed forward onto the steering wheel. He was shedding tears of helplessness and frustration, his body heaving. Even now, it seemed he was to be denied.

In desperation, he slammed his foot down on the accelerator again and this time the wheels dug in and spun away, catapulting the car forwards.

In that lurching moment, a ghastly grin spread across Graveney's face and then the ground began to fall away.

His stomach jammed his throat as gravity took merciless hold. The nose of the car dipped and it span in a great laboured somersault, down and down, seemingly for ever.

But eventually it hit the rocks hundreds of feet below and crumpled and flipped over onto its broken back. A split-second later, there was a terrible roar as the petrol tank ignited and the car was consumed in a murderous furnace.

Soon all that remained was a smouldering pile of wreckage.

No matter where he was in the world, Michael Conrad always had a sensitive finger on the pulse of his business.

Bleary-eyed editors and producers would be roused by long-distance calls; faxes requiring instant response would flood in from New York, Frankfurt, Hong Kong, Tokyo.

He had honed to perfection the disconcerting telephone technique of total silence. Compelled by this vacuum to keep talking, his minions would babble away all their secrets and insecurities. Only when they were denuded and exhausted would Conrad cut in with some devastating comment.

Conrad never sleeps. Throughout his sprawling media empire, that was the first axiom for self-preservation. No executive was safe from his probing, his occasional bouts of ruthless blood-letting.

Always he remained hungrily at the centre of his web. But this time, some wondered if he had travelled too far from the epicentre to remain in control. Where on earth was Bradcaster anyway?

Almost as soon as the prospect of a players' strike became overwhelming, Conrad had decamped to the unfashionable provincial city.

He knew the whole credibility of Spacelink was staked on his football deal. He reasoned he was in a better position to influence events from within the game itself, surrounded by its trappings and accoutrements, taking soundings, creating whispers.

The chairman's office at Bradcaster City became his war room. He conducted his campaign with a telephone jammed between chin and collarbone, barking instructions or cajoling gently.

Conrad's newspapers carried tub-thumping editorials about the greed of the players; hacks raked over their gilded lifestyles. As the moment of conflict approached, he grew confident that support for the strike was eroding.

For the first time in months, he started to relax a little, became less caustic. His managers were surprised by a newly genial manner as the crisis appeared to recede.

Increasingly, his attention focused on the football club itself, which he was beginning to shape in his own image. Casting off the ancient stink of liniment and old ledgers, it was becoming a gleaming corporate machine, antiseptic in its perfection.

Advertising, sponsorships, spin-offs, merchandising. None of these techniques was new but Conrad helped to fuse them together and drive them relentlessly in the pursuit of profit. Young marketing professionals moved in, all jargon and sharp suits; old retainers were ruthlessly dumped.

One morning, Conrad found himself taking a call from South America on his cordless 'phone. He was roaming restlessly around his office, grunting replies, when he halted at the window and gazed outside.

Normally at this stage of the season, the stadium was quiet and deserted, a little eerie. But even through the glass, the noise of heavy machinery was humming in the air.

Huge bulldozers and JCBs were clambering over the rubble of the Southside terrace, shunting aside great lumps of concrete, rusty metal railings and decades of tradition. Conrad stared down in satisfaction at the transformation he had wrought.

Of all his achievements, the takeover of Bradcaster was perhaps the most visible and visceral. It ached in some secret innermost place he had never reached before.

The voice at the other end of the telephone line became simply a hiss of static, as if he were holding a shell to his ear for the sound of the sea. Conrad mumbled absently from time to time but the exchange had long ceased to be a conversation.

For a long time after he finally clicked away the antenna, he remained at the window lost in thought.

Suddenly, a voice behind him knifed into his consciousness: 'Conrad, I've got a bone to pick with you.'

Swivelling, he glimpsed Gus Simmons advancing towards him with eyes blazing.

'When I want to talk to somebody, I don't send my wife.'

Conrad registered the anger, the bunched muscles of the athlete, and for a second was touched by physical fear.

'Gus,' he said uncertainly. 'What's the problem?'

Simmons halted a yard from him and the space between them became electrified, as each tingled with the presence of the other. Even in his rage, the footballer sensed Conrad's aura of authority.

'You used me,' he said accusingly.

By now Conrad had recovered his composure; he lolled easily against the window sill, smiling.

'What the devil do you mean? You seem to have done rather well recently.'

Simmons thrust his face nearer to Conrad, who stiffened perceptibly although the smile still played around his lips.

'I was your meal ticket, wasn't I? You used me to buy your way in here and you bribed Steve Wilde just to make sure. Like I didn't have a mind of my own. I was just a piece of property, some dumb nigger off the street.'

Conrad saw the pain in Simmons' eyes and his voice was soothing: 'Gus, don't listen to malicious gossip. When you're big enough, everyone wants to drag you down. I have many enemies who would like to spoil things for me here. Pay no attention.'

Simmons' mouth twisted in a sneer.

'Wilde is raking in a lot of money from Spacelink. That was the price on my head, wasn't it? Don't bullshit me.'

'Look, have you asked him about this? He is your agent, after all.'

'Not any more.'

Conrad's eyes widened in surprise.

'Is that wise? He's made you a rich man.'

'He milked me, that's all. Of course he backed you up. You bought him off, didn't you?'

A hardness and arrogance was beginning to creep into Conrad's expression. He was tiring of playing the diplomat.

He waved a dismissive hand and said curtly: 'I'm sorry, but this conversation is going round in circles. Don't let me detain you from your training.'

Conrad turned his back and walked towards his desk. Simmons stared after him in astonishment and fury.

'Is that it?' he yelled. 'Is that really all you have to say?'

Conrad settled into his chair and regarded the footballer with contemptuous indifference.

'Gus, I bought you to score goals. I paid the market rate as for any other commodity. I'm really not interested in this breast-beating.'

There he sat in his cocoon of power. Immediately, an image forced itself into Simmons' brain: of Alexandra throwing back her head and screaming in ecstasy, urging him deeper inside her.

At that moment, an iron resolve was forged in the heat of his vengeance. For he had more at stake, and more ammunition, than Conrad imagined.

In the garden of her lonely house, Melanie Simmons was sweltering as the midday sun grew incandescent.

The air was still and heavy; in every direction, rising heat was creating shimmering patterns of haze. Myriad fields, almost supernaturally green, tumbled away towards Bradcaster.

Sheep grazed lazily on the slopes; a tractor chugged along a hedgerow, too far away to be heard. The day was rich with bird song, which seemed to swell from all directions at once and weave a gauze of sound.

Melanie watched this burgeoning summer landscape with dull eyes, hardly noticing. She wore a tatty pair of dungarees knotted crookedly at the shoulder. Her feet were bare and a pair of secateurs dangled from her hand.

The fragrance of roses was rich and musky in her nostrils, cloying her senses and making her ache for sleep. The rose beds, planted generations before, were in their glory: an explosion of vibrant reds and pinks, intense yellows and pure white.

As if in a trance, she moved among the flowers, snipping away the dead and withered heads. Thorns were clutching at her clothes and scratching the flesh of her arms but she paid no attention.

The wounds began to look ugly and bleed. With incurious eyes, she gazed down at the dripping crimson trails across her skin. She hardly knew what she was doing anymore.

She spent every day and many nights alone. Time passed so slowly for her that each hour contained an infinity of nothingness. Instead of reaching out, she compounded her unhappiness by withdrawing completely.

She stopped writing to her parents in Bristol; she allowed the telephone to ring itself into silence. The loneliness and sense of dislocation was worse, much worse, when her husband was in the house.

Ever since the night of her attempted seduction, a great chasm had yawned open between them which could not be filled by words. So they remained silent: Simmons restless and fidgety, as if being in her presence was a kind of torture; Melanie listless and passive.

Her days stretched away endlessly. There was no future, only an eternal here and now, a debilitating uniformity.

The scent of the roses sickened her as she continued pruning, tossing aside dozens of brown and shrunken flowers as insects buzzed angrily at the disturbance. Her actions became more and more violent, severing the stems with a twist and snick of the gleaming secateurs.

Soon all the dead heads had been discarded but a rising inner rage drive her on. All around her were blooms of fiery red, fading to pale yellow at the base of the petals. Some were fully blown and crawling with bees, others just bursting from their tight green buds.

The colour and stink of them was maddening. In a frenzy of destruction, Melanie slashed at the flowers and petals flew and fluttered in the air.

She was panting in the heat and sweat started to trickle down her back. But she didn't rest until every single rose bloom lay in the dirt of the flower beds, their crimsons and yellows still glowing.

She paused and stared around her. The rose bushes thrust their brown denuded stems skywards, the lopped and scattered flowers shone like stars on a dark night.

Melanie watched appalled, fascinated. In such a way, the trophies and treasures of her past had been ripped from their life-giving root.

Silently, in the teeth of the drought, she prayed for a new season and heavy rains.

'Groin strain? We all know how he got that. Too much horizontal gymnastics.'

Gregory was leaning back in his chair and laughing, telephone propped beneath his right ear. He was scribbling Pitman's shorthand into a shabby notebook.

'So who are you playing up front?' he asked. 'Christ, that's a bit of a risk, isn't it? Is he fit?'

He gave a cynical chuckle and added: 'Well, you would say that. Confident about the game?'

Just then the bulky frame of Harry Walters hove into view, making a frantic winding motion with his hand. Gregory nodded.

'Look, Joe, gotta run. Thanks for your help. Yeah, and you.'

Gregory replaced the receiver and gave Walters a quizzical look.

'This had better be good, Harry. I don't like giving contacts the bum's rush.'

'Something came up on police calls you might be interested in.'

There was a shuffling, apologetic air about the editor.

'A couple of hill walkers found the wreck of a car this morning, up near Hazel Fell. It had gone over the edge of a cliff.'

'So?'

'Our boys checked the registration. It belongs to your mate Sid Graveney.'

The reporter's face dropped.

'Jesus Christ, was he in it?'

'The coppers aren't saying much until forensic have finished poking around. There's a body in there but it's burnt to a crisp.'

There was a look of horror in Gregory's eyes. As a reporter, he had seen terrible things, witnessed death and violence, bulldozed his way through the grief of others. But this was different, closer to home.

He fumbled for a Marlboro and lit it with unsteady

hands, sucking in a great draught of smoke that somehow tasted of nothing.

'Have we tried to trace him?' he asked faintly, clearing his throat.

'His wife hasn't seen him since yesterday. Likewise his office. Identification is just a formality.'

Gregory felt sick to his stomach. He had been chasing the Bradcaster story so hard, he had lost sight of the human element. All along there had been far more at stake than column inches.

'I presume it wasn't an accident,' he said heavily.

Walters shook his head.

'No way. He was well away from the nearest road and there were no skid marks. He just pointed the car at the edge and drove over.'

Walters eyed the reporter with something akin to embarrassment and added: 'I'm sorry, mate. You were right, there's something fishy about this whole business. Keep pushing and I'll keep the old man off your back.'

Gregory smiled wryly.

'I never stopped pushing, Harry,' he said.

The BBC's 'Spotlight' was the leading current affairs programme on British television. Fronted by a combative Ulsterman, Gavin McGarry, it ran live three nights a week and pulled upwards of ten million viewers.

'Spotlight' was a spicy mix of celebrity chat and hard-edged investigative reporting, attracting the best home talent and the biggest stars from Hollywood. Gus Simmons was in very illustrious company.

A tight knot of fear was clutching at his guts as a pretty make-up girl fussed over him, dabbing at his forehead to prevent reflections from the studio lights. She was chatting merrily away but Simmons hardly heard, just grunted occasionally when she paused.

His mind was far away: on the patronising smile of Michael Conrad, husband of the woman Simmons thought he loved. He hated Conrad for treating him like trash, some unthinking lump to be bartered over. He despised his power games and machinations, his brutal revolution at Bradcaster.

But above all, he could not bear Conrad's possession of Alexandra. Even in the white heat of their passion, there was a part of her that still belonged to Conrad and was untouched by the conflagration.

He knew what it was like to be bought by the man, to feel the shackles and humiliation of his ownership. On the field and in the illicit pleasure of his bed, he could not escape Conrad's malignant influence.

Now it was time to strike back.

A few minutes before broadcast, Gavin McGarry edged into the make-up room. Normally genial and broad-smiling, he was growing more taciturn as the seconds ticked away.

His voice was as tight as a bow string: 'Everything all right?'

Simmons stared at his own reflection in the mirror, the girl flicking at his hair. He realised he was clenching his jaw so hard it had begun to ache. He nodded.

'Yeah.'

'Just make sure you're with the floor manager in plenty of time. She gives you the nod and you make your entrance just like we rehearsed. OK?'

The room was charged with tension. McGarry snatched back his sleeve to look at his watch.

'Yeah, yeah,' snapped Simmons. 'I'm not stupid.'

'I want to go straight in and talk about the strike,' said McGarry, ignoring the display of temper. 'We might as well grab this thing by the balls. You happy with that?'

'That's why I'm here, isn't it?'

McGarry regarded the footballer contemplatively for a moment. His journalist's instincts told him this was going to be an interesting interview, not just another cosy plug. Simmons had something to say and McGarry was going to give him his head.

'One thing puzzles me,' said the Irishman. 'When our researchers called you a week ago, you said you didn't want to do the show. Suddenly you changed your mind. Why?'

'Sheer bloody spite,' replied Simmons grimly.

McGarry laughed and clapped the footballer's shoulder. 'Fair enough. Good luck and I'll see you in a couple of minutes.'

At precisely seven o'clock, the director cued the 'Spotlight' theme music and McGarry stepped purposefully onto the studio floor, the audience breaking into obedient applause. He halted before two vacant black leather chairs, smiling in acknowledgement.

As the acclaim died down, he delivered his introduction straight to camera with easy charm: 'Good evening and welcome to "Spotlight". My first guest tonight is famous for baring his body in an aftershave advertisement. His debut single rocketed to the top of the pop charts and stayed there for weeks.

'He also happens to be Britain's most talked-about football talent. Less than a year ago, he cost three million pounds but now they say he's priceless. Ladies and gentlemen, Gus Simmons.'

The applause swelled again, punctuated with cheers and whoops, as McGarry gestured towards the wings where Simmons was huddled. Blinking under the studio lights, the footballer appeared in a white linen Hugo Boss suit.

He strode across the floor to McGarry and the pair shook hands before sitting down. Simmons felt a sharp pain in the base of his throat, as if he were choking. He fidgeted in his seat and smiled wanly.

Sensing his discomfort, McGarry launched into a long preamble, hoping that Simmons would absorb the atmosphere and relax a little.

'Gus, football is in a wee bit of a mess at the moment,' he began. 'The Super League starts this weekend and everyone is at each other's throats. Your union has called for a boycott of Bradcaster's opening fixture and, as usual, you're in the spotlight. Are you going to strike?'

There was an expectant hush in the studio.

Then, as steadily as he could, Simmons said: 'Yes, I am.'

A tremor ran through the audience and McGarry followed up quickly: 'Why is that, Gus?'

'Because the deal between the Super League and Spacelink is going to destroy the game.'

Simmons dug a nervous finger into his shirt collar and took a deep breath. McGarry was experienced enough to let the silence build, despite the shrill voice of the producer in his earpiece.

'It's all down to greed,' continued Simmons at last, unprompted. 'Spacelink were talking silly money and the clubs sold out. But it will be the fans who suffer.'

'What do you mean?' urged McGarry gently.

'Look,' said Simmons, growing more passionate. 'Times are hard, right? But the fans either get stiffed at the turnstiles or ripped off by Spacelink. They just can't afford to watch football anymore.'

'So what's the effect of that?'

'We shouldn't take these people for granted. They aren't stupid. Sooner or later, they are going to wake up to what's going on and see that nobody really gives a stuff about them. They'll just reject the game. But take the fans away from football and it becomes pointless.'

Still McGarry was probing skilfully: 'You really think that could happen?'

'Sure, why not? I can see the day when games will be played in empty stadiums just for television. It already happens in the States. Spacelink only care about the fans who can afford dishes. Why else would they insist on so many Monday evening games?

'Don't forget, we're talking about saturation coverage, maybe 50 or 60 matches a season. So the fans who've got satellite will become bored and the rest will lose interest because they can't see anything at all. It's a total bloody farce.'

'So you're going to strike,' said McGarry. 'But isn't there a serious conflict of loyalty here? It must have cost you a lot of sleepless nights.'

Simmons nodded vigorously. By now he had forgotten the cameras and the watching millions. He was leaning forward and gesturing with his hands for emphasis.

'Bradcaster pay my wages and they expect me to play football. I'm also aware that our chairman, Michael Conrad, has a special reason for wanting the game to go ahead. But I felt it was time to take a stand.'

'What could that mean to you personally?'

'Refusing to play when I'm fit contravenes the terms of my contract. So the club could sack me or sue me. But this is a bigger issue than a single player or a one-off strike. I think much more could be done to bring these people to their senses.'

McGarry's eyes widened in surprise. Far beyond his wildest expectations, this interview was turning into a major scoop.

'What do you suggest?'

Even at this stage, Simmons wasn't sure what he wanted to say.

But in the end, the words came quite naturally: 'I feel all the players should withdraw their labour now, right across the board. And it's time for the fans to show their anger. They've stayed on the sidelines too long. The game is being stolen from them and they need to do something before it's too late.'

Throughout the exchange, scattered voices in the audience had been muttering in agreement. Suddenly, the whole studio broke into a wave of spontaneous applause. The noise rang around the enclosed space and grew into a cacophony.

A nerve had been hit.

Elated, Gavin McGarry struggled to make himself heard above the din: 'So there you have it,' he shouted. 'Gus Simmons has thrown down the gauntlet to football's fat cats and the fight is on for the soul of our national game. Until we meet again in the "Spotlight", goodnight.'

As the credits rolled, the roar was undiminished. Only as the adrenalin faded from his bloodstream did Simmons realise quite what he had done.

Already he had the feeling of kick-starting an engine he could not control.

SIMMO SPARKS STREET REVOLT

Conrad under pressure as fans show anger

by Colin Gregory

THOUSANDS of angry Bradcaster City fans took to the streets in protest after an emotional TV appeal by rebel striker Gus Simmons.

They marched through the city yesterday chanting for the resignation of club chairman, Michael Conrad. Dozens were arrested after violent clashes with police.

Elsewhere in the country, there were scores of smaller rebellions, including pickets and sit-ins at many football grounds.

The scenes were triggered by the shock appearance of Simmo on Gavin McGarry's peak time 'Spotlight' chat show and his pledge to miss Monday's game against Sheffield City.

The black ace slammed the

terms of the Super League's television deal with Conrad-controlled Spacelink and urged fans to make their voices heard. Most controversially, he also called on his fellow players to launch an all-out strike.

The move was roundly condemned by his Bradcaster City employers and bosses of the satellite station.

'Gus Simmons should remember where his loyalties lie,' said club secretary Harold Robinson. 'He has become a household name at Bradcaster and this is how he repays us.

'Unless he falls into line, he could cost us a great deal of money. At the moment, he is banned from setting foot here and we are looking very closely at the wording of his terms of employment.'

Spacelink managing director Tom Haslam launched a blistering attack, claiming: 'This stupid and vindictive young man is not only jeopardising his own future. He is going out of his way to destroy football in this country.'

Simmo even caught his own union on the hop. Privately, UPF chief executive Graham Wright is said to be furious at the striker breaking ranks. He was hoping to avoid an all-out confrontation with Spacelink and the Super League.

Now the row has spilled into open warfare, with many of his members joining the call for action, Wright has been swept reluctantly along.

'Simmons articulated deep-rooted fears about the state of the game,' he said. 'No wonder people found themselves marching on the streets in sympathy. I still feel a total players' strike would be inappropriate at this stage. But we need some concessions quickly to allay public concern.'

As chaos threatens to engulf English football, the man whose comments caused the trouble remains strangely tight-lipped. Simmo has taken refuge in his luxury country house on the outskirts of Bradcaster, refusing to comment to a besieging army of reporters and photographers.

Mystery still surrounds the reasons why the highly-paid star is prepared to lay his career on the line. But one thing is sure: the fans have found a new folk hero and they are fighting back.

We can only guess at the dark feelings of Michael Conrad. He was unavailable for comment yesterday after jetting back to Spacelink Towers for crisis talks with his management team.

It began peacefully enough. About a dozen abreast, the marchers wound through the streets of Bradcaster, brandishing their home-made placards and chanting songs of defiance.

The uniformed bobbies lining the route were discreet yet watchful; some exchanged jokes with the protestors. There were few signs of the anger that had caused this human spillage, indeed there was almost a carnival atmosphere.

Yet as the throng drew nearer the football stadium, passing through the most desolate and derelict parts of the city, the mood grew darker and more violent. The chanting became harsh and repetitive: 'Conrad out! Conrad out! Conrad out!'

The idea had been to force a meeting, to talk things through. But when they reached the ground, they discovered all the entrance gates padlocked against them. They were confronted by hundreds of police, some in riot gear, others with snarling Alsatians.

Through a megaphone, the crowd was ordered to disperse. Instead, a rumble of displeasure quickly swelled to outright fury. From somewhere a bottle was lobbed into the air and shattered just yards in front of the police ranks.

A shower of bricks and stones and glass began to rain down and the crowd surged menacingly forward. For a moment, the police wilted and retreated under the barrage.

But at a barked instruction, officers with riot shields massed to protect the cordon. Then, in terrifying unison, they charged the crowd, which splintered and scattered in all directions.

In the tumult and confusion, blows from fists and batons were exchanged. One policeman was felled and kicked around like a football as he screamed for help. A bewildered middle-aged man who just wanted to escape the terror had his face gashed open by a shield.

There was a brief and bloody struggle but in the end the fans had no stomach for the fight. Soon the police were merely mopping up, dragging men into waiting black Marias, tending to their wounded.

Once again, football had turned the city of Bradcaster into a battleground.

With a sudden click, the scene collapsed into a blank screen.

'So,' enquired Conrad. 'What do you make of that?'

Back in his eyrie at Spacelink Towers, he was jabbing his remote control device viciously at a bank of VDUs.

Tom Haslam had never seen his boss so discomfited. For perhaps the first time in his life, Conrad had been exposed to the hatred not of newspapers or business rivals but of ordinary people. He had watched the news footage of the street protests several times over.

'It doesn't look good,' said Haslam warily. 'But these things have a habit of blowing over.'

Compulsively, Conrad paced the floor of his office.

Jerking his head from side to side, he muttered: 'No, Tom, it's a bandwagon. Everyone's jumping on and they're trying to run me down.'

'So maybe it's time the PR agency started to earn their money.'

Conrad snorted.

'Wilde wants me to do some interviews but I'd just get

236

torn apart. They've all been waiting for this for years, an excuse to sink their teeth in. Even my own editors can't ignore it. I mean, Christ, this is a big story.'

Haslam watched in alarm from the leather sofa as Conrad continued to prowl around the room.

'Michael, trust me,' he urged. 'People have very short memories.'

'Not with Gus Simmons stirring things up, they haven't. What the hell has got into him?'

'Have you upset him in some way?'

'Oh, not really,' replied Conrad airily. 'He came to see me the other day bleating about something or other. I thought he was being damn silly and told him so. Seemed that was the end of the matter.'

'Evidently not,' said Haslam evenly. 'But how can one man scupper the whole project? It's just not possible.'

'You saw the TV pictures. He's got the fans on his side and if the players strike, our cash flow is shot to pieces. Advertisers will lose faith, subscriptions will go through the floor. If Simmons keeps opening his mouth, we're dead in the water.'

'Can't you talk some sense into him? You pay his wages, after all.'

Conrad's eyes blazed.

'Tom, the man is unstable, anyone can see that. He won't listen to reason.'

Haslam's voice was icy: 'Then something will have to be done.'

'What the hell does that mean?'

But Haslam made no reply. The room lapsed into a brooding and malevolent silence.

The death of Graveney confirmed Redwood's isolation from the world. Despite his betrayal, Graveney had remained the only man who truly understood him.

More than ever, Redwood turned in upon himself. Over and over in his mind, he imagined Graveney's car in flames on the rocks, its sickening descent. He saw the desperation and futility in his eyes and found an echo of his own despair.

Redwood remembered their last meeting, Graveney's strange intensity and gnomic words. Now it all made sense. He had indeed been settling his accounts.

So Redwood mourned. Not just for his friend but for something that had been snatched from them both.

At first he grew torpid and melancholic. But as his memory revolved, he recalled Graveney's urgent plea: someone has to be the voice of Bradcaster's conscience.

The thought took root in his brain. Then came the terrible television footage of the rioting outside the stadium and Redwood was persuaded at last. He could not simply walk away and see everything he had worked for ground into the dust.

The next day he woke early and spent hours grooming himself. He bulled his shoes and the metal buttons of his blazer to a mirror shine. Painstakingly, he scraped a brand-new razor across his stubbled face and calmed his grey-white hair with oil.

Later, as his Daimler dawdled through the commuter traffic, a piquant sense of anticipation rose inside him.

Approaching the Bradcaster stadium, he was waved through the main gates by a cheery steward, who called out: 'Good to see you back, sir!'

There were moments of absurdly tangled emotion as he mounted the stairs to the top floor, resentment and exhilaration scrapping for supremacy. Despite everything, this was where he belonged.

He moved along the corridor with its familiar landmarks: the photographs and paintings, memorabilia behind glass. Unconsciously, he quickened his step as he passed the chairman's office, which now bore an ostentatious brass plaque with Conrad's name.

Soon he found the small yet comfortable room he had originally been promised. He turned the knob but the door wouldn't budge. With a lurch of his stomach, he noticed that his nameplate had been removed.

Increasingly frantic, Redwood dashed down the corridor bursting into the other offices. Staff greeted him with puzzled deference but he didn't acknowledge them.

Flushed and humiliated, he finally found what he was looking for on the ground floor between the administration office and the caretaker's storeroom. On the door, in stencilled letters which were already rubbing away, were the words: Arthur Redwood Vice President.

He pushed it open and the stink of stale air rushed into his nostrils. The room was windowless and dank. A tatty desk was pushed up in a corner and a telephone sat on the bare floor. The solitary filing cabinet had burst its hinges.

'Welcome home,' Redwood said aloud with bitter irony. 'You bastards.'

Gingerly, Melanie lifted aside a corner of the curtain and peered outside. Already early morning sunshine cloaked the room in warm and golden light.

She screwed her eyes against the glare, rubbing the gum from her lids, and gazed down the driveway to the gates beyond.

But before her mind could focus, a faraway cry rang out: 'There he is!'

Dozens of figures were milling excitedly in the road outside, pointing up at her, sunlight glinting from telephoto lenses that were raised like weapons.

Panic-stricken, she dropped the curtain and tugged her dressing gown tighter around her body. She swept the fronds of hair from her face with a nervous twitch.

'For God's sake, Gus,' she called out. 'I can't stand any more of this. They think I'm you.'

For a few moments, there was silence. Then Simmons appeared from the bathroom, already dressed in a dogtooth jacket and silk patterned waistcoat. Tension was etched in every detail of his face.

'Look, don't fuss,' he snapped. 'When they see me go, they'll just disappear.'

Melanie saw the savagery in his eyes but didn't understand. More than ever, she felt estranged from him.

'Where are you going?' she asked quietly.

'Nowhere you need to know about. Just drop it, OK?'

'Please yourself. You always do.'

He flashed her an irritated glance and disappeared from the room without further comment, adjusting his tie. She heard him clattering down the stairs and then the soft thud of the front door. She pressed her eyes to a crack between the curtains to scrutinise the waiting horde of reporters.

The cough of the Mercedes' engine aroused them. Shaking off the torpor of their all-night vigil, they started cursing and jostling for position. By the time the car reached the gates, they were blocking the entrance and spilling into the drive.

Simmons heard the whirr of cameras, saw the mad forest of arms brandishing microphones. They all seemed to be yelling at once, the sounds blurring into babble. He saw the face of Colin Gregory leering towards the driver's window, mouthing like a stranded fish.

Face set, he revved the engine and nosed the Mercedes slowly into the bodies. The crowd parted as it had to before the weight of the car, stumbling backwards, shouting obscenities.

He saw clear space and rammed the gas pedal to the floor. Tyres screeching, the Mercedes burst away up the road. In his mirror, Simmons saw the media gang break up and dash for their own cars but by then he was disappearing into the haze.

After a while, confident he had shaken off his pursuers, he relaxed a little. As he kept driving, the landscape changed gradually from lush pasture to bleak moorland purpled with gorse.

The altitude rose sharply through knolls and foothills until he was ascending the great jagged back of a mountain range. The air grew thin and the scenery increasingly desolate, populated only by a few bedraggled sheep.

At the very top of the highest peak was a television mast, gaunt against the skyline. As he drew near, Simmons saw the smooth white shape of a car nestling in its shadow.

It was an Alpha Romeo Spider and it belonged to Alexandra Conrad.

Simmons eased his car alongside the shining flanks of the Spider but there was no one inside. Casting his eyes around, he saw a distant figure at the very edge of a steep escarpment. He flicked open the car door and stepped outside, stomach churning.

Even on this glorious late summer morning, the wind was like a knife. In the mountain air, the sun seemed to blaze more fiercely but without heat. His face and hands grew numb with cold as he strode towards her.

She was staring out across a landscape as blank and inhospitable as the surface of the moon, her long black coat flapping at the knees, her hair tugged and tousled by the wind. As he approached, he scuffed a stone with his foot and she flinched and turned.

Her beauty was murderous. She wore an expression of both yearning and anguish, as if a battle was raging in her brain, and for a moment he was stopped dead in his tracks.

Then he stumbled towards her, desperately. She waited

for him with her arms limp at her sides. He engulfed her, covering her face and neck with kisses, and suddenly she responded, holding him as tightly as she could and kissing him back passionately.

But instead of being consumed by desire, slowly they grew less urgent, their caresses less searching, until finally they were still and separate. Alexandra resumed her gaze across the featureless terrain.

'I can't stay long,' she said. 'I'm supposed to be staying with friends in Cheshire.'

'All right,' he muttered.

There was a moment of silence and then, without looking at him, she asked quietly: 'What are you trying to do?'

His voice was clogged with emotion: 'I'm tired of being pushed around, being someone's plaything. I want to make him suffer.'

'Is this because of me?'

'Not completely.'

She swung around to face him, dark eyes aflame.

'I never promised you anything. I never said I would leave him. You have no right to do this.'

'He's got to understand he can't carry on like he does,' said Simmons doggedly. 'It's time somebody stood up to him. He thought I was some thick footballer with his brains in his boots.'

She grabbed his arm and shook him hard, her voice strident: 'You fucked his wife, isn't that enough?'

'No.'

'For Christ's sake, what else do you want?'

Prompted by the darkest and most secret corner of himself, he replied: 'I want him to know. I want the whole fucking world to know I had you.'

Her jaw dropped as if she had been slapped. Incredulity spread across her face.

'What are you talking about?'

242

'I'm going to give the story to the tabloids.'

She gave a short and bitter laugh.

'You're not serious, you can't hate him that much.'

But she looked into his face, saw the strength of his resolve and was appalled.

'What about me?' she pleaded. 'What have I done to you?'

'I'm trying to cut you loose.'

Almost hysterical, she spat back at him: 'I'm happy as I am, you stupid bastard.'

Alexandra saw her world, all the sheen and splendour of it, dissolving before her eyes. She could not bear the thought of the hostile whispers, the knowing and malignant eyes. And she was terrified of Conrad's retribution.

'I'll deny everything,' she cried. 'You have no proof, no one ever saw us alone together.'

Simmons watched her disintegrating before him with a freshly dispassionate gaze.

'You're so scared, aren't you?' he said. 'That's why you dragged me all the way out here. So scared.'

'No one will believe you. You can't prove a damn thing.'

'What about the photographs?'

She gaped and blanched.

'You didn't . . . ?'

He nodded slowly.

'I took the film from the camera in the studio, when your back was turned, because it meant something to me then. It was careless of you to forget.'

He smiled ironically and added: 'Perhaps you just got carried away.'

Alexandra stared at him in disbelief. She felt sick and giddy.

'You wouldn't. Gus, please.'

She reached out imploringly but he swayed back, snarling: 'Keep your hands off me. You're as bad as he is. You think you can take anything and just forget about it. But not this time.'

This was the moment when everything came to an end. Leaving only bare sands and rotting debris, the all-embracing waters of their passion had simply ebbed away.

In a voice that was suddenly still and flat, Alexandra said: 'You know I can't let you do this.'

Simmons turned to go.

'You can't stop me,' he said.

But as he walked back to the car, a tiny lost speck amid the louring landscape, she realised that anything was possible.

'I'm telling you, Harry, that old bastard knows more than he pretends.'

It was a slack day in the northern newsroom of the Daily World. Journalists hate the summer: everyone on holiday, even politicians, a kind of dull lethargy cocooning the country.

Normally sub-editors spend their days shaping, slashing or spiking the reams of copy from staff reporters, stringers, agencies, freelances. But in the summer, this great flood dries to a trickle.

So papers have to manufacture the news. Stories that would barely have merited two paragraphs at the bottom of a column are pumped up to page one splashes. Every tip-off, no matter how lunatic, is followed up and squeezed dry.

Because there is so little hard news, summer is the time for the bizarre and outlandish. Small wonder hacks call it the silly season.

But Gregory had not succumbed to the general air of boredom. He was chasing the biggest and most elusive scoop of his career.

'Redwood could be the key to the whole thing,' he urged. 'He knows more about Bradcaster than any man alive.'

Harry Walters scowled. At the insistence of his doctor, he had just stopped smoking and was even more snappy and irritable than usual. His mood was not enhanced by the Marlboro dangling from the corner of Gregory's mouth.

'Why the fuck should he talk to you? He's kept his mouth shut so far.'

'Well, he won't say anything if I ask him directly.'

'So drop it.'

Gregory paused to take a long drag at the cigarette, leaning back in his chair and blowing the smoke from his nostrils. Walters stared at him in angry longing.

'We just need another peg to hang the interview on, that's all,' said the reporter.

'Like what?'

'Redwood is 70 next week, I checked. Great excuse for a profile and I could get him to talk about the glory days. That's his one soft spot, he's as vain as buggery about it.'

'Sounds fucking boring to me,' muttered Walters. 'He'll rabbit on and on about that and we'll be none the wiser about the takeover.'

'Maybe,' admitted Gregory. 'But I reckon I can sucker him, catch him off guard.'

Walters pulled a doubtful face and, losing interest, started to wander off towards his office.

'Look, Harry,' the reporter called after him. 'At worst, we'll get a nice nostalgia piece. You know how the punters love that shit and it ties in with the start of the season on Saturday.'

Gregory fixed his editor with a look as close to pleading as his temperament would allow.

'Come on, you miserable old bastard,' he said. 'Trust me.'

Walters smiled wearily and in that instant Gregory knew that he had got his way.

Now he had to make it count.

Inside the Bradcaster City stadium, the noise was deafening. But it was not the roar of a crowd, its blend of tribal loyalties and raw emotion, that assaulted the eardrums.

Rather it was the harsh clanking of heavy machinery, still busy on the Southside terraces. Slowly the skeleton of a new stand was rising from the rubble, great metal stanchions were being riveted into place. Men in orange jackets and hard hats tried to scream above the din and scrambled over the wreckage.

When Bradcaster's players swarmed towards the Southside, they felt the passion of the crowd, like a lover aching for consummation. But for the whole of the next season, it would be empty and scoring goals a desolate fulfilment.

With sad eyes, Redwood watched the demolition of his memories. He stood in the very centre of the pitch, with the stands and the floodlights towering over him and the noise of the machines pounding his senses.

Beneath his feet, the turf was firm and flawless, edged with lines of vibrant white. All was in readiness for another campaign, there was a tangible atmosphere of renewal. But Redwood knew it could never be the same again.

He turned away and from the corner of his eye glimpsed two figures striding across the grass towards him.

'Arthur!' yelled Colin Gregory, cupping his hands to make himself heard. 'Top of the morning to you!'

The reporter approached and they shook hands. Gregory jabbed a thumb in the direction of his companion, a youth with a heavy camera slung across his shoulder and the sharp, sly face of a weasel.

'This is Kevin,' he said. 'Shall we do the pictures first, so the lad can get off?'

Redwood shrugged disinterestedly.

'As you wish.'

'How about a shot in front of the new stand?' asked Gregory. 'Could be nice and dramatic. Shows that, even at your age, you're still looking forward.'

A dark cloud passed across Redwood's face.

'No,' he said shortly. 'Think of something else.'

Gregory exchanged glances with the young photographer, who tutted impatiently and scanned the stadium for an alternative.

'How about the goals over there?' muttered Kevin, jerking his head. ' 'Course, it's all been done before.'

As they wandered towards the goal mouth at the north end, the noise from the machinery receded slightly. Gregory pulled out his notebook and started chatting about the old days, past successes.

At first diffident and monosyllabic, Redwood gradually unwound. The experienced reporter played him like a fish, applying a gentle and coaxing pressure.

All the time Kevin was swapping lenses or wriggling on the ground for a better angle, Redwood reminisced about cup finals and championships and last-gasp winners. He was hardly aware of the constant clicking of the shutter, the orders to turn his head a few degrees or thrust a hand into his pocket.

After a couple more rolls of film, Gregory murmured: 'All right, son, that'll do. On your way.'

Kevin packed up his kit and slouched away. Immediately, the reporter adopted a more conspiratorial tone.

'You seem a bit edgy about the new stand, Arthur,' he said. 'Don't you like it?'

Redwood was wary: 'It's a necessary evil. As you know, we're constrained by the terms of the Taylor Report.'

'Still, bloody shame though,' persisted Gregory. 'Being forced to throw a piece of history on the scrapheap like that.'

Redwood didn't reply but instead began prowling restlessly up the touchline. Gregory followed a yard behind, sensing his discomfort.

'That doesn't bother me so much,' said Redwood at last. 'But I can't accept making fans pay through the nose before it's even built. The policy is deeply unfair.'

The reporter was scribbling away in his notebook, desperate to remain unobtrusive.

'That was Conrad's decision,' he said. 'Does that mean you regret selling out to him?'

Stung, Redwood turned on his heel. For the first time, Gregory saw in his ravaged face a terrible weariness and frailty. But the ice-blue eyes were blazing with passion.

Redwood grabbed the notebook and dashed it to the ground, shouting: 'I'll regret it to my dying day. But do you seriously think I had any choice?'

Momentarily taken aback, Gregory gaped at the older man and then bent to retrieve the pad.

'Leave it,' snapped Redwood. 'This isn't for publication.'

For a second, the reporter was caught in two minds. The last thing he wanted was an off-the-record interview. But otherwise he could be left with nothing, a snapped line.

Silently cursing, he straightened his back and said quietly: 'Why did you have to sell?'

Redwood was breathing hard, struggling to control himself.

In a voice that was cracking at the edges, he whispered: 'Conrad put up four million pounds for the transfer of Gus Simmons and like a damned fool, I took it. Then he simply threatened to recall the loan unless I sold him my shares. It was blatant blackmail.'

'Good God, Arthur,' said Gregory incredulously. 'Couldn't you see it coming? What made you think someone like Conrad wanted to play Father Christmas?'

Redwood refused to meet his gaze, staring at the turf in humiliation.

'He was convincing,' he muttered. 'No doubt I'm not the first man he's duped.'

'Nor the last,' agreed Gregory. 'What about Sid Graveney?'

He held his breath for the reply: could this be another revelation, a further piece of the jigsaw?

'All I know,' said Redwood, 'is that Sid would never willingly have sold out. Conrad must have had something on him.'

'But you don't know what it was?' demanded Gregory, unable to keep the disappointment out of his voice.

Redwood shook his head and said: 'I was one of the last people to see him alive, you know. He was different somehow. Now I know why.'

A brooding silence descended as Redwood grew more withdrawn, face clouded by remembered emotion. He almost forgot that Gregory was there at all.

'Do you hate him?' nudged the reporter after a while.

'Who?'

'Conrad.'

'He robbed me of everything I tried to build here. Just like the war robbed me of my best years as a player,' said Redwood in a voice like flint. 'But no, I don't hate him. You can't really hate someone like Conrad. He is just a dark force, it would be like cursing the sea or shouting at the moon. But I hate what has happened to this club.'

'So who do you blame?'

Redwood laughed bitterly, mouth contorting. It lasted much longer than it should have, collapsing into the echo of itself. The sound was convulsive, eerie. Without quite knowing why, Gregory shuddered and the nape of his neck went cold.

'Everyone,' said Redwood, choking off his laughter abruptly. 'Myself for being such an old fool, Graveney for having a skeleton in his cupboard. Television companies who want to bleed the game dry, spineless administrators who let it happen. Greedy players and stupid fans.'

His lips parted in a brittle smile.

'I'd like to put a match to everything,' he said, his face becoming expressionless. 'Purge it all in the flames. That's the only answer.'

Gregory peered deep into the older man's eyes but found no reflection.

'Bloody hell, Arthur,' he said at last with a trace of embarrassment. 'I think you need a rest. Why don't you go home?'

Redwood was already stumbling away to the tunnel, shoulders hunched, leaning forward as if into a stiff wind. Yet not a breath of air disturbed the lush summer grass.

Gregory watched him go, shaking his head in bewilderment, then bent for the notebook that Redwood had snatched from him.

He wiped the dirt off the page and cursed aloud.

Simmons had slept fitfully, drenched in a clammy sweat. It wasn't until well after dawn that his body finally rebelled and he fell into a deep slumber.

Midday sunlight was flooding the bedroom by the time he woke. Squinting and still barely conscious, he hauled his heavy limbs out of bed, a plan of action already coalesced in his brain.

He crept stealthily to the window and looked outside. Melanie was on her hands and knees at the bottom of the garden, tugging weeds from an overgrown flower bed. She had the impenetrable concentration of a child.

Simmons stared at the telephone for a long time, as if it were no longer a box of electrical components but a nexus with another life. To somewhere, anywhere, but here and now.

With a final decisive lunge, he plucked the receiver from its cradle and punched in a seven-digit number.

'Come on,' he muttered as it rang out, his heart thumping sickeningly.

A switchboard cut in and he blurted: 'Colin Gregory, please.'

He waited for what seemed an eternity while Wagner's 'The Ride of the Valkyries' was piped into his eardrum. The tension inside him tightened to such a pitch that he was on the brink of hanging up.

Suddenly Gregory's voice barked: 'Yeah?'

Silence hung heavy on the line.

Then the striker said: 'This is Gus Simmons. I want to talk.'

'What about?'

'Michael Conrad and his wife.'

Simmons heard the rasp of a match and a sharp inhalation of breath as Gregory dragged on his cigarette.

'Go on,' said the reporter in a colourless voice.

'You were right when you said Conrad bribed my agent to get me transferred to Bradcaster.'

'I know. Can you prove it?'

'No,' admitted Simmons.

'Shame. What about Conrad's wife?'

Trying to keep his voice steady, Simmons murmured: 'I'm having an affair with her.'

'Jesus!' burst out Gregory, his poise shattered. 'Er, hold on.'

For a few moments, the line went quiet.

Then, in a different tone, Gregory added: 'Conrad's lawyers will be sharpening their knives over this one. I've got to be sure.'

'There are photographs,' said Simmons hesitantly. 'Pictures she asked me to take. She's . . . she's naked. I'm in one of them as well.'

'Gus, we've got to meet. Can you come straight away?'

'Yes. But not to your office. I don't want anyone to know about this except you and me, OK? Not even your editor. Conrad's got everyone in his pocket.'

'Sure, sure,' muttered Gregory quickly. 'You know the monument at St Stephen's Park? Can you be there in half an hour?'

'Sooner.'

'Great. Oh, and Gus?'

'What?'

There was a trace of yearning in the reporter's voice: 'Bring the bloody photographs, all right?'

By now Simmons was shaking uncontrollably, the telephone still clamped to his ear.

Struggling to compose himself, he heard a soft click on the line and a wave of nausea engulfed him as he realised its significance.

'Oh God,' he said aloud.

He dashed from the room and skidded to a halt at the top of the stairs. Hardly daring to look, he bent precariously over a banister to scan the hallway below.

Melanie stood hunched with her back to him, a telephone dangling from her numb fingers, head bent into her chest.

Suddenly, out of her stillness, a heaving sob racked her body and the telephone clattered to the floor.

'Mel,' he said, his voice thick and indistinct. 'I didn't know . . .'

She was weeping bitterly. She slumped to the ground, clasping her head in her hands, and rocked slowly backwards and forwards.

'I knew,' she was repeating to herself. 'I knew, I knew.'

Everything fell apart: the chat show appearances and flashy adverts, the photo shoots and the adulation of the fans. Confronted at last by reality, he could no longer avoid her pain.

Somehow he had not expected it. In his fantasies the newspaper was not real, had no power to hurt, and he and Melanie could have carried on just as before.

But she had heard the betrayal from his own mouth and it changed everything. Now there was no hiding.

Slowly, as if he took long enough the situation might evaporate, Simmons came down the stairs. He had the disturbing sensation of floating outside his body, watching himself.

She was still rocking and whimpering like a child when he reached her. He stared at her in appalled fascination. Her hands were clasped tightly at the nape of her neck, her back crabbed so he could see the lumps in her spine through the thin blouse.

With trembling fingers, Simmons reached out to touch her but could not bring himself to stretch the final inches. His hand hovered above her shoulder as if she were electrified.

Then his face crumpled and collapsed and tears ran unhindered down his face. He wept silently, knowing he had no right to mimic her grief.

Without turning around or ceasing the repetitive motion of her body, Melanie said: 'How long, Gus? How long has it been happening?'

She had stopped crying and there was something in her bitter and contemptuous voice he did not recognise. Paralysed by guilt, he was unable either to take her in his arms or tear himself away.

So he remained motionless above her and mumbled: 'Not long, just a few weeks. I . . . never meant it to happen. I'm so sorry.'

'You're pathetic,' said Melanie flatly. 'You think you're such a bloody bigshot. Don't you realise these people are poison?'

She paused for a moment and, more hesitantly, added: 'Do you love her?'

Simmons felt his mouth go dry. Even now, the question was revolving endlessly in his head. He stared down at his wife, who had grown still and tense, and at last something cast itself adrift.

'No,' he said. 'No, I don't.'

She turned her tear-stained face towards him for the first time. Her eyes were candid and unblinking.

'So why did you do it?'

He wanted to run away and hide. Everything was crashing down around him but somehow he could not escape the devastation.

'I don't know,' he murmured. 'She was so lovely, I was flattered. It made me feel like I was somebody.'

'And I just made you feel ashamed,' she said quietly.

He said nothing because the bare truth had corroded his power to speak.

Wordlessly, Melanie rose to her feet and went upstairs. Simmons heard her rustling and clattering in their bedroom and, reluctantly, he dragged himself after her. Suddenly overwhelmed by exhaustion, he could hardly force his brain to focus on this fracturing of his marriage.

He watched her packing with dull eyes. She was throwing some essentials into a suitcase with angry gestures: underwear, cheque book, lipstick, shoes.

'Don't go,' he managed. 'Please don't go.'

She clicked down the suitcase lid and swung to face him.

'I'm going home,' she said. 'I should have done it months ago. There's nothing for me here. She can have you, for what you're worth.'

With set jaw, she strode across the floor but he moved into the doorway to block her exit.

'Don't go,' he pleaded again, feeling his lips begin to quiver.

'You sad bastard,' she snapped in a voice of steel. 'Just get out of my sight.'

Without waiting for him to move, she thrust roughly past him, spinning him round. He wanted to grab her and hold her until she stopped kicking and went still in his arms.

Instead he simply watched as she left.

With an unpleasant and deepening sense of anticipation, Gregory strode through St Stephen's Park towards the war memorial.

He knew he was early for the rendezvous but had been quite unable to remain in the office after Simmons' call. Yelling at the Rubensesque rear of Walters that he was 'going to see a man about a dog', he had fled the building.

St Stephen's was the vibrant heart of Bradcaster, a park modelled, somewhat optimistically, on the gardens of the Palace of Versailles. It was in its late summer splendour: roses were spilling over their rigid borders, rhododendrons made great blasts of colour with their trumpet-shaped flowers.

The intensely green lawns spreading away in every direction made the eyes ache and the heat of the sun was merciless.

As Gregory approached, the huge stone obelisk towered overhead, topped by a depiction of Christ on the cross, head dangling limply on His chest.

Lowering his eyes, Gregory saw there were hundreds of

names carved around the plinth and a great inscription which read: 'To the praise of God and in glorious memory of the men of Bradcaster city who laid down their lives in the struggle for righteousness 1914-1918.'

He glanced fretfully at his watch and sat down on the stone steps, drumming his fingers on his knee. He rummaged for a cigarette and lit it inside cupped hands.

'Gotta give these bloody things up,' he muttered, then drew in a lungful of smoke.

Squinting into the sun, he cast his eyes around the park, searching for the dark figure of Simmons. Couples were spooning on the grass; their laughter carried to him on a light, warm breeze. Sweaty middle-aged men jogged past idling youths and mothers with pushchairs.

Brushing a lock of damp hair from his eyes, Gregory wriggled out of his jacket and rolled up his shirt sleeves. He leaned back against the monument and felt the cool stone between his shoulder blades.

For a moment, he almost forgot why he was there. But half an hour and several cigarettes later, the landscape had been engulfed in a red mist of nervous fury.

'Where are you?' he kept repeating to himself. 'Where the bloody hell are you?'

He prowled around the memorial like a hungry beast. Something had gone wrong, horribly wrong.

For whatever reason, Simmons was not going to show up and the story of a lifetime was melting away in the sun's glare.

'Fuck it,' he spat out aloud and strode quickly away in the direction of his car.

A terrible sense of emptiness had overwhelmed Simmons as he heard Melanie start her car and drive away.

Suddenly everything had fallen away: his passion for Alexandra, the urge to punish and humiliate Conrad, his thirst for chaos and destruction. All that was left was the chilling silence of Melanie's absence.

He felt numb, unable to goad his mind into coherent thought. Nothing in this predicament seemed familiar, as if he had woken to find himself in a dream.

Dully, he recalled his planned meeting with Gregory, the promise of the photographs, but could not fathom the point of the disclosure. He no longer wanted the roof of his world to cave in, merely to crawl away and lick his wounds.

He could not compete in these power games of blackmail and brinkmanship. He was used to a public conflict in which all the participants knew the rules, where no enmity spilled beyond the final whistle.

Instead he had strayed into a secret arena where no law prevailed and only the undertakers or the bankruptcy courts decided the game was over. He no longer had the stomach for it.

By now Gregory would be waiting for him and the assignation had to be kept. Otherwise, in eagerness or frustration, the reporter might write the story anyway. Simmons had to retract, turning the truth into a lie he could live with.

In the bedroom was a chest of drawers which held his football kit, a place where Melanie was forbidden to trespass. Tugging open the bottom drawer, Simmons rummaged through a pile of shin pads, tie-ups, tubes of Vaseline, elasticated bandages.

Finally he uncovered a large plain white envelope. He took it downstairs and removed the photographs inside, unable to resist gazing at them one last time.

Alexandra's nakedness was both painful and compelling, her eyes boring into the very quick of him. He felt his lust rising again, like a recurring nightmare.

With deliberate gestures, he tore each of the pictures in

half and set them alight. As they shrivelled and crumpled into ash, his heart lifted a little. He glimpsed an image of his own hand, reaching out into nothing as blue flames curled around the fingers.

Surely this was the moment of a new beginning, a sort of rebirth. A sense of exultation surged inside him.

He left the house with a lighter tread than for many weeks. Outside, the sun burned fiercely and cast an intense golden hue over the gardens and the shimmering hills in the distance.

Simmons breathed the air, savouring its freshness, and a slow smile began to spread across his face. Absently, he delved into his jacket pocket for the key to the Mercedes.

A dark shape disengaged itself from a yew tree and caught his eye. He turned, recognised the figure and in that instant realised something awful was happening.

He shrank back in terror, mouthing words he could not hear. With absolute clarity, he saw the dull metal of the gun barrel and the hammer poised to descend.

At first he did not feel the pain, even as the first bullet tore into his body, spinning him round. He was conscious only of the deafening report of the gun, a mad and murderous stuttering. But then, as he fell, his senses convulsed into a wincing agony.

By the time the crows ceased their alarmed cawing, he had been released from this torment into blackness. Beneath him, a ruby pool seeped wastefully into the gravel.

With savage acceleration and neck-wrenching use of the brakes, Gregory was struggling to circumvent Bradcaster's gridlock of traffic. He urged his battered Astra up narrow sidestreets, sent it squealing and protesting over kerbstones and cobbles.

Finally he escaped the clogged arteries of the city and, with the gas pedal to the floor, clattered through the suburbs into the countryside beyond. He wasn't going to let this story go without a fight.

As the car flashed down the long lane to Simmons' house, gouts of brown mud, dried to powder in the summer heat, erupted in a cloud. Startled by the roar of the engine, a thousand starlings hurled their gorged bodies from a cherry tree.

'Right, you bastard,' snarled Gregory, car lurching through the gates of the house. 'Where are you?'

At first, he thought the dark crumpled shape in the driveway was a pile of old clothes or a sack of refuse. But then he saw a hand, outstretched as in pleading, clawing at the gravel.

The truth dawned like a blow at the base of his skull.

He scrambled from his car and dashed over to the prone figure of Simmons. Kneeling, he placed two fingers on his neck and felt a weak and irregular pulse.

Grunting with the effort, he managed to turn the footballer over and stared helplessly at the blood-soaked shirt, the lolling head.

'Christ,' he muttered in rising panic. 'Jesus Christ.'

He stumbled back to the Astra and leaned inside for the car 'phone. Punching in the number, he saw with horror and disbelief that his fingers were stained with crimson.

'Yeah, yeah,' he stammered. 'I need an ambulance, a man has been stabbed or shot or something. He's covered in blood. What? Last house at the end of Mountain Rise. That's right. Just hurry, OK?'

Gregory struggled to yank his tattered senses back together. He stared at the still shape of Simmons on the ground but knew there was nothing he could do.

His lungs were aching for a cigarette but he fought the urge. Instead, he keyed another number into the telephone with an unsteady hand.

'Walters,' he snapped at the Daily World newsdesk.

'Look, I don't care if he's meeting the fucking Pope, just get him.'

The line went dead. Gregory's heart was pounding at his ribs as the adenoidal Cockney voice of his editor cut in.

'Look Harry, shut up for a minute, will you?' urged the reporter as Walters launched a tirade of abuse. 'I'm sitting on the biggest story of the fucking decade here.'

As calmly as he could, Gregory explained the sequence of events, Walters barking questions at him.

'No, he never showed, that's what I'm trying to tell you . . . It looks like he's been shot . . . No, I haven't seen them . . . How the fuck should I know? . . . He's still alive but only just.'

Then, so faint it was almost imperceptible, Gregory heard the distant whine of sirens.

'Listen, I've got to go,' he said hurriedly. 'This place will be crawling with bluebottles in five seconds flat.'

His face turned to stone as he added: 'I want the byline for this one, Harry. You got that? This is my story.'

Gregory slammed the 'phone into its cradle and ran back to Simmons. Ignoring the seeping blood, he rifled the footballer's pockets for the promised photographs. Simmons stirred and a bubble of saliva appeared between his lips.

All the time, the noise of the sirens had been growing louder until finally an ambulance swung into the driveway with a screaming phalanx of police cars at its rear. Gregory sprang guiltily to his feet, drenched in blood from hand to elbow.

He was thrust aside as a pair of medics crouched over Simmons, clamping an oxygen mask over his mouth. The air was filled with the synthetic screech of the sirens.

Gregory's arms were pinned to his sides in an iron grip and two constables subjected him to a ruthless body search.

A big man with a face like weathered granite appeared

and said: 'Looks like you've got some explaining to do. Let's go where we'll be a little more comfortable.'

A knot of dread already tightening in his stomach, Gregory was dragged struggling to a waiting police car and driven away.

Bradcaster's rush-hour traffic parted miraculously before the braying ambulance. Shoppers and loiterers turned their heads to watch; a dark shadow passed across their faces as they tried to peer inside, at once inquisitive and appalled.

Inside Gus Simmons was teetering on the edge of oblivion, medics struggling to staunch his wounds. He seemed as small and helpless as a child. Only the snaking tubes maintained his fragile grip on life.

Finally the ambulance hurtled through the wrought-iron gates of Bradcaster Royal Infirmary. Visitors hopped onto the grass to evade its noisy progress to the casualty ward.

A group of nurses and a white-coated doctor was already waiting anxiously at the entrance and sprang forward as the ambulance halted. The back doors swung open and the stretcher carrying the unconscious footballer was disgorged.

At the same time, another figure materialised with a camera pressed to his face, clicking furiously. Harry Walters was marshalling his troops.

Medical staff surrounded the stretcher as it burst through the swing doors of the ward, the doctor yelling instructions.

'Christ, what a bloody mess,' he exclaimed as the stretcher was wheeled furiously down a corridor. 'Take him straight to theatre.'

At first, no one noticed the photographer chasing after them, still banging off shots. But then he made the mistake of getting too close, actually elbowing a nurse aside for a clearer view of Simmons' face.

The doctor turned with an expression of disbelief and rising anger.

'For God's sake, man!' he snapped. 'What the hell do you think you're doing?'

The photographer made no reply but carried on clicking. With an oath, the enraged doctor made a grab for the camera and wrenched it free.

'This patient is dying! Don't you understand that?'

He hurled the camera to the floor with a resounding crash and the lens splintered, the back of the case burst open. Light flooded in and all the images were lost for ever.

'Right,' he shouted, dashing to rejoin the stretcher. 'Let's see if we can save him, shall we?'

Inside the police interrogation room, Gregory took a long nervous drag of his cigarette.

'Look,' he said in a querulous voice. 'How many more times? We'd arranged to meet earlier at St Stephen's Park. He didn't show up so I went to look for him. When I arrived, he was on the ground bleeding.'

'Yes, I know you said that. But I don't believe you.'

A tape recorder hissed on the table. Opposite Gregory, the big man sat with fingers steepled beneath his chin. Detective Inspector Jack Marshall was turning the screw.

'I called the ambulance, didn't I?' yelled Gregory, voice rising an octave. 'Why would I do that if I'd shot him?'

'So he was shot, was he?'

The reporter sighed and passed a hand through his hair.

'That's what it looked like,' he said sullenly.

'So you've seen it before, have you, Mr Gregory? People who have been shot.'

Gregory was frightened and exasperated.

'No, of course I haven't. There was . . . blood coming from lots of different places, that's all.'

'So you called the ambulance,' said Marshall more kindly.

'That's right. I turned him over and I could see he was in a bad way, so I dialled 999 from the car 'phone.'

'I see,' murmured Marshall.

For a moment, Gregory thought he was getting somewhere, that this nightmare might soon be over.

Then the policeman added: 'Of course, it wouldn't be the first time a killer had called for an ambulance. It's a rather crude device, isn't it?'

Gregory buried his face in his hands. The interrogation had been going round in circles for over an hour; he was becoming tired and disorientated. Sooner or later, he was going to have to tell all he knew.

'Why were you going to meet Simmons?' demanded Marshall.

'Just for an interview. About the players' strike, nothing important.'

'If it was so trivial, why did you go racing over to his house when he didn't appear?'

'I didn't want to lose the story.'

Marshall scowled and snapped: 'Don't insult my intelligence. Nobody does an interview in the middle of a park. You decided to meet there because you didn't want to be overheard. Why not?'

'No reason.'

Marshall leaned across the table and speared Gregory with a pitiless gaze

'Look Gregory, we found you with blood on your hands next to a dying man. Think about it.'

The reporter shook his head and remained silent. He still had the chance to bust this story wide open. Once he squealed to the police, every hack in Fleet Street would be chasing it.

'You were going through his pockets, weren't you?' said

Marshall softly. 'What were you looking for, Colin?'

'Nothing. I was just loosening his clothing.'

'How considerate.'

Gregory stared at the table, the cigarette between his fingers burning away to a precarious plume of ash.

Marshall was growing impatient: 'Come on, is that really the best you can do? Don't piss me about.'

'It's the truth.'

'I doubt it, laddie, but have it your own way,' said Marshall, gesturing to a uniformed constable. 'We'll see if being banged up all night jogs your memory.'

Gregory jerked up his head and laughed nervously.

'You can't do that.'

'Watch me.'

'You haven't even charged me.'

Marshall smiled sardonically.

'Do you want me to? I'd be happy to oblige.'

The reporter's last vestige of resistance was swept away. He couldn't file his copy from a police cell.

'All right, you win,' he said wearily. 'But you mustn't make this public for another 24 hours, OK?'

'I'm listening.'

'Is that a promise?'

Marshall's voice was frosty: 'I said I was listening. You're not in a position to make deals.'

Gregory paused for a moment and, realising he had no option, plunged in: 'Simmons claimed he was having an affair with Michael Conrad's wife, Alexandra. He said he had some nude pictures of her. That's why we were meeting.'

The cold eyes of the policemen didn't betray a flicker of surprise.

'Surely you are the last person he would have told.'

'I think he was trying to hurt Conrad. He's a proud boy and he thought Conrad had used him.'

'In what way?'

'You'd better ask him that.'

'If he ever wakes up,' said Marshall evenly. 'Did Conrad know about these photographs?'

'I don't think so.'

'What about his wife?'

Gregory shrugged and replied: 'She's in them, isn't she?'

Marshall absorbed this information silently. Before he could speak again, there was a tentative knock at the door. He nodded to a constable to open it and a fresh-faced young detective sidled into the room.

'Beg your pardon, sir,' he said hesitantly. 'There are some, er, developments I thought you should know about.'

There was an awkward pause as Marshall remained rooted in his seat.

'I . . . don't know if you want to come outside, sir.'

'Just tell me.'

Marshall exchanged a glance with the reporter; this was the pay-off for coming clean.

'There's no sign of the gun at the scene, sir,' said the detective, eyes darting. 'The wife of the victim is also still missing, along with her car.'

'Anything from the ballistics boys?'

'Yes, sir. They say that five rounds were fired, four of which hit the victim. The other bullet was embedded in the brickwork of the house. There were no spent cases.'

'Type of gun?'

'An Enfield .38 No. 2 Mark 1 revolver, sir.'

A hint of a smile played briefly around Marshall's lips.

'You're sure you can't be more specific?'

'No, sir,' replied the young man, flustered. 'That particular model is double action, which means the hammer cocks automatically when you pull the trigger. Not terribly accurate, which accounts for one bullet missing the target despite the short range.'

Marshall pursed his lips in thought.

'Bit old-fashioned, isn't it?' he mused.

'Very much so, sir. In fact, it was standard army issue for commissioned officers during the war.'

Marshall waved a hand in dismissal and turned to Gregory.

'You didn't hear any of that,' he said curtly. 'On your bike.'

As the reporter stood up to leave, he added: 'Stay where I can get hold of you and keep out of my way. Got that?'

Night was falling by the time Gregory emerged from the police station, rubbing his eyes in fatigue. He glanced at his watch and cursed: the deadline for the Daily World's last edition had expired an hour ago.

Millions of copies would already be heading for the streets, with the story of the shooting emblazoned across the front page. He hoped Harry Walters had kept his promise about that byline.

But something else was preying on his mind, a vague suspicion that was slowly evolving into certainty.

'It's got to be,' he muttered to himself. 'It's bloody got to be.'

Grimly determined, he raised his arm to hail a passing taxi.

SOCCER ACE GUNNED DOWN

Horror attack on top striker Gus Simmons

WORLD EXCLUSIVE

by Colin Gregory

SOCCER super-striker Gus Simmons was fighting for life last night after being shot down in a ruthless attack.

I found him sprawled unconscious and covered in blood on the driveway of his luxury home after he failed to turn up for an interview with me.

As Simmo battles on a ventilator in the intensive care unit of Bradcaster's Royal Infirmary, where his condition is described as 'critical', mystery surrounds the brutal shooting.

Police investigating the attempted murder said they were anxious to trace the soccer star's wife Melanie, who has disappeared without trace.

'We are anxious about her safety,' said a spokesman. 'A serious crime has been committed and in those circumstances her absence is most worrying.'

The always colourful career of the £3 million striker grew increasingly controversial in the run-up to the launch of football's new Super League.

Now speculation is mounting that the shooting was prompted by his call for an all-out players' strike, to break Spacelink TV's stranglehold of the national game.

Said Graham Wright, boss of the Union of Professional Footballers: 'Gus Simmons' fearless stand has made him some bitter enemies.

'It would be a tragedy for football if this dreadful incident was in any way related to his involvement in legitimate industrial action.'

No one at Bradcaster City or Spacelink was prepared to comment last night.

Slumped in the back of a Hackney cab, Gregory felt waves of exhaustion lapping at his brain. He would never have believed a police interrogation could be so draining; his nerves still felt raw and exposed.

Night had descended but a full moon cast the cab's

interior in a silvery, ethereal glow. Through gaps in the towering hedges, Gregory saw clusters of sleeping cattle.

The car turned sharp left, jerking him from the onset of blankness. With a supreme effort of will, he struggled bolt upright and tried to focus his mind on the events of the evening. He was still unable to shake off a sense of utter incredulity.

A little further on, the cabbie leaned back and inquired: 'This where you want?'

Gregory grunted and told him to swing into the driveway of Simmons' house.

As they straightened up, the driver blurted: 'Bloody hell, what's been going on here?'

Sodium lights illuminated the house and gardens so it was like daylight in a blazing summer noon. Half a dozen police cars were still scattered around, some with their blue lights flashing.

Constables scrabbled on hands and knees in the gravel, others combed the rose beds and shrubbery. Figures were moving in every visible room of the house.

As the cab approached, a policeman ran towards them flapping his arms.

He stuck his head through Gregory's open window and demanded curtly: 'Who are you?'

'I found him,' said the reporter. 'I've come for my car.'

He nodded towards the Astra, which remained where he had parked it several hours earlier, and a suspicious glare dawned in the constable's eyes.

'Hold on,' he muttered.

Withdrawing a few paces, he turned his back and with hunched shoulders started whispering into his walkie-talkie.

After some moments, still wearing a grim expression, he wandered over and said: 'Just get in the car and drive away. The chief doesn't want you poking around and disturbing anyone. All right?'

Gregory got out of the cab and paid the driver. As he walked towards his car, he couldn't suppress a shudder as he recalled Simmons lying bleeding on the ground. There was still a patch of red in the stones. He looked away.

By the time Gregory span the Astra noisily around, his hands were shaking uncontrollably. Delayed shock, he thought to himself. Giving it a name seemed to help. He sucked in lung-bursting draughts of air to calm himself.

At last, his mind began to work. He punched in the number of the Daily World newsroom on the car 'phone. After several rings, it was answered by Walters himself, who never left before midnight.

'How's it going?' asked Gregory. 'Did we make the front page all right?'

The editor's voice crackled over the loudspeaker, ignoring the questions with one of his own: 'Colin, where the fuck are you?'

'Coppers hauled me in for questioning. They've only just let me go.'

'Thought as much,' grunted Walters. 'You'd better get your arse over here so we can check out the angles.'

'Sorry Harry. I'm on to something, no time to explain. Talk to you later.'

Walters' protesting voice was silenced at the touch of a button and Gregory pointed the Astra back towards Bradcaster with a renewed sense of purpose.

It was the gun that made him sure. A standard wartime issue Enfield .38, a relic from the past.

Arthur Redwood, ex-army officer, former chairman of Bradcaster City, had finally snapped.

Gregory remembered the hatred in his eyes as he had stalked the pitch at Bradcaster, his usurped domain.

Somehow in Redwood's bitter and twisted imagination, Gus Simmons had become a target.

At first, it didn't occur to the reporter to be frightened. But as the Astra nosed into a quiet cul-de-sac in the city's leafy suburbs, anxiety tugged at his guts. Redwood was a desperate man and no story was worth getting shot for.

Gregory killed the headlamps and engine of the car and drew up in a dark corner. With exaggerated stealth, he clambered out and stared up at Redwood's house.

All the lights were blazing. As Gregory crept across the lawn, he noticed that the front door was slightly ajar and Redwood's Daimler was missing from the drive.

Ears straining for sounds of life, he reached the door and waited in silence for several minutes. Then he finally summoned up his courage and gave the door a gentle push. It swung inwards to reveal an empty hallway and a flight of stairs.

Gingerly, he stepped inside and moved towards the living room. He peered round the door jamb with painstaking slowness but all that caught his eye was a half-empty whisky bottle on a low table. Heart still pounding, he stole into the next room and suddenly his eyes widened in shock.

'Jesus,' breathed Gregory as he took in a scene of devastation.

Every single one of the glass-fronted cases which lined the walls had been smashed and their contents strewn over the floor. Among the shards of glass were bent and twisted trophies, torn shirts, shredded pennants.

Photographs had been yanked from the walls and ripped to pieces. Stepping forward, shoes crunching on the debris, Gregory saw one picture still intact. It showed Redwood at Wembley holding the FA Cup aloft in triumph, being mobbed by supporters.

As the reporter bent to pick it up, he saw the word

'betrayal' had been scrawled right across it in jagged red letters. His stomach did a long slow somersault.

It took another half an hour of breathless creeping before he was sure the house was empty. By then he was sick of the thudding pulse in his neck, the enervating tension. He just wanted to crawl into a corner and go to sleep. But the long night wasn't over yet.

He forced himself to run back to the car, legs heavy, brain protesting. In a strange way, he understood the troubled mind of Arthur Redwood and had a hunch where he might be.

No one was going to snatch this story away from him.

Conrad gave little of his day to sleep. Perpetually besieged by jet lag, his body had become resilient and resourceful.

He travelled further and worked harder than anyone else in his organisation. He had grown accustomed to snatching cat naps, a kind of watchful slumber. But for the last few weeks, he had not slept at all; his insomnia was like a tightening knot.

Thoughts revolved in his mind until they became obsessions. There was no relief from the demons eroding his self-belief, no welcoming oblivion.

He was beginning to ask questions about the nature of his empire, his reasons for carrying on, what in essence made it worthwhile. Wasn't he simply bellowing in the wilderness?

Above all, he tortured himself with rage and shame every time he thought about Alexandra. Was the purpose of his acquisition of power merely to cloak his own inadequacy, his failure to love her as a man?

Conrad sat upright in his bed staring at his sleeping wife. Her face was turned towards him and in repose had lost all its calculation and hardness. Scrubbed free of make-up, it seemed instead younger, more vulnerable.

Her mouth was parted slightly; one pale arm was stretched out on the pillow as if she were clutching for something. Her legs were drawn up beneath her like a baby's in the womb. Conrad felt her bony knees pressing into his hip. He leaned towards her to deepen the pain.

Alexandra stirred and her eyelids flickered.

'Michael?' she murmured drowsily. 'What's the matter?'

By now she had opened her eyes and was glaring at him for disturbing her sleep. Moonlight turned her dusky skin milky-white, softening her anger into a child's petulance.

She saw the pain in his face and her voice changed.

'Is everything all right?' she asked with a tinge of worry. 'Can't you sleep?'

Conrad shook his head heavily. In silence, he reached out and brushed the wisps of hair from her forehead. Instinctively, she grasped his hand and kissed the fingers softly.

It was the most hurtful thing she could have done. Unshed tears burned in his eyes and misted his vision. A hundred questions rose in his throat but he could not bring himself to utter them.

For some minutes they remained staring wordlessly at each other. Then, shattering the silence, the bedside telephone began a nerve-jangling bray.

Conrad snatched it up and barked into the receiver.

It was the security man at the main gates: 'Sorry to bother you so late, sir. But there are some policemen here to see you.'

'For God's sake,' snapped Conrad. 'Can't they come back in the morning?'

'Apparently not, sir.'

'What's so bloody important it won't wait until tomorrow?'

'They won't say, sir.'

Conrad sighed in exasperation.

'All right, you'd better let them through.'

He sprang from the bed and started dressing. Alexandra followed his movements with concerned eyes, an indefinable fear swelling inside her.

'What's going on?' she asked, as Conrad hauled himself into a polo-necked sweater.

'Sounds like trouble,' he grunted. 'Police want to see me.'

'I'll come down with you,' said Alexandra firmly.

She swung her lithe and naked body from beneath the sheets and wrapped a towelling robe around herself. It had been neatly folded by her maid, ready for an early-morning swim.

'There's no need, I'll deal with it.'

His voice was dismissive but he made no protest as she followed him from the room. As they reached the end of the landing, there was a thunderous knocking at the front entrance.

Conrad swung back the heavy door to reveal two men in suits standing atop the great stone steps. One was middle-aged, running to fat; the other barely out of his twenties, with a lean and watchful face.

Behind them, Conrad caught a glimpse of three police cars, one of which was empty.

The younger man spoke first in a clipped Scots accent: 'Good evening, sir. I am Detective Inspector Moncrieff of the Metropolitan Police, this is Detective Sergeant Simpson. We are pursuing certain inquiries on behalf of the Greater Bradcaster Constabulary. May we come in?'

'Do we have a choice?' asked Conrad sourly.

Moncrieff gave a faint smile.

'Not really, sir.'

'Then you'd better come in.'

Moncrieff's eyes widened for a second as he walked into

the hallway and saw Alexandra for the first time. Her hair was unruly and she was barefoot.

'This way,' said Conrad shortly, leading them into his study. 'Now what's this all about?'

Moncrieff's voice was frostily polite: 'Are you aware that one of your players, Augustus Simmons, was shot earlier today?'

Alexandra gasped and clutched her mouth. Conrad merely looked bewildered.

'No, I wasn't,' he said.

'Is he . . . is he dead?' stammered Alexandra, her face suddenly pallid.

'He is critically ill, madam. It was a particularly brutal attack.'

Alexandra looked for a moment as if she might faint.

'God, how awful,' she said weakly.

'Indeed,' said Moncrieff without emotion. 'Is is true, madam, that you were having an affair with Mr Simmons?'

Alexandra stared at the policeman in disbelief; then her eyes darted to Conrad, whose face was quivering.

She looked quickly away and said: 'Absolutely not.'

'We understand the victim had some photographs in his possession at the time of the incident,' persisted Moncrieff. 'They were of a rather intimate nature. Were you aware of that?'

This was becoming a waking nightmare.

'I don't know what you're talking about,' she muttered.

'But Mrs Conrad, it was you in the photographs, wasn't it?'

The corners of her lips began to twitch. She sent a desperate glance to Conrad, searching for some kind of support. But in his cold eyes, she saw only bitter hatred.

'What about you, sir? Did you know about these photographs?'

He replied with weariness: 'No, no. But perhaps I should have done.'

Balefully, he stared around the room: its exquisite regency furniture, the Gainsborough on the wall, delicate porcelain and finely-wrought silver. He blinked.

Although the outward opulence of his world remained undimmed, Conrad knew that everything now lay in tatters.

It was almost one o'clock in the morning by the time Gregory neared the Bradcaster stadium. Through a dense cobweb of backstreets, the Astra's headlights illuminated piles of litter and boarded-up shop fronts.

Every road was eerily deserted. Gregory began to curse himself for not ringing the police and washing his hands of the whole affair. A nameless dread was settling over him like a shroud.

Another left turn and he was running alongside the huge grey perimeter wall of the football ground. He squinted into the long shadows cast by the street lamps and slowed the car to a crawl.

Then he glimpsed something in the car park near the main entrance gates. His heart leapt into his throat. Even at that range and cloaked in darkness, the smooth shape was unmistakable: Redwood's Daimler.

As Gregory swung in, car pitching and swaying on the pitted surface, his lights picked out a still figure at the wheel.

Cautiously, he halted some way off and sat for a while in silence. This was the stupidest, most dangerous thing he had ever done in his life. But he did it anyway.

He climbed out of his car and walked slowly across towards the Daimler, conscious of his crunching footsteps on the loose stone. By now he could see the back of Redwood's head quite clearly, still motionless.

Now there was no turning back. Gregory crept to the passenger door and peered in through the window. Quite oblivious, Redwood was staring straight ahead and moving his lips as if he were talking to himself.

The reporter felt for the handle in the darkness and gave it a gentle tug. As the door swung outwards, a strident male voice and the roar of a crowd assailed his startled ears.

After a moment of panic, he realised it was the commentary to an ancient football match: 'Culverhouse with the ball, deep inside Bradcaster's own half. He finds Pettigrew in space, that little imp of a winger. The Blues searching for the goal to break the deadlock . . . '

He moved into the seat next to Redwood and clunked the door shut behind him. Glancing over, he saw the old man's worn profile, still mouthing the words on the tape.

The situation had the curious logic of a dream.

'You found me then,' said Redwood colourlessly.

All the fear had suddenly evaporated; Gregory felt merely awkward, blundering among someone else's stale dreams.

'Malone makes the timely interception, the rock on which wave upon wave of Bradcaster pressure has foundered. He looks up, probing for an opening. Wilkins is screaming for the ball on the left flank . . . '

Redwood's voice was misty: 'Nineteen fifty nine. Another world. When they played the national anthem at the start, you could have heard a pin drop.'

'Great times,' said Gregory dully.

For a little while, neither man spoke. In spite of himself, Gregory began to absorb the rising tension of the commentary as the BBC man's vowels grew ever more strangulated.

Then Redwood asked softly: 'Is he dead?'

'I don't know.'

Still the tape blared away: 'Extra time is looming now

but here come Bradcaster for one last surge. Surely they've left it too late. The crowd are roaring them on . . . '

The reporter looked again at Redwood and was astonished to see his cheeks were damp with tears.

'Why did you do it, Arthur?'

'He was the cause of all of it. He let Conrad in,' said Redwood in a thick voice.

He shook his head, bewildered.

'All those chat shows and advertisements. In my time, footballers knew their place. He thought he was bigger than the club. Who did he think he was, calling for a strike? I couldn't let that happen, I just couldn't.'

'So you shot him? Jesus Christ, Arthur.'

'No choice,' murmured Redwood, his face crumpling. 'I had no choice.'

With immense weariness, Gregory pushed open the passenger door and stepped outside. This was a sad and squalid end to his odyssey and he just wanted it to be over.

As the door thudded shut, he heard a voice calling out across the decades: 'He's through, Pettigrew is through. The linesman's flag stays down. He steadies himself, Thompson advances to meet him. He's scored, he's scored. Bradcaster have snatched it in the very last minute . . . '

Head bowed, Gregory walked back towards his car. He had no option; he had to call the police and tell them everything. There would be a trial, he would be hamstrung by the laws of contempt. Everything was lost.

Just at that moment, a single sharp crack rang out across the deserted car park.

Melanie had been on the M5 just a few miles short of Bristol when she was flagged down by a police patrol car.

She had cried scalding tears for the whole of the journey, revolving the bitter fact of Simmons' adultery. She imagined him in the extremity of his passion, the sounds he made in the back of his throat as he approached climax, the urgency that had been so long absent from their own relationship.

Interrupted in this poisonous fantasy by the lights of the police car, her first thought had been that she was driving too fast. But the sombre face of the officer told her immediately that something was very wrong.

He had driven her all the way back to Bradcaster without telling her why; yet she knew with terrible clarity that a tragedy was unfolding. Crouching still and small in the back of the car, she had wept in fearful anticipation.

When the news was finally revealed, she could find no surprise or further sorrow. She simply shook her head from side to side and murmured inaudible words.

At first, the police took this as a sign of guilt. They kept her shut up in an airless room for more than an hour, battering her with questions until her head ached. By the time they were convinced, she felt herself swaying at the edge of a great drop into blackness; her whole body was screaming for release.

They drove her to the hospital just after midnight, past the casualty ward which was clogged with bleeding drunks. In her fevered imagination, the towering Victorian buildings looked like a great prison where she would be incarcerated for ever.

Insisting on being alone, she stumbled down endless corridors which stank of sickness and disinfectant. Eventually, her chalk-white complexion and vacant eyes alarmed a passing nurse and she was ushered into a day room and told to wait.

A few minutes later, a doctor appeared. His face had a quality of stillness which went beyond tiredness into another dimension. He looked at her without compassion.

'Mrs Simmons?'

She nodded, unable to disentangle a squirming knot of emotions.

'Your husband is a very lucky man. In a relative sense, of course.'

He rummaged in the pocket of his white coat and pulled out a peppermint. With an expression of great concentration, he tugged at the rustling paper to release the sweet.

'Would you like one?' he inquired.

Melanie shook her head. Somehow this didn't seem real.

'He was hit by four bullets,' said the doctor, sucking hard.

The mint clattered disconcertingly against his front teeth and muffled his speech: 'Remarkably, given the short range, they all missed vital organs, although we had to remove a kidney. He was most at risk from loss of blood but transfusions have stabilised his condition. He's still very ill but not in immediate danger.'

A tremendous sense of relief flooded her body. She had not known until that moment that she had been prepared for the very worst.

'Is he conscious?' she murmured.

'Of course not,' snapped the doctor. 'He's on a ventilator and still under anaesthetic.'

'Can I see him?' she asked.

'In time, yes. Please understand that you may find the extent of his injuries upsetting.'

'Yes, I realise that.'

She made to stand up but the doctor held out a restraining arm. As they touched, his face softened slightly.

'There is one more thing, Mrs Simmons,' he said. 'One of the bullets was lodged near his spine and there is some evidence of paralysis in his lower body. It is too early to say if the damage is permanent.'

Melanie's face went rigid.

She stammered: 'But he . . . he could be all right, couldn't he?'

The doctor hesitated for a moment, then said slowly: 'He might make a full recovery. But a subsequent blow to the spine would put him in a wheelchair for life. I'm sure you understand the significance of that.'

Melanie stared at him, her ravaged mind unable to function. She shook her head dumbly.

'Your husband's career as a footballer is over, Mrs Simmons,' said the doctor. 'That's what it means.'

REDWOOD TUMBLED!

Bradcaster boss confesses to Simmo shooting

WORLD EXCLUSIVE
by Colin Gregory

TODAY the World reveals the amazing identity of the man who shot soccer superstar Gus Simmons.

It was 70-year-old Arthur Redwood, ousted former chairman of Bradcaster City and the man who brought Simmo to the club.

He confessed the attempted murder to me just moments before blowing out his brains in a deserted car park outside Bradcaster's stadium.

Twisted by bitterness and the thirst for revenge, he blamed Simmons for the ruthless takeover of the club by multi-millionaire media baron Michael Conrad.

And he believed Simmo's orchestration of the players' strike was the final nail in the coffin of the game he loved.

I found Redwood hours after discovering the blood-stained footballer in the driveway of his home. Police were still pursuing the red herring of his missing wife Melanie.

Slumped in his vintage Daimler, Redwood was listening to a commentary of his team's triumph in the FA Cup final more than 30 years ago.

This sad old man has never been able to come to terms with the changing face of football.

'In my day, players knew their place,' he told me. 'I couldn't let Simmons destroy everything I stood for.'

Moments later, as I left to call the police, a single shot rang out and his torment was at an end.

The vital clue was an Enfield revolver used in the shooting. The gun was standard army issue during the Second World War, when Redwood served with distinction with the Cheshire Regiment.

The football world has been stunned by the revelation that one of its most respected figures was a would-be killer.

'I just can't believe it,' said Bradcaster secretary, Harold Robinson. 'This has to be the

saddest day in the history of
the club. None of us had any
idea what Arthur was going
through, how disturbed he was.
    'We'll just have to try and pull
ourselves together for the start
of the season.'

The moment she saw him, any trace of bitterness or resentment simply fell away.

It was like the myth of Frankenstein's monster, his
inanimate body awaiting some burst of energy to jolt it
back to life. Except this was horribly mundane and real.

His mouth was lolling open as though he were drunk.
His eyes were closed. Covered in ugly purple bruising and
swathed in bandages, his body seemed small and fragile.

Computer screens blipped and hummed. Tubes and
needles had attached themselves to him like the tendrils
of some carnivorous plant.

'We took him off the ventilator,' said a young nurse,
smiling brightly. 'He's breathing by himself now.'

But for three long days and endless nights, he remained
in his world of blackness. Refusing all offers of food, she
stayed in a chair at his bedside, just watching him.

Occasionally, drowsiness nibbled at the edges of her
mind but she did not sleep. When she could no longer
bear to see his face, she turned and watched the square
of light in a high window fading and brightening as the
days progressed.

Finally, the end of her vigil approached as she saw
his eyelids flutter for the first time. A jackhammer heart
pounded at her ribs and she scurried away to fetch a
nurse.

For an hour, he made no further sign. Then he shifted an

infinitesimal inch in his bed, his lips twitched. Gradually, as if they were oppressed by an invisible weight, his eyelids struggled apart.

Melanie was clutching at his hand, massaging the fingers and urging him into consciousness with a soft voice.

When he opened his eyes, they were blank and unseeing. But the light of recognition began to sharpen in them as Melanie placed her face next to his. He felt her warm breath.

Suddenly there was an answering pressure when she clasped his fingers, so tightly her tendons ached. With her other hand, she caressed his face and the tears coursed down her cheeks.

'Mel,' he managed, tongue clogging his mouth. 'I don't remember . . . '

His voice tailed away. For the next few minutes, he drifted in and out of consciousness, each time growing stronger and more lucid. The doctor with the peppermints dashed in to check his condition and nodded with satisfaction.

'Let him talk if he wants to,' he ordered curtly. 'But don't tire him out.'

But now there was no need for words. In a warm and cocooning silence, they sat for hours, she cradling his head in her breast and rocking him gently like a child.

'You've come back,' she murmured. 'I always knew you would. I always knew.'

Just then, on the other side of the city, thousands of voices fused in a deafening roar. Arms were thrown skywards in triumph and vindication.

In the stillness of a late summer evening, among the floodlit shadows, Bradcaster City had just won their first game of a new season.

At first the crowd had been diffident. The stadium

had cradled a huge awkward space like the interior of a cathedral, every noise grotesquely magnified.

The silence from the razed Southside terrace, hidden behind a wooden barricade, seemed to have infected the supporters.

But as the match wore on, they discarded their dark emotions like superfluous clothing. The stadium began gradually to throb with life, the players were urged on with increasing passion.

When the goal came, it was as though the final barrier had been breached. The ground was swamped with joy. Fans embraced and punched the air, laughter gushed from them in a torrent of release.

Everything had been forgotten by the final whistle; victory, at that moment, was sufficient.

No one noticed that the directors' box was almost empty. Only a couple of sad-faced old men stared silently down at the celebrations.

Before the game, someone had spent hours making a banner with the words 'Simmo Get Well Soon' emblazoned across it. When the crowd streamed away, it was left flapping disconsolately against an advertising hoarding.

From the narrow streets outside, sounds of laughter floated across the deserted stadium.

The End

SEX BY ROYAL APPOINTMENT

Girl runs vice racket from Buck Palace

By Julian Desser

A beautiful but wayward girl is banished to England from her home in New Delhi, India, only to embark on a sexual adventure into the domain of high-class prostitution that takes her to the very doorstep of the world's most famous royal residence.

When the tabloid press becomes infatuated with her, she seizes the opportunity to fulfil her life-long ambition of fame and fortune . . . but terror is lurking in the shadows of her past.

ISBN 1–874652–02–3   £4.99